Edward Sullivan

Stray shots: Second series

Edward Sullivan

Stray shots: Second series

ISBN/EAN: 9783337278557

Printed in Europe, USA, Canada, Australia, Japan

Cover: Foto ©Andreas Hilbeck / pixelio.de

More available books at **www.hansebooks.com**

BY

SIR EDWARD SULLIVAN, BART.

AUTHOR OF 'FREE TRADE BUBBLES' 'PROTECTION TO NATIVE INDUSTRY'
'HAPPY ENGLAND' 'THE FROTH AND THE DREGS'
'OUR ECONOMIC CATOS' ETC.

SECOND SERIES.

London:

PUBLISHED BY JOHN DAVIS, AT 24, QUEEN VICTORIA STREET, E.C.

1888.

CONTENTS.

WHO KILLED CHARLES GORDON?

WHO killed Charles Gordon?
 I, said the Nation,
With my vacillation,
I killed Charles Gordon.

Who saw him die?
No friendly eye;
Only his enemy,
He saw him die.

Who caught his blood?
I, said the dog:
Dog of a Christian!
I lick'd his blood.

Who made his shroud?
Spurned by the crowd,
None made his shroud:
Honour's his shroud.

Who'll be chief mourner?
I, said Saint George,
Champion of England,
I'll be chief mourner.

Who'll be the parson?
I, said Hypocrisy,
With "exub'rant verbosity,"
I'll be the parson.

Who'll dig his grave?
I, said the slave,
He died me to save;
I'll dig his grave.

Who carried him to his grave?
So noble, so brave;
Deserted—betrayed,
None carried him to his grave.

Who'll sing a Psalm?
I, replied Fame,
Crimson'd with shame,
I'll sing a Psalm.

Who'll toll the bell?
I, said John Bull;
Because my heart's full.
So brave Gordon, farewell!

PRIDE OF RACE.

" IF I were not a Frenchman, I should wish to be an Englishman," said a French Minister, with a complimentary bow, to an English Minister. "If I were not an Englishman, I should wish to be one," was the blunt reply. Here spoke the pride of race, the proud feeling of superiority, the conviction that England was the greatest nation in the world ; that her mission, her motives, her policy were for the good of civilization and of mankind. Pride of race has been the birthright of Englishmen for 300 years, handed down from father to son as a priceless heirloom. For the time it is gone, vanished out of sight. If any of the mighty dead—Chatham, Pitt, Canning, Palmerston, Russell, or even peace-loving Aberdeen —were to revisit the House of Commons, they would scarcely recognise the English breed. They would see defeat, disgrace, humiliation to our arms and our diplomacy, condoned without a murmur, treated with absolute apathy and indifference. They would see a class to whom the glory of the British Empire is a distasteful theme, who look upon it rather as an incubus to be got rid of, who shudder at the strains of " Rule Britannia," as Mephistopheles shudders at the church bells ! They would find the age of patriotism dead, and in its place an age of sophisters, economists, and calculators. If they should inquire what has caused this great wreck of national pride, they will learn that during his Midlothian campaign Mr. Gladstone and his followers set themselves to undo everything that Lord Beaconsfield had done, whether it was working well for the country or not ; every stone of the edifice he erected with so much care and forethought was to be destroyed, not because it was working badly for the country, but because it was the work of Lord Beaconsfield. By exaggeration, by inaccuracies, by passion, by insinuation, Mr. Gladstone so distorted the aspect of the Imperial policy of Lord Beaconsfield that the people began to believe that the Empire was a curse rather than a blessing to them ; that it existed for the benefit of the rich alone at the expense of the poor ; that it was a Tory institution, in which the rest of the community had no share. It is this feeling that has caused the present alarming apathy on all national matters. But this feeling cannot last. A nation cannot change its skin like a snake. It cannot be completely transformed in two years. It may be confused and bewildered by sonorous verbosity, by mock sermons on humanity and national humility, and fancy it has got rid of the old Adam, but it has not. As sure as the sun rises, England will soon awake again, and the awakening may be dangerous. Spite of the new promises made by our Radical godfathers at our Midlothian baptism, the English race will always hear with pride the stories of Plassy and Assaye, of Waterloo and Trafalgar ; the name of Clive and Hastings, of Howe and Jervis, of Collingwood and Nelson, and others, "feared for their breed, and famous for their birth," who have made the name of England ring throughout the world, will still be household words ; and Englishmen will still make pilgrimages to the Abbey to gaze on the effigy of England's greatest War Minister, that "seems still with eagle face and outstretched arm to bid England be of good cheer and hurl defiance at her foes." More than ever they will tell their children of the gallant deeds of the warriors of their race—

> " How Horatius kept the bridge
> In the brave days of old."

The British Jingo owes his existence to the British "Nihilist." Jingoism, Chauvinism, Nationalism, Patriotism, call it what you will, is the national protest against Nihilism, against incivism, against Gladstonism, in fact, against the cry of perish India, perish British interests, against the clap-trap of St. James's Hall, against those who rail at the over-burdened Empire of England, who denounce her colonies as encumbrances, who are resigned to her decadence. It is a protest against the spirit that dictated " kin over sea," against the spirit of national defamation than can never sufficiently foul its own nest, that proclaims no conduct too base, too cowardly, for British statesmen, no statements too false, no reports too exaggerated for British officials ; that sees in the monstrous ambition of Russia, in the despotism of a military oligarchy, a holy mission ! It is a protest against the spirit that would keep the flag of England half mast, and hoist in its place the spurious flag of cosmopolitanism. It is, in fact, the natural rebound of the pendulum of English pride against those who have pulled it over too much the other way. It may seem to many foolish, but there is nothing to be ashamed of in it ; it is natural to the English breed, it is the spirit that animated Cromwell, Chatham, Pitt, Palmerston, Russell ; it is the spirit that, please God, will always find expression when the effacement of England is advocated. Certainly there will be a reaction, a violent oscillation of the pendulum. May it come soon ; it cannot come too soon. When the reaction comes, it will come from the country, not from the House of Commons. In the present House of Commons there will be no reaction. The constituencies sent members to Parliament to support Mr. Gladstone, for no other object, and support him they will to the bitter end.

So long as the present Parliament lasts Mr. Gladstone, surrounded by flatterers, will.

> " Like Cato, give his docile Senate laws,
> And sit attentive to his own applause."

But the House of Commons is not England. The time will come when the members will have to give an account of their stewardship. Then the constituencies will say to them, " It is true we sent you to Parliament to support Mr. Gladstone, because he told us, and you told us, that Lord Beaconsfield was ruining England, and that only Mr. Gladstone could save it. But we find now, after two years' trial, that it is Mr. Gladstone that is ruining England. We see Ireland in almost open revolt, our European influence gone, our Eastern Empire threatened, our officers insulted and killed in time of peace, &c. We sent you to Parliament in order to assist Mr. Gladstone to save the Empire, not to assist him to reduce it to a fifth-rate power." The foreign policy of Lord Beaconsfield was the hereditary foreign policy of Great Britain. It was natural, and national, and straightforward. It was dictated by the requirements of the British Empire. Nobody objected to this policy. France, Germany, Austria, and Italy thought it reasonable, and approved of it. But the foreign policy of Mr. Gladstone is the very reverse of the hereditary foreign policy of England. It is not national in any sense. It is personal—personal to Mr. Gladstone, and to him alone. It is originated and directed by influences of which nobody can guess the sources. Mr. Gladstone hates the Austrians, and hates the Turks (and, it is whispered, is not over fond of Prince Bismarck); but why he hates the Austrians, and why he hates the Turks, nobody knows. What, alas! we do know is, that this hatred of his, outspoken and demonstrative, has converted two of our oldest and most trustworthy allies into scarcely covert enemies. Every sense of national duty should have induced Mr. Gladstone to control his hatred to the Turk ; to check any violence of language or action that could convert into an enemy the spiritual suzerain of 40,000,000 of our fellow-subjects. We have heard of great men sacrificing themselves for the good of their country ; it really looks as if in his treatment of Austria and Turkey Mr. Gladstone has not hesitated to sacrifice the interests of his country for his own pleasure. Mr. Gladstone is a great humanitarian, but the humanity that is effusive about Italians and Bulgars, and draws a line at the sufferings of Turks and Jews, that passes over without notice the treacherous slaughter of British troops, and to avoid "blood-guiltiness" hands over 900,000 natives to the tender mercies of the Boers—this is only "electioneering" humanity after all, humanity snatched up as a rapier to pierce your enemy with.

> " *Lucius.*   His enemies confess
> The virtues of humanity are Cæsar's.
> *Cato.*   Curse on his virtues ! They've undone his country,
> Such popular humanity is treason."

Do not let us deceive ourselves. The same national spirit, the same qualities of heart and hand that built up the British Empire are necessary to support it. It was built up by deeds, and "deeds are the sons of Heaven." It can never be saved by words, however copious, which are the "daughters of the earth." "Be bolde, be bolde, and everywhere be bolde," was the motto of our Elizabethan ancestors, and it is that has made us what we are. If we cease to be bold, if we are no longer ready, even eager, to "fight for our own hand," our kingdom will not and cannot stand.

It is certain that England must, at all times, boldly and determinately maintain her own rights and interests, peaceably if she can, forcibly if she cannot. "I give you a toast," said Stephen Decatur, speaking in Norfolk, in 1816, "Our country ! in her intercourse with foreign nations, may she always be in the right ; but our country, right or wrong."

GLADSTONISM.

I F a public company that had attained great credit, wealth, confidence, and respect, by following for a hundred years certain lines of moral and commercial policy, was suddenly to reverse this policy absolutely and entirely, *ab ovo usque ad malum*, simply because a new chairman and board of directors entertained a personal dislike for their predecessors in office, should we not look out for a smash ? Should we not say the directors were throwing away a fine business and doing very badly for their shareholders ? Well, this is exactly what is happening, or rather what has happened, with the Great British Empire Company (Unlimited). Under the chairmanship of Chatham, Pitt, Grey, Peel, Russell, Palmerston, and Beaconsfield, the British Empire (Unlimited) has attained extraordinary credit, wealth, confidence, and respect, by following certain fixed, and straightforward, and well-understood lines of foreign and Imperial policy, by championing British interests openly and boldly, by speaking in the " Scythian phrase," by calling a spade a spade, in fact.

Well, Gladstonism has entirely reversed this policy: it minimises British interests, it discards the " Scythian phrase," and insists on calling what everyone in his senses sees and knows to be a spade, and nothing but a spade, by some other name. It is seriously maintained by many honourable men that Gladstonism is so noble, so grand, so cosmopolitan, so self-denying, so inexpressibly superior to any former or existing political gospel, that it is sheer blasphemy to decry it. But this is childish. If many other equally honourable men believe that this new gospel has emasculated the national character, watered down its noblest qualities, that it is rapidly reducing their country to the position of a subject Power ; that it is destroying before their eyes everything they most venerate and love ; that it has made the name of England a byword for folly, for indecision, for hypocrisy, and now, indeed, for bloodguiltiness, are they not to say so ? Gladstonism is a policy of noble sentiments, of superfine professions, of exalted motives, of plausible platitudes ; it appeals to the ear alone, it professes to believe that the world is better than it is, and that we are better than the world. Of course this is all nonsense, sham, hypocrisy. It is self-illusion in the most fatal form that can ever affect a nation—the power of seeing things as you wish them to be, not as they are. Gladstonism has made Britannia appear before the world as a hypocrite.

> Together lie her prayer-book and her paint,
> At once t' improve the sinner and the saint.

" Look," cries Gladstonism, with affected piety, "look at our prayer-book." " Yes," replies the world, " but look at your paint." " It is so hard," whines Gladstonism to incredulous Europe, " that you will not believe we are the one unselfish nation in the world ;

that in spite of all our assurances you will still assume we had selfish motives in going to Egypt. Indeed we had not. It is so distressing to men actuated by such noble motives as we are to be doubted. We destroyed the forts of Alexandria, we burnt the city, we slaughtered Egyptians at Tel-el-Kebir, Arabs at Teb and Tamanieb, we have made the land smell of blood, and have raised up a spirit of most bitter animosity against us in Egypt, not in our own interest in any way, but for the sake of Egypt, of Europe, of civilisation, of humanity. Is not this noble? Is not this grand? Can we give a greater proof of our disinterestedness?" Gladstonism professes to sink all national feeling, to mistrust national sympathies, to prefer treaties written on the " fleshly tablets of the heart " to those written on parchment, to appeal to the verdict of civilized mankind, &c., and a deal more similar nonsense. Well, we have appealed to the verdict of civilised mankind about Egypt, and what is it? Simply that we are a nation of fools: that the British lion, like the very gentle beast of Snug the joiner, is "a very fox for his valour, and a goose for his discretion." I declare, when I read the magnificent sentiments of Gladstonism, compare the motives it professes with the acts it performs, reduce to plain English all the sound and sonorous verbosity that preludes and accompanies its every act of legislation, when I mark the unbounded arrogance of the humble, the Old Bailey quibbles of the conscientious, the wastefulness of the economist, the bloodguiltiness of the humanitarian, the incivism of the patriot, the illiberality of the Liberal, I begin to sicken at the very name of virtue. "Le bon maréchal Louvois était toutes les vertus mêmes, mais peu réjouissantes, et avec peu d'esprit; après une longue visite, Ninon d'Enclos baille, le regarde, puis s'écrie: ' Seigneur! que de vertus vous me faites haïr !' "

"Clericalism is the enemy," cried Gambetta. " Gladstonism is the enemy," cry most Englishmen who are out of the party traces. It is Gladstonism that will bring the mighty Empire of Great Britain to ruin. There is no danger in Radicalism, Imperialism, Republicanism, Socialism, Nihilism even. Italy, France, Germany, Russia show us that each and all of these are compatible with patriotism, with pride of race, with the permanence of empire. Gladstonism is not. It is vestryism and methodism in national affairs. It denounces patriotism, it sneers at pride of race, it accepts defeat, it condones disgrace, it ignores an Imperial policy, it is absolutely inconsistent with the permanence of empire. "Virtus post nummos " is its motto.

> Get money, money still,
> And then let virtue follow if she will.

Bah! go to your consols, to your counters ; that is your business. What have you to do with Imperial interests, with Imperial duties, with honour, glory? What have you to do with generosity, with liberality, with science?

> A tradesman thou, and hope to go to heaven !

But, indeed, is it really money only that has made England what she is? Not a bit of it. It is not the bankers, the brokers, the manufacturers who have made the great name and honour and plain words, the incessant employment of language to conceal the truth; it is the perpetual hair-splitting and torturing of words, childish distinctions between " beleaguered " and " surrounded," between " wars " and " military operations," between a " prohibitory" telegram and a " dissuasive " one that are more suited to

> Some peaceful province in Acrostic Land,
> Where they might wings display and altars raise,
> And torture one poor word a thousand ways,

than to the vocabulary of statesmen!

The Northern half of America said to her wayward sister, "You shall not go; you shall not break up the grandeur of the Empire." Gladstonism said to Ireland at Kilmainham, and says it to her again now, "Do as we tell you, and you shall go; you shall break up the Empire. There is a thing that is much more odious to us than Repeal, than Disunion, than severing the ties between Great Britain and Ireland, and that is Imperialism, Toryism, Conservatism; only help us to crush out this pest, and you may have what you like—even to half the kingdom!"

Gladstonism has no vigour, no backbone. It knows no hard-and-fast line between order and disorder; between what is within the Constitution and what is without it, between national dignity and national humility; between common sense and sentimental nonsense; there is nothing in it to rouse the pride of our race; the refrain of " Civis Romanus sum " jangles on its ears as the church bells do on those of Mephistopheles; it is unnational, humble, undecided, squeezable, and above all things it is apologetic; it apologises for anything and to anybody; it apologises to the peace enthusiasts for maintaining a sufficient army and navy to keep off invasion; to the Dissenters for maintaining an Established Church; to the Democrats for maintaining a House of Lords; to Republicanism for preserving the Throne; to Mr. Parnell for maintaining the Union; to the Baboos of Calcutta for retaining India; to the Boors for remaining in South Africa; to Mr. Stansfeld for the Contagious Diseases Act; to Mr. Hopwood for the Vaccination Act; and soon, apparently, it is going to apologise to Europe for the ruin of Egypt and to pay the bill.

1884.

THE WEAK-KNEES.

THE "weak-knees" are a large family. They represent the moderate opinions of the educated minority of the country, and a very considerable portion of its wealth ; their heads and pockets are all right, but their knees are weak. I don't suppose the "weak-knees" will ever govern the country (though, God knows, we are now apparently governed by those who have no knees at all !), but if those who call themselves Whigs and those who call themselves Conservatives would only agree occasionally to put the drag on they could check the dangerous pace of the coach. But they will not. Directly one tries to put on the drag the other begins to flog the horses ; of course the coach goes faster ! Instead of the two weak bodies combining to make one strong one they prefer to weaken each other still more by fighting. We know what happened to the frog and the mouse when they took it into their heads to fight —the kite eat them both up. In the present crisis the attitude of Whigs and Conservatives towards each other is astounding : it really looks as if their heads were as weak as their knees. A candidate advocates the confiscation of the land and its division amongst the labourers, and Whig landowners wring their hands in despair and their weak knees shake ; but the opposing candidate is a Conservative, and Weak-knees actually cries out, "Not this man but Barabbas." It is astonishing. Nothing will attract public attention to the absolute extinction of the Whig party as a power in the State so much as the reception given to Lord Grey's letter of the 26th ult. Here is the foremost Whig in England, the most distinguished, the most consistent, the most honourable, accusing the Prime Minister of deliberate misrepresentation, and his accusation does not attract even a passing notice. Whigs are those unfortunate Liberals whom an unkind Providence has endowed with a knowledge of good and evil, right and wrong, honour and dishonour, and a few trifles of that kind, very subversive of party discipline, and if they venture to criticise the acts of the great apostle of Radicalism they are immediately, like Adam and Eve, driven out of the Liberal Paradise into the limbo of the weak-kneed. But though naked they need not be ashamed. Palmerston, Russell, Clarendon, Cornewall Lewis would keep them company if they were alive. It is sad to witness the dependent and deprecatory *rôle* of this once independent and militant party. How are the mighty fallen ! "Quantum mutatur ab illo." How changed are the Whigs of to-day, without leaders, trembling at the little finger of the Caucus, gulping down their principles with a ghastly grin, from the sanguine, confident Whigs who, 15 years ago, marched to victory under the famous banner—Free speech, free thought, free votes. Poor fellows, their antecedents are all that remain to them. They have a past, but certainly no present, except dragging the triumphal car of their conqueror; and evidently no future. They hesitate like Hercules between Vice and Virtue, or, rather, like a jackass between two bundles of hay; they can't quite harden their hearts to sacrifice their country to their party, or their party to their country; and, of course, as is usually the case, they sacrifice both. Alternately, "they roar like bears and mourn like doves:" they swagger as robust Radicals in public, and wring their hands as weak-kneed Whigs in private! But, pitiable as is their case, they are not alone in their misery—weak knees are by no means confined to the Old Whigs. They are almost as common in the ranks of the Conservatives. In fact it is difficult to say in which party political timidity most prevails. Æsop tells us that the hares being very miserable, by a common consent went to the river to drown themselves, but when they got there they met a company of frogs more fearful than they were, and so they took courage and comfort again. At one moment the Whigs are deterred from self-destruction by the greater misery of the Conservatives; at another the Conservatives are deterred by the greater misery of the Whigs. Poor Whigs! Poor Conservatives! They will soon be numbered with the Lost Tribes. Their fate reads like a Greek tragedy. They have actually fallen victims to the unnatural cruelty of their own parents. Medea like, Lord Hartington led his Whig children into the Radical den; whilst Sir Stafford Northcote compassed the destruction of his offspring by not leading them at all! Just now party warfare rages round Mr. Gladstone; the country is divided into two camps— those who worship and those who denounce him. The *argumentum ad hominem* is very monotonous and very unsatisfactory: but how can it be avoided when his worshippers insist on attributing every act of his Government, bad or indifferent, to him alone? He is what Jack calls a G.C.B.,—gunner, carpenter, and boatswain in one; he does everything, or does nothing, or undoes everything everyone else does. The attacks on Mr. Gladstone are intolerable, say his supporters; but if the attacks of his enemies are intolerable, what are we to say to the attacks of his friends? It is the old story. No man is a hero to his *valet de chambre*, and it is because his old friends and colleagues know him so well, I suppose, that they are so severe upon him. "Mr. Gladstone will ruin England," &c., &c., said his old friend and colleague, Lord Palmerston, thirty years ago. "Gladstone, my old friend and colleague, will bring to ruin everything we now venerate and love in England," said Sir James Graham a few days before his death. "Mr. Gladstone's foreign policy has lowered the British name and tarnished British honour," wrote his old friend and colleague, Lord Russell, shortly before his death. What would he have said if he could have seen the ruin and disgrace that now attends his foreign policy? And now his old friend and colleague, Lord Grey, distinctly charges him with what is either the "fabula" or "lie direct;" or the "fabulosa narratio," or "simple fib." Certainly Mr. Gladstone has cause to exclaim, "Save me from my friends." There is no accounting for taste. What is lovely in one man's eyes is hideous in another's. "If you could only see with my eyes you would see she is lovely," exclaimed the ardent lover of a very plain headed mistress. Love, political or

physical, will turn a frog into a goddess, as the poet tells us.
"Quisquis amat ranam, ranam putat esse Dianam." "Demandez
à ce crapaud," says Voltaire, "ce que c'est la beauté il vous repondra
que c'est sa crapaude:" and so robust Radicals, "Pro Junone
nubem," embrace a cloud for Juno, worship verbosity for wisdom,
and see in Mr. Gladstone the very beauty of political holiness."
"You would treat Mr. Gladstone as the Athenians treated Aristides,"
say the Radicals. "You would ostracise him because you are tired
of hearing him called 'the Just.' He is too good for you!" But
our old friend Cornelius Nepos gives the story quite another turn.
"Why do you wish to ostracise Aristides?" inquired Aristides of
the man who asked him to scratch his name on the oyster shell.
"Because he takes so much trouble to be called the Just," was the
reply; so this illiterate citizen, who apparently had not attended
his Board School, was not simply a fool, or a mere hater of virtue!
It is not only in Athens that there is a desire to ostracise those who
take too much trouble to be called the just, or the pious, or the
humane. "Lord Beaconsfield will ruin the Empire," said Mr.
Gladstone five years ago, "turn him out," and the country turned
him out. "Mr. Gladstone is ruining the country" now say all
sensible men, "turn him out." But "No" is the reply of those
who are not sensible men, "we will not turn him out: very likely
he is ruining the country—indeed, we think he is—but we prefer to
be ruined by him to giving a blank cheque to you." And so the
game goes on. Party counts for everything; country for nothing
at all. England is not in the position she was five years ago.
One side says she has gone up like a rocket, the other that she is
come down like a stick; but both sides agree on one thing, that
whether she has gone up or whether she has come down it is the
work of one man. and one man only. "Five years more of Mr.
Gladstone's foreign and Imperial policy will," say the Radicals,
"place England on the highest pinnacle of prosperity and virtue it
is possible for any nation to attain." "Five years more of Mr.
Gladstone's foreign and Imperial policy," reply most people with
two eyes in their heads, "and all that will remain of the British
Empire will be a mere *nominis umbra*, the shadow of a great past."

Compare the promises of Midlothian with the results. Then we
heard of "Happy England," the "Fleshly tablets of the heart."
Peace on earth, goodwill towards men. Ambrosia was not sweeter
—and what is it now? Bloodshed, red ruin, broken faith, dishonour—
a policy without shame and without pride. Black hellebore is not
so bitter. "Nonsense." say the Radicals, "England won't be
ruined because she loses her empire. Thank God we have completely
educated the people out of that Jingo notion. They are beginning
to understand that the British Empire is an empire of fraud and
force, and that in many ways they will be better without it. As for
what other nations think of us, let them mind their own business
—we don't care twopence what they think—let those laugh who
win." Exactly! but we are asked to laugh who lose.

1885.

HODGE AND THE SQUIRE.

HODGE has got the vote and has plumped against the squire. This is the burning question of the day—Does the squire realise the significance of the incident? "Hodge is a fool," he says: "he has listened to designing persons." "Not such a fool as you think," says Hodge, with a wink: "I listen to those who promise to improve my condition. Isn't it very natural? I will vote for you if you will talk to me in the same way." Hodge has plumped against the squire because he has no sympathy with him, and believes the want of sympathy is mutual—probably it is. "You have had your turn," says Hodge, "and you have taken precious little interest in me, probably less than you have taken in your pheasants and hares, and now it is my turn, and I am inclined to take precious little interest in you. The voice of the 'carpet-bagger' is more attractive to me than yours; he pledges himself to do something for me, you pledge yourself to do nothing. I should, indeed, actually be the fool you take me for if I plumped for you against him." This appears reasonable. In 19 cases out of 20 Hodge only knows the squire on the bench, when he fines him 10s. for killing his hares, or in the shooting season, when he gives him 2s. for beating his coverts. This is not good enough to induce Hodge to vote for the squire. Few intelligent agricultural labourers really believe in the actual "cow and three acres," but they take it as an earnest of the intentions of the Radicals to do something for them. They are under the impression that the Radicals wish to improve their condition, and that the Tories wish to keep them as they are. Very possibly they are wrong; but that is their impression, and many impressions often cause sinister results.

The responsibility of restoring the *entente cordiale*, or of creating it, rests with the squire, and it will not be an easy task. Hodge, though slow, is cunning. He is a wary bird: he is not to be caught with chaff unless he thinks there is some grain mixed with it. He is beginning to realise the immense difference the franchise has made in his position. He has no longer to pull his forelock to the squire if he wants some small favour; the squire has to go to him, hat in hand, to ask him for his vote. He is now in a position to make terms with the squire. "Scratch me," he says, in his homely but expressive language, "and I'll scratch you; but I won't scratch you if you won't scratch me." Hitherto the squire has had no direct interest in scratching Hodge—now he has a very direct one indeed. His whole political future is in Hodge's hands. Hodge can send him to Westminster as a knight of the shire, or he can outvote him and send the "carpet-bagger" in his place. Now, I think it cannot be denied that the squire is far more responsible for their present strained relations than Hodge. Hitherto Hodge has never been in a position to do the squire a service, perhaps if he had been he might have neglected the opportunity. That is possible, but he can claim the benefit of the doubt. On the other hand, the doubt will not assist the squire. He has been in a position to do Hodge many services, and he has neglected the opportunity—an effort of self-denial, no doubt, but a fact nevertheless. Unfortunately squires, like virgins, vary in intelligence ; some are wise, some are foolish. Virgins seem to be better off in this article than squires, for amongst them the wise and the foolish are equally divided, whereas amongst squires the foolish certainly predominate.

Take the " cow and three acres," the " quadruped and the tri jugera," for instance. Every wise squire and every intelligent Hodge knows, that in this climate, and with our soil and existing agricultural values, it is.impossible; but if it is impossible, why should the squire stick himself like a lion in the path to oppose it ? especially as he must have known his opposition was needless. A live lion that can roar and lash his tail, might keep the path, but a live lion stuffed with straw would go over at the first kick, and that unfortunately was the position of the squire at the last election. The foolish squire said " The cow and three acres is a sham, and I will never be a party to imposing a sham on Hodge. I love him too much. I will stand like a lion in the path." Foolish squire ! The cow " went for " him, like the donkey at the Aquarium, and knocked him over. On the other hand, the wise squire says : " This three acres and a cow is a sham ; but it amuses Hodge, and it can't hurt me, and if it leads to any improvement in Hodge's condition I shall be very glad. How can I expect Hodge to vote for me if I deliberately vote against him ?" If the advice of the wise squires had prevailed, if they had supported the principle of the " cow and three acres," or if they had proposed some alternative scheme, they would have got Hodge's vote. They would have taken the wind out of the carpet-bagger's sails and dropped them astern. Unfortunately, the wise squires were in the minority, and Hodge's vote was lost. It is ridiculous for the squire now to turn round on Hodge and accuse him of ingratitude for voting against him. Hodge is not a bit more ungrateful than his neighbours. Like his neighbours he looks to see on which side his bread is buttered. As he finds the carpet-bagger has put lots of butter on one side, and the squire has put none at all on the other, he naturally prefers the former. Never was there such a complete transfer of political power ; never was there such a leap into the dark. The land-owners had some knowledge and experience. The tenants had also some knowledge and experience ; but the labourers had no knowledge and experience. or at least very little ; and, therefore, our wise men have taken all power from the landowners and tenants, and given it absolutely to the labourers. Whether it is wise, or just, or fair on the community to disfranchise knowledge in favour of ignorance, whether it is wise or just, or suicidal, it is too late now to inquire—*actum est*. Right or wrong, it is an accomplished fact. The good of the country has never been the question : it has been solely and entirely a question of party tactics. Feeble-kneed Whigs and rampant Radicals combined to disfranchise the landowners and tenants in order to dish the Conservatives and get office. And they have succeeded. But now comes the Nemesis. The "feeble knees," who only wished to dish the Conservatives, now find to their dismay they have dished themselves also. "Good God," they say, "we only intended our agricultural Orson to club the Tories, and now he is beginning to club us also." "Yes, indeed," says the triumphant Radical, "of course he will. We knew this long ago, and were only afraid you would find it out before you were committed too far. How you were such fools as not to see it we can't understand. However, it is all right now. You, my dear credulous Weak Knees, have very kindly taken the chestnuts out of the fire for us, and now we have no further use for you. May the devil have you in his good keeping." Silly Whigs! What is the use of bleating now? it only excites ridicule. As you placed yourselves in the hands of the shearer you had better be dumb. But to return to our muttons, or to our friend and Master Hodge. The squire has to recover Hodge's vote from the carpet-bagger. He has to prove to him that "Codling's his friend, not Short." How is he to do it? It is certain he can do it if he sets about it the right way. Owning the land, living in his midst, more or less understanding his wants, he has it in his power to be fifty times more useful to Hodge than the carpet-bagger who lives in London, or Manchester, or Liverpool, can ever be. But he will have to take some time and trouble about it, and put his pride in his pocket. But he must do it. It is of no use his becoming suddenly effusive, holding out both hands, and saying, "Welcome, dear Hodge, to the franchise. I have always tried to give you the vote, and now that I have succeeded in doing so, I hope you will give it to me." Hodge will again have recourse to his agricultural vocabulary, and mutter "Gammon." But if he says to him, "Good Hodge, I never thought you fit for the franchise, and so I never tried to give it to you; but now you have got it I don't grudge it to you. Let us see if we cannot work together for our common good," Hodge may listen to him. Hodge is practical and does not like a prig. He wants something more substantial than good advice. What he wants is intercourse, sympathy, and generosity, the helping hand, with something in it now and then. His burdens are heavy to bear—occasionally intolerable. At these times the man who assists him to bear them, whether squire or carpet-bagger, is his true friend. This is the business of the squire. He deserves no commiseration for it, but he deserves political extinction if he leaves it to the carpet-bagger. Hodge is very recognisant of kindness. It was proved beyond any doubt at the recent elections, that in every case in which the squire was resident, and in which he or his family had shown any sympathy with Hodge or his family—in fact, in every case in which Hodge had come to the conclusion that the squire was his friend he plumped for him and let the carpet-bagger slide. This does not look like want of gratitude; it looks like common sense. The recent election in the counties was the victory of the Dissenting minister and the labourer over the established minister and the squire. If, therefore, the tables are to be turned at the next election the squire must get the Dissenting minister as well as Hodge on his side. How is he to do it? Happy thought. The Primrose League. This mighty organisation has always been a mystery to me. I neither could understand its origin or comprehend its object. Now I see it all, and am in amazement at my own stupidity, and at the prescience of its founders. "Wherever any particular herb grows," says Sancho, "there is the ass to eat it." Wherever the Dissenting minister grows there must come some dainty Dame or Damoiselle of the Primrose League to nibble him up. Happy Dissenting minister! Victorious Primrose League! Of Sidney Smith's three sexes— men, women, and parsons, it is evident that Providence intended the women to subjugate the parsons. The Dissenting minister is certainly not exactly like the minister of the Establishment: but the difference is chiefly in exteriors. He is a parson all the same. He may be stern of aspect, but he is amenable to female influences, or he is not a parson. I feel convinced the Dissenting ministers are destined to go down before the Dames of the Primrose League. But then it is of no use the Dames purring in their own Habitations. They must become a militant body, they must attack the enemy in his stronghold. Every Dame and every Damoiselle must mark down a Dissenting minister, to whose conquest she must devote her time, and the perfection of her Siren art, with eyes, with phrases, with braces, with slippers, in the drawing-room, at the squire's table, on the lawn-tennis ground, in the school-room, in season and out of season, at his going out and his coming in they must attack their enemy. He must have no peace—

> " Till the stern parsons, gulled by acts like these,
> Grow gentle, tractable, and tame as geese."

If they do this their success is certain, they need not expect any very violent opposition; on the contrary, I am inclined to think their enemies will rather like it. " I am only a man, or at any rate a parson," says the Dissenting minister; " don't be afraid of me ; don't suppose I am anything very superior. Only treat me as you have treated my Established *confrères*, and be assured you will find me equally tractable. I have not yet tried the squire's port wine and three-year-old mutton, but I have an internal conviction that I shall like them very much when I do; and as for worked slippers and braces they have been the dream of my life. I may be a little awkward at first at lawn-tennis, my shoes generally creak, and my tread is heavy, and insect life flies my approach, and I am quite aware that I don't look lordly without my coat and waistcoat. But who knows, fair Dames, better than you what a transformation your graceful coaching will effect ? My action will improve, I shall skip like the roe, my tread will become so elastic that even the ' azured hare-bell ' will not suffer; and perhaps, who knows, I may in time employ a London tailor." What a promise this confession opens out. And when, at the next general election, each Fair Knight shall lead to the poll a captive Dissenting minister, then, indeed, the glorious mission of the great League will be accomplished. The squire will enjoy his own again, and the carpet-bagger will be up a tree.

1885.

THE HORN OF ASTOLPHO.

M ERCURY was the god of Eloquence and of Deceit.

> To Mercury Autolycus she brought,
> Who turned to thefts and tricks his subtle thought :
> Possessed he was of all his father's sleight,
> At will made white look black, and black look white.

Venus, Bacchus, and Mercury, some cynic tells us, compose the Pagan Trinity that share between them the worship of civilised mankind, but, powerful as are the two former, I am inclined to think that the most powerful of all is Mercury ; for do not mankind pass the greater part of their lives in deceiving and being deceived ? To doubt the omnipotence of Eloquence is absurd, but it would be very easy, I imagine, to prove that it has brought more ill into the world than good. "L'eloquence est une espèce de friponnerie," says one of the subtlest of philosophers. "C'est l'art de surprendre les hommes : c'est une manière delicate de les séduire." This is why some of the wisest of mankind have so mistrusted the power of words. Pythagoras taught his followers to love "silence, retirement, and contemplation." When Carneades, the most eloquent man in Greece, came to Rome on an embassy, Cato, the censor, demanded that he should be immediately sent back, "because it was very difficult to discern the truth through the arguments of Carneades." He apprehended danger to the public conscience from the wit and strength of argument with which he made "white look black and black look white ;" one day proving that justice was right, and the next day proving that justice was wrong. Moreover, the ancients understood that the talent of eloquence is seldom combined with great wisdom. Demosthenes was twenty times as eloquent as Aristotle, but Aristotle was twenty times as wise as Demosthenes. Eloquence is irresistible, omnipotent ; it even deprives its worshippers of common sense. The Athenians, we are told, would rather hear Alcibiades speak, even when he was drunk, than hear anyone else. His speeches had the effect on them of the enchanted horn of Astolpho that when it was sounded made mad all who heard it. But human nature does not change. There are hundreds of thousands in this country now who would rather hear Mr. Gladstone than anyone else, though, as Cato said, they "find it very difficult to discern the truth through his arguments," and know that he is for the most part only engaged in a dialectic delight of making "white look black and black look white." What else but the sounds of the Enchanted Horn could have compelled the people to rave as they have done during the past five years, shouting for justice one day, for injustice the next ; for war to-day, for peace to-morrow ; for humanity and inhumanity ; for honour and dishonour ; for economy and extravagance, almost in the same breath ?

It is said when lovers swear Venus laughs. I am sure that when Mr. Gladstone orates Mercury must laugh at the success that attends his duel art—Eloquence and Deceit. Various and versatile as have been many of the great masters of rhetoric, or eloquence, or verbosity, or whatever it is called, none have ever approached Mr. Gladstone in the facility with which he can almost at the same moment "make white look black and black look white." He appears to be under the influence of some "Dual Control:" to be constituted like Millie-Christine, the two-headed nightingale, with two heads, two voices, two hearts, and two souls: one soul that (we were told eight years ago) requires a good deal of looking after, and another soul that evidently is perfectly able to look after itself. The conclusion is inevitable that there are in reality two Mr. Gladstones, and it is only enchantment that makes us fancy there is only one. There is the Mr. Gladstone who reads the lessons, and the Mr. Gladstone who gives delightful dramatic breakfasts; the Mr. Gladstone who hurries to morning service, and the Mr. Gladstone who hurries to the theatre; the Mr. Gladstone who denounced the Bulgarian atrocities, and the Mr. Gladstone who inspired the Soudan massacres: the Mr. Gladstone who declared in Parliament that the authority of the Crown must be asserted in the Transvaal, and the Mr. Gladstone who immediately scuttled out of the Transvaal: the Mr. Gladstone who declared the Madhi must be smashed up at Khartoum, and the Mr. Gladstone who is now scuttling out of the Soudan: the Mr. Gladstone who ten days ago declared the book of the Penjdeh incident could not be closed without an explanation, and the Mr. Gladstone who has now apparently closed the book without any explanation at all: the Mr. Gladstone who has bit by bit pulled to pieces the foreign and Imperial policy of Lord Beaconsfield, and the Mr. Gladstone who is now, bit by bit, piece by piece, trying to put it together again, &c., ad infinitum. Is there anything that one Mr. Gladstone now supports the other Mr. Gladstone has not before opposed? and is there anything that one Mr. Gladstone now opposes the other Mr. Gladstone has not before supported?

Mr. Gladstone's Jingo speech is described as the best he ever made; as having, indeed, fairly taken the House by storm. But what raised this enthusiasm? The earnestness with which he urged the members to do their duty. Not a bit of it. It was the earnestness with which he assured the House that he would do his duty. They really believed the time had come at last when his "Yes" actually meant "Yes," and his "No" actually meant "No." How miserably they have deceived themselves the last twenty-four hours has shown them. Praising Mr. Gladstone for his skill in making a speech is very much like praising Mr. Roberts for his skill in playing the spot stroke at billiards. Apparently he can't help it: neither can Mr. Gladstone. Long practice has made speech-making as easy to him as playing the spot-stroke is to Mr. Roberts—in fact, he can't help it. A man who feels very proud when he has delivered himself of half a dozen consecutive sentences, listens to the rolling river of Mr. Gladstone's oratory with enthusiasm: every succeeding speech he declares is the most splendid he has ever heard. And so the man who "fancies himself" uncommonly if he can make three consecutive spot strokes, watches Roberts make 150 consecutive spot strokes with enthusiasm, and declares each stroke the best he has ever seen. Why Mr. Gladstone's admirers should have been so delighted with this speech I cannot imagine. There is nothing very grand or very heart-stirring in seeing a venerable statesman of seventy-five don the white sheet of repentance, and make as complete a recantation of his entire policy as it is possible for any man to make. For what do Mr. Gladstone's words mean when translated by common sense?—Gentlemen of the House of Commons, when I turned out the Tories five years ago I had no foreign policy, none whatever. Foreign policy is the one thing, the only thing I believe, that I do not understand : but I was inspired ; I decided at once to adopt as my foreign policy the exact and complete antithesis of the foreign policy of Lord Beaconsfield, and I remember with what enthusiasm you cheered my decision. I found Lord Beaconsfield had taken steps to punish the insult offered to the British Crown, and the treacherous murder of British Troops in the Transvaal, so I immediately withdrew the troops from the Transvaal. I found Lord Beaconsfield, at great cost, had arranged a scientific frontier that would safeguard the gates of India, so I immediately abandoned it, retired from Candahar, and sent the railway plant to Jehanum. I found Lord Beaconsfield had cemented most friendly relations with Turkey, Austria, and Germany, so I at once insulted Austria, put pressure on Turkey, cold-shouldered Germany, and made most gushing advances to France and Russia. In all this I followed the advice of a very clever lady, who I felt understood these questions far better than I did. I know my enemies argue that because I have now sent troops to South Africa ; am rebuilding the railway to Quetta : am about to re-occupy Candahar : have, hat in hand, sought the friendship of Germany and Austria, have shaken hands with those odious Turks ; am rebuilding bit by bit, stone by stone, the structure of Lord Beaconsfield's policy that I have with such labour and cost pulled to pieces, that therefore my policy has been a failure. But this is only because they do not understand it. Believe me, my foreign policy has been and is an absolute success. You, my advanced supporters, have always maintained that the proper position of England is that of a third or fourth rate Power ; that the burden of her present empire is too great for her to bear. "Perish India," "Let the Colonies go," have been your cry. I have never contested the reasonableness of your views ; but it has always appeared to me a question of grave difficulty how England could descend from the perilous position of the first Power in Europe, to the safer one of a third or fourth rate Power, without going through the ordeal of war or revolution. But I think if you will consider the events of the last five years, and carefully examine the position we are in now, you will see that without war—for you know that I deny emphatically that we have been at war in Egypt and the Soudan, "military operations" is the term I insist upon—or revolution, we are already entering the haven of our hopes. The skill with which I have retired England from the perilous position of being the head of the Great Powers of Europe to the far safer one of a third or fourth Power is a page of our history that must, I am sure, command your admiration. You will easily understand that the task was not an easy one. I was quite aware that, in spite of my five years' rule, the odious spirit of Jingoism was still rife in the country. I knew the change could not be accomplished suddenly without exciting that contemptible spirit of ignorance and prejudice that fools delight to call the " Pride of Race : " the people have yet to learn that the real value of defeat in diplomacy or war is to teach us we are not humble enough ; but, as I have told you, I was inspired, and it occurred to me that if I could get on bad terms with the Great Powers of Europe, and with one after another get England between the horns of a dilemma, in which she must either fight or apologise, my object would be gained. I knew a little gentle pressure from you would always make fighting impossible, when apology would come as a mater of course. Fortune favours the brave. The colonial question gave us an opportunity of quarrelling with Germany. At the proper moment we apologised. The *Bosphore Egyptien* incident gave us an opportunity of quarrelling with France. At the proper moment we apologised, and apologised, too, I am proud to say, in a spirit of humility that England has never adopted before. The Penjdeh incident gave us an opportunity of quarrelling with Russia, and already we have amply apologised and have referred our just rights, or the just rights of our ally, to our good friend the King of the Sandwich Islands and the Mikado of the Savoy. Naturally after each apology we heard the now familiar phrase, " Friend, go down lower," and each time, without shame, we began to take a lower place. Five years ago we were first amongst our comrades at Dame Europa's School. In the most natural way in the world, almost without a struggle, in fact, we have gone down till we are now in the secure position of fourth boy. Could Machiavelli himself have done better ? Of course, my advanced Radical Friends, I appreciated at its real value the cheering that greeted my great speech about Herat. The Jingoes cheered, because, when they expected to hear only the hated voice of Jacob, they heard again, or fancied they did, the loved voice of Esau. You, my friends, cheered because you knew that though the voice might on this occasion sound like Esau's voice, it was indeed the very voice of Jacob ; and you were right. Did the subtlety of Jacob exceed mine ? The Jingoes cheered because they thought that the £11,000,000 would go to increase the army and navy : but, be assured, as little as possible shall be wasted in ships and guns : we have better uses for it ; and, moreover, secure in the position of a fourth-rate Power, relieved from the burden and responsibilities of empire, with neither India, Ireland, or Colonies to excite our anxiety, we may fairly hope that the storms and rivalries that at all times affect the peace of a first-class Power may rage with impunity over our heads, and that, in company with Belgium, Holland and Portugal, we may henceforward represent the non-combatant portion of the European family.

1885.

A RESPONSIBLE STATESMAN.

"HUMPTY Dumpty sat on a wall," &c. Now there is no doubt that a short time ago Humpty Dumpty did sit on a wall, and, equally, there is no doubt he does not sit on it now. His enemies say he has had a great fall, and that he will never sit on the wall again ; that all his horses and all his men will never put him back again ; for one very good reason that they do not intend to try. "That is sheer blasphemy," say his friends. How can Dumpty the Infallible, Dumpty the Inspired, Dumpty the Semi-Divine ever fall ? He may have descended from the wall for strategic purposes ; but fall, never ! Semi-divines never fall ; but, nevertheless, there are reasons why many people think that his friends would rather see him off the wall than on it. Infallibility and Inspiration are all very well when things go right, but are of no use at all when they go wrong, and even in the best regulated families things so easily go wrong. Now I do not think Mr. Gladstone will get on the wall again. I believe this is his final fall, and I'm sure I hope it is. I believe the Empire can only be saved by his keeping off the wall. Much is forgiven in a party leader ; but to break up the party, with a large majority, three times in a few years, is not forgiven. It becomes tiresome. It suits no one. Of course he assures his friends that he will soon be back again, more powerful than ever. But many look upon this as nothing more than the irrepressible confidence of age. The fact is certain that if Mr. Gladstone determines that he will never retire, he must sooner or later fall. He cannot go on for ever ; but even if this is his final fall, it is not sudden. It has long been recognised as inevitable. He has listened too eagerly to the ridiculous assurances of his flatterers that he could do anything. He began to think that, like the famous inventor of the axe, he could fly ; but it was evident to all that if he tried he would come to the ground with a bump, and he has done so. He thought he could carry the people with him in a *coup d'état*, and rush the country into revolution ; but the people declined to be rushed. His *coup d'état* has failed, and when a responsible states-man tries a *coup d'état* and fails it is a serious matter for him. He spared no efforts to succeed, but he failed—failed absolutely. Cer-tainly during the last five years the belief of most educated people —the despicable classes, as he considers them—in Mr. Gladstone has been very much modified. The feeling in the country about him is not at all what it was. Somehow or another, the gilt has come off the gingerbread. The Egyptian War did it. The extraordinary indifference, and even cheerfulness, with which he heaped disgrace after disgrace on his country—beginning with the bombardment of Alexandria, and ending with the desertion of Gordon—the blood-guiltiness and wanton cruelty, the immense cost, and the utter and complete failure of his policy in every detail, induced people to ask themselves whether he was still a responsible statesman—whether he was in his right mind—whether he "understood judgment," and knew what was going on? And then it was whispered, in his defence, that he did not know what was going on. That it was considered better not to tell him anything that would worry him. His fall was inevitable, as inevitable as Cæsar's. He was no longer a party leader, he was Imperator. It was I and my Cabinet, I and my Parliament, and he consulted one just as little as he consulted the other. It was no longer party government but autocratic government; and the one condition necessary, absolutely necessary, to autocratic government is success —failure kills it at once. Well, Mr. Gladstone's autocratic government brought failure after failure, each one was more disgraceful and more alarming than the last. When the criminal attempt was made to wash out the blood of Gordon in the blood of thousands of Soudanese who had never seen him, or heard of him, the public conscience was deeply hurt; the cup of national shame flowed over. Those who ran could then see the handwriting on the wall that foretold the fall of an incapable Minister.

It is the inevitable fate of everyone who lives long enough that sooner or later he must begin to *radoter*—struggle as he may, sooner or later he must reach the point where great age impairs judgment, and induces him to say and do silly things. Well, to many of us—in fact to most educated persons, those horrid classes again—it has come home as a sad but undeniable fact that Mr. Gladstone has begun to *radoter*. There is nothing wrong in saying this; it must come to all men. Neither infallibility nor inspiration will prevent the dot-and-go-one stage, mental and physical, overtaking us all. Happy is the man who recognises the inevitable, and retires from action with his colours flying. When Mr. Gladstone wrote his two articles last year, the "Dawn of Creation" and "Genesis," observing people shook their heads. "Cela sent la Radotage," they said. No man who had not begun to *radoter* would have ever put his name to such a tissue of folly and fallacies. Good natured, and indeed unwilling, critics made it evident to every one that Mr. Gladstone did not know the simple A B C of natural science, and that he had distorted facts and misquoted authorities in order to bolster up impossible views. Like Le Sage's immortal Archbishop, he no doubt honestly believed that the "Dawn of Creation" was the most brilliant and convincing article he had ever written. "Learn, my young friend," said the Archbishop to Gil Blas (who ventured to hint that his sermon *sent l'apoplexie*, and that he should think of retiring)—"learn that I never composed a more brilliant homily than the one that has not your approbation. My wit, thank Heaven, has yet lost nothing of its vigour." But the public thought otherwise. "Mr. Gladstone," they said, "has begun to talk and write nonsense—he is no longer a responsible statesman." The (Political) Rake's Progress to Home Rule points a moral, but scarcely adorns a tale. Three years ago he denounced Mr. Parnell as steeped in treason to the very lips, and imprisoned him without trial because he advocated Home Rule. He imprisoned 1.000 persons, men and women and children, without trial, because they advocated Home Rule. He passed the severest Act of repression against Home Rulers ever known in Ireland. He was on the very point of asking Parliament to renew this Act when he went out of office. He threw over Mr. Forster. He was reported to be going in for Home Rule. He indignantly denied the charge. His friends were furious that such a shameful report should be circulated. It was declared by them to be impossible. Whilst his friends were still denying the possibility of his becoming a Home Ruler he declared for Home Rule. Thereupon his friends immediately declared for Home Rule too. He declared he had always been a Home Ruler, and his friends at once declared they had always been Home Rulers too. He denounces Mr. Pitt as a blackguard, and the Act of Union as a second massacre of St. Bartholomew. His friends denounce Lord Hartington as Judas. He receives a deputation of Home Rulers at Hawarden Castle. He describes himself as a " humble individual " (ye gods !) " dwelling in his humble private residence " (how the devil must have grinned !). He complimented the gentlemen he had denounced as steeped in treason to the very lips and imprisoned without trial on their " singular moderation and temperance of expression." " Threats of force, gentlemen, have not proceeded from you," &c. (here Mercury, the god of deceit, burst into a laugh). He promised Home Rule to Scotland and Wales. He denounced the English. Repudiated Liverpool as his birthplace, and declared himself to be entirely of Scottish blood. He denounced the selfishness of the classes, and held them up to the hatred of the masses. At present there is a pause. He is editing his explanations, but he would be a sanguine man indeed who would say he has no more arrows in his quiver. Most men would have found it rather awkward to explain away the speeches, and arguments, and denunciations and ridicule of 50 years. But Mr. Gladstone did not find it awkward—not a bit of it. He can explain anything away. When it was proposed to marry Garibaldi to a rich Englishwoman it was objected that there was an impediment, that he had already got a wife. " Oh, that does not signify," said Lord Palmerston, " Gladstone will explain her away." In this case he boldly took the bull by the horns. His explanation was very simple. He was not a Unionist at all. He had always been a Home Ruler. All the Unionist sentiments he had uttered for 20 years were false. God only knows what it had cost him to utter them. But now *liberari animum meum*. Thank God he was free. The situation required decision. He had two horses in the race, " Infallibility " and " Veracity." He declared to win with Infallibility, and Veracity was not persevered with. Never have words been so unscrupulously employed to conceal thoughts ; never has veracity been so cynically repudiated. It is the most stupendous public deceit that has ever been practised or attempted. That of the Claimant was a joke to it. He claimed to be a baronet, knowing all the time that he was the butcher's son ; Mr. Gladstone claimed to be a Unionist, knowing all the time he was a Separatist. But the one imposition only lasted 10 years ; the latter through a long life. It was shocking, almost brutal, but it did not answer. It gave every one a shock, set everyone's teeth on edge.

Explain as he may, the fact still remains that if he has been a
Home Ruler for 20 years, for 20 years he has been living with a lie
on his lips. " Il y a des mauvaises examples qui sont pires que des
crimes ;" and here was one of them. We have not had long to
wait to see its demoralising effects.

> " With other echo late I taught your shades
> To answer, and resound far other song,"

Mr. Gladstone says to his followers. " Yes, you did, certainly,"
they reply, " and we thought your echo was true, but now we find
it was not, that all the time you were preaching Union to us you
were cherishing Separation in your heart ; but it is all right, we are
Separatists now, always have been, like you, don't you see ?" (with
a wink).

But it is not the apparent want of veracity in these gentlemen
that is so startling; it is their extraordinary effrontery. Lord
Hartington still repeats the echo Mr. Gladstone taught him, and
because he does so he is received by those turn-coats with cries of
Judas ! It may be a very good masher's joke to call the man who
shows you an example of honour, honesty, and self-respect, Judas ;
but in this case it does not seem to apply. Judas betrayed his
Master ; but here his master betrays Judas ! There is no doubt
of it. Lord Hartington stood firm to the principles and professions
of his master, and his master ratted, ratted abominably ; beyond
example past or present. A few years ago Mr. Gladstone illustrated
the absurdity of the demand for an Irish Parliament by the argument
that if Ireland had a separate Parliament Scotland and Wales
should have separate Parliaments also. Now he is prepared to
grant separate Parliaments to all three. But now London puts in a
claim, and London has three to one the population of Wales. How
can London be refused ? The fact is that separate Parliaments, as
now advocated by Mr. Gladstone, means disintegration of the
Empire—absolute, entire, complete. It would in a very short time
reduce a great United Kingdom to a very small dis-United States.
People are beginning to understand this at last—very slowly, it is
true, but fast enough, I hope, to save the Empire.

The fact is that the prospect of Mr. Parnell as uncrowned King
of Ireland, of Mr. Gladstone as uncrowned King of Scotland—and
who shall we say ?—the members for Northampton, perhaps, as
uncrowned Kings of England and Wales, is not a view of national
felicity that fills all hearts with joy. Cicero relates of Carneades,
the Greek orator, that out of hatred to the Stoics he not only contradicted the rest of the Academics with regard to the *summum bonum*,
or Supreme Good, but even contradicted all that he had ever said
on the subject himself. All his life Mr. Gladstone has maintained
that the unity of the kingdom was the *summum bonum* of national
existence. Can it be true, as is supposed by many people, that it is
only his bitter, sour detestation of the Tories that induces him to
contradict all that he has ever said, and argue that the *summum
bonum* of national life is in Separation ? Of course, every public
man is more or less of an actor. Mr. Gladstone is more of an actor
probably than any public man that ever lived. He is miserable
when he has not got an engagement, and he has to pass a day

without appearing before the footlights.. He can play a great
number of characters, from Plato to Pecksniff, and from Cicero to
Catiline. There is only one part he will not play, and that is an
unpopular part. He always plays to the gallery, and the moment
he sees his part is not popular with the gallery he chucks it up,
even though it is in the middle of a run. In these matters he
consults nobody's interest but his own. It has become a necessity
with him to hear Demos purr every day. If he misses this treat,
he, like Titus, feels he has lost a day, and he tries to arrange for a
double purr the day following.

Many people have wondered what can have been the cause of the
extraordinary accession of bitterness and recklessness that has
marked the political utterances of our responsible statesman during
the last year. Why has he become so bitter against England?
Why has he so deliberately encouraged class animosities? "The
embers of hatred, which have been cold for years," says Mr. Goldwin Smith, "are rekindled by the religious statesman for the
purpose of exciting the hatred of Scotland, Ireland, and Wales
against England." This is true—absolutely true—but why does he
wish to excite the hatred of Scotland, Ireland, and Wales against
England? Is it only because England has disappointed his vanity
and his ambition? Scotland, Ireland, and Wales played into his
hands, but the English trumped his game. He seems to have
come to the conclusion that the fact of 86 Irish members having
given him their votes was more than a sufficient cause for breaking
up the Union between Great Britain and Ireland, and he was very
angry with the English because they did not think so too.

If the masses had followed the advice of our responsible statesman, the country would now be in the full swing of revolution.
For the time we have escaped the storm, but undeniably he has
sown the whirlwind. How are we ever to believe him again? How
are we ever to know what he really is at any one time? For 20
years he has been loudly professing Union principles, and now tells
us that during all that time he has been a Home Ruler! In one
sentence he extols the greatness and unity of the Empire, and
exhorts all classes to work together for the common good; and in
the next he advocates separation, and urges the masses to shake
themselves free from the selfish tyranny of the classes! And Mr.
Gladstone is a responsible statesman! What does he mean! The
voice, indeed, is Cicero's voice, but the hand is the hand of Catiline.
The clouds are very threatening, but yet there is just a little bit of
silver lining. Hitherto Mr. Gladstone has periodically declared he
would retire, and he has babbled about green fields, and repose, and
all that sort of thing: but the more he babbled the less he seemed
inclined to go. Well now he has dropped all this, and at the age of
nearly four score he declares he will not retire. I really believe this
means that he intends to go.

1886.

AARON'S ROD.

AT length we hear the solemn tones of the "Voice that breathed o'er Hawarden." It is a lugubrious strain certainly, and decidedly monotone : but we are told it celebrates the wedding of Whigs and Radicals, and sends them on their way rejoicing to spend their honeymoon in the "Paradise Regained" of office. It makes one, indeed, more inclined to weep than to rejoice : but nevertheless it comes as a relief. It is not an hour too soon. The "stump" is played out. The political priests on both sides have exhausted their stock of misrepresentations and satire ; they have, in turn, "cast down each man his rod," and there they are darting about all over the place, in every direction, some more or less venomous, some perfectly harmless. But nobody has taken much notice of them, because everyone knows that the Great High Priest himself must sooner or later cast down his rod, which will immediately begin to swallow all the rest, and it is of no use taking interest in any particular rod that we know is on the point of being swallowed by some other rod. Well, he has done so. He has cast down his rod, and a most enormous serpent it has become, probably the biggest on record. Many think that it is too heavy and too unwieldy, and will never be quick enough to swallow up the other rods. I think so, too. I don't believe Aaron's rod will swallow all the rest. The position of the Great High Priest of the Radicals is a very exceptional one. Twice in ten years he has indulged in the excessively foolish and puerile amusement of taking off his shoes before he was going to bed : in other words, he has twice thrown up the sponge when he might have won the fight. He has twice relinquished office when he had more than a necessary majority to keep it, and on each occasion that he has voluntarily resigned office he has tried to resume it again the next day. Now surely this is acting more like a spoilt child than a serious statesman. If it was any other man, the Liberal party would be angry ; they would say : "our leader is like Hannibal, he throws good dice but does not know how to use them" ; he gains victories but does not profit by them ; he is the grandest advocate possible, but the worst possible judge. This is what they might say, and what in any other case they would say. What they do say is this. Our leader is very unreliable ; he throws down his cards when he has the game in his hands ; he turns us out of office unexpectedly, but he brings us back in triumph quite as unexpectedly ; he has what no other man amongst us has—the ear of our masters ; he is the withy that binds all our troublesome sticks together ; with him we are strong, without him we go absolutely to pieces. And this is quite true. Thrice in ten years Mr. Gladstone has wielded the axe that has brought the Liberal majority to the ground, but nevertheless on each occasion the Liberal party has, like the sandal tree, shed perfume on the instrument of its destruction.

The situation is a very complicated one. The Radicals openly advocate a radical reconstruction of everything—a complete transfer of the governing power. The Whigs desire to avoid all Radical reconstruction—to keep the governing power where it is ; to follow a policy, in fact, in all things moderately Conservative. The aspirations of Whigs and Radicals are indeed as opposite as the Poles—divergent, and every hour more diverging. The only person that can make the resultant of these diverging forces work for the good of " the Party " is Mr. Gladstone. " Opifer per orbem dicor," he says to Whigs and Radicals. I am the great Liberal Physician ; come to me and I will put you in office again. And they go after him straightway as an ox goeth to the slaughter ; or shall we say rather, " as a fool to the correction of the stocks." The party *mot d'ordre* at present is that there is not and never has been any real split in the Liberal camp, but this apparently leaves them on the horns of a dilemma. If there was no divergence of opinion two months ago, why on earth did they throw up office with a majority of 70 ? And if there is no divergence of opinion now, why do Lord Hartington and Mr. Chamberlain hum such strangely different tunes. There is a split no doubt, and the only possible cure for it is to resume office, and the only possible way to resume office is to assemble under the umbrella of Mr. Gladstone. Mr. Gladstone at this moment stands between Plutus and Plebs. He says to the former, " I am for the rights of property, for primogeniture, the Church, and everything you care about ; but remember Plebs has a vote, and to secure that vote we must dissemble." He says to Plebs, " I think, and I have always thought, you ought to have a great deal more of everything that Plutus has got than you have got ; but remember Plutus is timid—Timidus Plutus the poets always call him—and he has got a vote, and to secure that vote we must dissemble ; " and therefore " to dissemble " is the necessary policy of the hour. It is rather illogical, certainly, to throw up office without any sufficient reason one day, and to make any sacrifices of consistency or conviction to regain it the next ; but such are party politics. In office the Whigs think they can dish the Radicals ; in office the Radicals think they can dish the Whigs. Out of office the Radicals can do very little ; they cannot make landlord soup till they have caught their landlord, and they cannot sell the Church's skin till they have killed the Church, and to do both, or either of these things, they must be in office. " To everything there is a season," we are told, "and a time to every purpose under the heaven. There is a time to embrace and a time to refrain from embracing." Well, this is the time for Whigs and Radicals to embrace under the great umbrella.

The Liberal programme is to kiss and take office again, and from a party point of view, and of course the party view is the only one professional politicians can afford to take, it is simple common sense. The situation admits of no other. There is little doubt that it will recommend itself to all who follow politics as others do the church, the bar, the army, medicine, trade as a profession. But what will Plebs say ? That is the question. They may argue in this way : " We don't benefit personally by your return to office. You fortunate sons of Levi divide the contents of the fleshpots amongst yourselves, but don't give us any. We therefore go for those who promise to give us most, or who, at least, we hope will give us most. You, Mr. Gladstone, tell us that we ought to have a great deal more of everything that Plutus has, but you do not tell us exactly how we are to get it. You lead us to suppose your sympathies are with us, with partition, Disestablishment, and all that sort of thing, but that you are restrained by certain great economic laws. Now Mr. Chamberlain also tells us that we ought to have a great deal more of everything Plutus has ; but he goes further than you ; he tells us exactly what we ought to take, and how we are to take it. He entirely agrees with your theories, and, as he does not regard the great economic laws that restrain you, he actually points out to us how we should put your theories into practice. There is no difference between you, except that you prefer theory to practice ; he prefers practice to theory. You must not be surprised if, when the squeeze comes, we, as practical men, prefer the man who is prepared to act to the one who is contented to preach. In following Mr. Chamberlain we are in reality only trying to realise your hopes and wishes. ' A snatch from behind a bush is sometimes better than the prayers of good men,' and a snatch from behind Mr. Chamberlain's orchids will most probably secure us what we want much more quickly than your pious aspirations." Now, Plebs may say this, and very likely will, and if he does I do not see what Mr. Gladstone can say, or any of his followers. Without any doubt whatever his indefinite promises and exhortations have created immense expectations amongst the people. To catch the popular applause of the hour, as many think, he has somehow or other encouraged the desire for your neighbour's goods. To a certain extent it is his child. He cannot now put it on one side. It is rather awkward. But though the Manifesto has summoned all good Whigs and Radicals to the great umbrella, the game between Whigs and Radicals is not being satisfactorily played out. Accidents will happen in the best-regulated families, and in the Radical family an accident has happened, regretted, I believe, by all men of good feeling on both sides, that has deprived the Radicals of one of their most stalwart champions. As we all know, there is a great difference between a boat propelled by one man with a pair of sculls, and by two men with a pair of oars :—

> One doctor singly likes the sculler plies,
> The patient struggles, but by inches dies ;
> But two physicians, with a pair of oars,
> Waft him right swiftly to the Stygian shores.

Well, the Radical boat, instead of being propelled by two physicians with a pair of oars, is only sculled by one doctor singly. He is sculling away very pluckily no doubt, but it is a different affair, and he may not stay the course. It may be an excellent thing for the patient, however ; it may actually give Nature a chance, and he may steer clear of the Stygian shores altogether ; but it certainly for the time conceals from the country the true strength of the Radical party. I don't think Mr. Gladstone's elaborate apology for the absolute smash up of his foreign policy will influence many of his followers, either Whigs or Radicals. The " Please, mum, it's the other cook's fault " excuse becomes tiresome when we remember that the last cook left our service five years ago. She must, indeed, have bewitched all the pots and pans and demoralised the marmitons if all the horrible cooking and frightful messes of the last five years are still her fault. This new gospel of original sin is, of course, very convenient. It releases us from all responsibility for our actions. " My grandfather stole a duck 50 years ago, and therefore I am not to blame for stealing a chicken now—the blame rests entirely on that wretched old man who stole the duck 50 years ago." Time apparently has nothing to do with original sin. This may be very convenient in private life, but it is very inconvenient in the public service. Really, the heads of the parties should meet together and fix a " Statute of Limitations " as to when the responsibilities of one Minister must end and that of another must commence. According to the Hawarden Manifesto, Providence and Lord Beaconsfield are responsible for all the disgrace, and ruin, and slaughter, and extravagance of the last five years, more especially for the desertion of Gordon. It will surprise many of us to hear that Providence and Lord Beaconsfield were on such exceedingly friendly terms. I always understood that Providence resided permanently at Hawarden, and that it was quite another influence that was paramount at Hughenden. The only meaning of the apology that I can discover is this—that the Devil and Lord Beaconsfield got us into a horrid mess, and that Providence and Mr. Gladstone have made it ten times worse.

1886.

A "BALLON D'ESSAI."

YOUR readers all know what a *ballon d'essai* means. Well, this is one. I send it up in order to test the current of public opinion ; but balloons are very unsatisfactory. Like adults, they seldom do what they ought to do, and very often do what they ought not to do—or like spoilt children, refuse to do anything at all. Sometimes they travel with immense rapidity to the very point they are desired to go to, at another time they travel with equal rapidity to the very point they are desired not to go to, and sometimes they decline to travel in any direction whatever. They are painfully human. I am quite aware that in sending up my balloon I shall be reproached with bad taste, and shall be reminded that "Fools rush in where angels fear to tread," &c. And this, no doubt, is perfectly true as regards the angels and the fools ; but we must remember that the fools are the vast majority, that flats are born every minute, whereas angels' visits at the best are only few and far between. It is certain that if the fools always leave the initiative to the angels, the world will make very little progress in any direction, and besides, in this world, at any rate, the fools represent the men, and the angels the women ; at least, I don't at this moment know of any male angels except those little unfortunates who found it impossible to accept the Virgin's polite invitation to be seated—mais madame—nous n'avons pas de quoi ! —and as my balloon has particular reference to angels, perhaps they feel a delicacy in taking any direct part in the discussion. However, it is no use wasting any more time in preliminary remarks. My balloon is inflated. I have only to cut the string to let it go : and now at the last moment, let me confess that I fear I am treading on delicate ground—so delicate that probably only a fool would venture on it. But in whatever direction my balloon is carried by the breath of public opinion, I wish it to be distinctly understood that it is not a war balloon charged with ill-will to any person or nation, but essentially a peace balloon, freighted with goodwill towards men, and especially towards women.

The heir presumptive to the Throne of England has attained the age at which Royal Princes usually enter into the state that is especially described as "Holy," and many millions in and out of the British Empire are asking each other, "Who will he marry ?" "You should take a wife, sir," said a certain famous physician to a certain famous wit. "By all means," was the prompt reply, "but whose wife shall I take ?" This reply at the expense of that great fulcrum of modern society, "Other People's Wives," was rude, and the O. P. W.'s ought to have resented it, but they didn't. "You should take a wife, sir," John Bull may some day say to his presumptive Sovereign. "By all means," may be the prompt reply, "But where am I to find her ?" But here comes in my *ballon d'essai*—What will public opinion say? In which direction does England wish her future Sovereign to look for a wife? Of course all sensible people hope that when his Royal Highness does marry he will marry the object of his choice (object is the expression used in such cases, though when you say a lady is an " object," admiration is not always understood). But unfortunately for his Royal Highness the trammels that hedge in the Heir to the British Throne in the selection of a wife are very irksome, and I think very unreasonable ; whilst almost every other man in the world may marry whom he pleases (the Lord of Burleigh a dairymaid, King Cophetua a beggar maid, &c.), the Heir of the Throne of England must marry where he is advised. He is, by law, probably more restricted in the choice of a wife than any other person in the world. Is it not our duty to assist him in every possible way, and make his matrimonial burden as easy as we can ? At present the wife of the presumptive Heir to the Throne must be Royal or Serene, Royal for choice, and she must be a Protestant, and thus by a stroke of the pen, nineteen-twentieths of the Royalties and Serenities of Europe are scratched for the Royal Stakes. Hitherto, as we know, the Royal Family of England has sought and found husbands and wives amongst the Royal and Serene Families, great and small, of Protestant Germany, his Royal Highness the Prince of Wales's most fortunate selection being the one conspicuous exception.

I do not decry the German alliances. On the contrary, I admire the German character and nation very much, and I think it has grafted well on the Anglo-Saxon stock, but there is no doubt that there is a feeling in the country that there is already German blood enough in our Royal Family ; and it is, moreover, undoubted that the creation of the German Empire has made a great change in the rank and power of the Royalties and Serenities of Protestant Germany. They have sunk considerably more into a subject position. A Grand Duke or Prince in Germany is now just as much a subject of the Emperor of Germany as an English duke or earl is a subject of the Sovereign of England ; and the question naturally occurs to many of us if our future King may marry a subject in Protestant Germany, why may he not marry a subject in any other Protestant country ? The question is entirely one of common sense. Have not the growth of nations and the march of events rendered it desirable that the Heir Presumptive to the Throne of England should seek a matrimonial alliance outside the Royal and Serene families of Protestant Germany? That is the question. The English-speaking races number now over 80,000,000 of people. Cannot our Prince find a fitting bride amongst them ; one who speaks the English tongue ; has old English blood in her veins ? Of course he can—thousands !

Amongst the 80,000,000 of the Anglo-Saxons of our race there are thousands of women who for beauty, and wisdom, and nobility of nature would have graced the throne of the Great Alexander himself. It would be inconvenient, we are told, for his Royal Highness to marry one of his own subjects—English, Irish, Scotch, Canadian, Australian, New Zealand, or Hottentot. (I believe we already have a Hottentot countess.) This may be so. I cannot say; but, granted it is so, can there be any objection whatever to his marrying an American?

Again, I ask, and this is the object of my letter, why should not Prince Albert Edward marry an American, always supposing he wishes it—*bien entendu*? The Americans are a great people, a tremendous people, a wonderful people. Their empire extends from ocean to ocean—from pole to tropics. Their great eagle spreads his wings over the whole earth. Their great snapping turtle—but I forget, all this relates to American men, and our subject is a far more charming and attractive one, it is American women. Well, eagle and snapping turtle aside, are American women worthy of this wonderful race of men? Are they indeed? Does anyone doubt it? Why, yes, certainly they are, and a great deal worthier, too. Comparisons are always odious, and very dangerous, too, where ladies are concerned, so we will keep off the delicate ground, at any rate. But I think this much may be stated without fear of the consequences, that if the three goddesses—Europe, Asia, and America (I think the Hottentot goddess may be omitted from this competition)—were to contend for the apple, the last named would not be the last to catch the "Speaker's" eye—I mean the eye of the modern Paris. Without presuming to make any comparisons of female attractions throughout the world, it is certain the American women are very charming—very charming, indeed, and very clever; charming and clever, not only in the eyes of Englishmen, but of all nationalities. Charming and clever enough to monopolise half the diplomatists of Europe; charming enough and clever enough to adorn any throne in the world.

The French have a pretty little conceit about their pet, the Parisienne. They say that when the good fairy who served out female attractions to all the daughters of Eve, complexion to the German, grace to the Spaniard, expression to the Italian, &c., had exhausted all her treasures, an attractive little figure came tripping up and asked for her share. "And who are you, dear?" said the fairy, rather surprised. "Oh, I'm a Parisienne," said the little lady. "I am so sorry," said the Fée, "but I have given everything away to your sisters, I have actually nothing left." This caused great grief to the petitioner, so much so, that the good fairy took pity on her, and calling the other recipients of her bounty together, put it to them whether, as she had been so generous to them, they would not give a portion of her gifts to the little stranger, which they agreed to do. They each gave her a share of the Fairy's gifts, and so they made the Parisienne who, we are told, combines in a sufficient degree all that makes woman-kind delightful. The Americaine was not present when these good things were being served out, for the very good reason that "in that good fairy's time she hadn't been invented yet," but she was quite equal to the occasion. She had no idea of being left out in the cold. Like those fine old Milesian families who had a boat of their own at the flood, she got a fairy of her own, and told her to take the Parisienne for a model, and see if she could not improve upon her, hence the Americaine. Whether the American fairy was successful in fulfilling the instructions of her fair client, I must leave to better judges to decide, but there is no doubt that both original and copy are very nice. Many of your readers no doubt have heard a very irresistible champion in the lists of beauty recite the story of the only Royal alliance that, as far as I am aware, has yet been celebrated in America. I am bound to say it is not encouraging. " Better luck next time," as the dentist cheerfully remarked when he found he had pulled out the wrong tooth and proceeded to pull out the right one. A certain crowned head, from a kingdom that shall be nameless, came on earth to find a wife. First he visited England, where he found the ladies very charming, and he was just going to deliver himself into their hands when something induced him to try France. In Paris he found them still more delightful, and again he was on the point of offering his hand and his—I was going to say heart, but I suppose this article would be rather *de trop* where he came from—when he again changed his mind, and went to New York. Here he found absolute perfection—no drawbacks at all. He came, saw, and was conquered ; proposed, was accepted ; married, and—even perfection has a thorn somewhere— in a month he wished himself back in his warm, and, we will hope, comfortable (as so many of our friends seem bent on going there) home. Whether his bride accompanied him I don't think we are told. Probably she would prefer going to Paris.

But the Americans are not Royal we are told, nor Serene, not even noble : but noble is as noble does. Those who act nobly are noble though they are not even born so, and those who act ignobly are not noble though they can prove that their ancestors actually scrubbed the boots (they used sand paper in those days instead of blacking) of William the Conqueror. We hear a great deal in diplomatic circles of tangling alliances, and it is quite certain that in these unsettled days it would be very easy for our Prince to form an alliance that might ere long become tangling in the way the bramble is tangling. If he married an American he would form an alliance that might become tangling, too ; but it would be in the way the honeysuckle is tangling, binding together the two great English speaking nations of the world in its firm and fragrant coils. It is a pretty conceit, but actually not an exaggerated one. Would such a marriage bring about a closer intimacy and alliance, and a sense of common interest between Americans and English ? Would it make both nations realise that " blood is really thicker than water?" I believe it would. I believe that 50,000,000 (more or less) of people in America would hail with enthusiasm the prospect of one of Columbia's daughters sharing the throne of England, and I believe 34,000,000 in England would welcome with delight a Queen of their own blood, and breed, and speech.

From the stand of *haute politique*, is not this a subject deserving the most anxious and earnest thought of the nation? Can any other question be more so ? England and America are the two great divisions of the Anglo-Saxon race. If such an alliance would bring them into closer union and concord, is it not worth striving for ? Can any other alliance offer us such fair prospects ? We are told that the British Monarchy and British institutions are at their decline. It may be so; but the end is not yet. Certainly this year has seen incitement to revolution, a hounding of class against class, of the masses against the classes, that recalls the days of Catiline; but somehow or another, the powder only fizzed, the explosion did not take place. I suppose the public saw there was something not quite square when they recognised in the chief agitator against the classes the owner of a castle, the largest landed proprietor in his county, who has created more peers and drawn more public money than any politician living. The Americans are Republicans, and Republicans they will always remain, but Republican spells order and security in America, in England, as yet, it only spells revolution. It seems a contradiction, but it is a strong probability, that in the not distant future, the monachy of England may find its strongest support in the Republic cf America.

1886.

MY AWFUL DAD.

NO, it is not a joke at all—it is not a *mauvaise plaisanterie* in any way; it is an actual fact, that what England has been suffering from for the last six years, and is suffering from now, is the astounding indiscretions of her oldest statesman. He is the last of the past generation of statesmen; but he has a greater facility for getting into scrapes than the whole of the present generation rolled into one. In the words of one of his former colleagues, he is one of

> Those very persevering bricks
> Who bustle on at seventy-six.

His mental vivacity is phenomenal, his erratic impulse unaccountable, his capacity for scrapes illimitable.

Every succeeding year seems but to place him in a position of greater freedom and less responsibility. From the period of the Bulgarian atrocities to the present moment scrape has succeeded scrape, indiscretion succeeded indiscretion with bewildering rapidity, till at last he has out-Heroded Herod—actually out-Gladstoned Gladstone—by throwing up his hat for Home Rule. Irresponsible statesman! Perplexed England!

It is incredible. How will it all end; or, what is of more importance, who will it end? Him or the country? One must positively go. I think the country will stay the longest. Mr. Gladstone is again too late. It is too late for him to disestablish the Church : too late for him to break up the United Kingdom. He is too old.

> The game of life has got no nicks
> For him who plays at seventy-six.

In nine hundred and ninety-nine cases out of a thousand we are accustomed to see age restraining the impetuosity of youth; but in this sensational instance we see youth trying in vain to restrain the impetuosity of age. " Don't be in such a devil of a hurry, my dear boy," is the usual injunction of age to youth. " Who goes gently, goes safely." Instead of that, we hear youth on all sides calling out, " For God's sake, old man, don't be so rash. If you don't mind, you'll break your neck, and ours, too." Now, there is no parallel to this extraordinary rejuvenescence (except the case of the notorious Doctor Faustus, and there is a flavour of brimstone about him that is disagreeable), and it is so entirely contrary to all human experience that we are taken aback. We don't know where we are. An old head on young shoulders is bad enough—it generally means a prig, or something disagreeable; but the head of 20 on the shoulders of 76 is positively uncanny and dangerously misleading. As a rule, we listen to the voice of age without question. It is a case of misplaced confidence indeed when it proves to be only the irresponsible verbosity of youth. Every man becomes more

Conservative, or Preservative, as he grows older ; it appears to be a universal law of nature. Time has taught him that man is not infallible, not even the youngest—that there were strong men before Agamemnon, and wise men even before himself. We have no experience to guide us in dealing with a statesman whose belief in his own infallibility and whose contempt for past experience increases in geometrical proportion with his advancing years. And now can any of your readers explain the "Dual" mystery of Hawarden ? At Hawarden are Mr. Gladstone *père* and Mr. Gladstone *fils*, and recent events show us that occasionally these two are apt to get mixed. A true believer consults the oracle of Hawarden. "Oh ! " he exclaims with ecstasy, "That is the voice of Mr. Gladstone." "No, it is not," replies the attendant priest, rather sharply, tor he has heard the same mistake very often before, "it is the voice of Mr. Herbert." He listens again. "Oh ! that is the voice of Mr. Herbert," he says, somewhat disappointed. "No, it isn't," again replies the unsympathetic priest, "it is the voice of Mr. Gladstone." "Why, confound it," says the true believer, now really angry, "which is which ?" "I only wish you would tell us," answers the confused and now confounded priest, "we often don't know ourselves." And, indeed, who does know ? It is the old story. The voice indeed is Mr. Gladstone's voice, but the hands are the hands of Mr. Herbert. This "confounding the person and dividing the substance " is indeed very confusing and very inconvenient, as the Leeds journalists have discovered to their cost. Now, no doubt there are some of us who are content to follow Mr. Gladstone, and some of us who are content to follow Mr. Herbert ; but I cannot conceive it possible that the being exists who would be content to follow the two combined. Some of Mr. Gladstone's friends say he is pining for retirement, for religious meditation, for classical absorption, and all that sort of thing, and is only kept on the treadmill of party strife by the ambition of his surroundings. Other of his friends, on the contrary, say that his surroundings do all they can to induce him to seek the peace and repose that are necessary for his health, and which eight years ago he so passionately claimed as his right, but that since the elections such a fierce desire to return to office has taken possession of him, that they are helpless to restrain him. Possibly both statements are true, or neither of them, and it really does not much concern the outside public. What really does concern them very closely, what indeed they have apparently an actual right to know, is how much that emanates from Hawarden is inspired by Mr. H. Gladstone and spoken by Mr. W. E. Gladstone ; how much is inspired by Mr. W. E. Gladstone and communicated to the press by Mr. H. Gladstone.

The most disappointing and distressing feature of the condition "greater freedom and less responsibility" that influences Mr. Gladstone in his old age is the increased indifference—even dislike —it appears to develop in him for the institutions of his country. Certainly he never has said much in their favour during his long life, but of late years he has not had a good word for any of them. On the contrary, he is always on the look out for weak places ; and of course old institutions, that have stood the wear and tear of

centuries whilst all around have been swept away, must have many
weak places, and when he has found one he does not attempt to
mend or strengthen it, but sets to work tooth and nail to make it
worse and expose it to the censure of the world. " Your image is
made of gold and silver and brass," he says to us, " and no doubt
it is a very imposing image ; but after all it is a sham, its feet are
only iron and miry clay, and I will smite the image upon his feet
and break them in pieces, and then the iron, and the clay, and the
gold, and the brass, and the silver shall be broken in pieces together,
and become like the chaff of the summer threshing floors." It
really looks as if this is to be our fate. Mr. Gladstone is already
preparing to smite our image on the feet, to pick out the iron from
the clay, to cut the withy that binds the Imperial sticks in the bundle.
He will give independence to Ireland, and Scotland, Wales,
Australia, Canada, and India will soon take it for themselves ; and
the withy will be cut and the bundle will fall to pieces, and the
débris of the great British Empire will soon be as " the chaff on
the summer threshing floor." This is really no nonsense, no mere
nightmare—it is a fact, as certain as that the sun will set to-night,
that if Mr. Gladstone is given *carte blanche* to try his destructive
experiments on the unity of the kingdom, it will be the beginning
of the end. I see Mr. Gladstone has written what is called a
" Proem : a plea for a fair trial," on that unfortunate slip of the
pen, " The Dawn of Creation."

> So gloz'd the tempter and his Proem proved,
> Into the heart of Eve his words made way.

More than they will do into the heart of Professor Huxley, I
imagine. Does it never occur to him that the United Kingdom,
the British Empire, may also claim its " Proem," may also put
forward a " plea for a fair trial ? " If England is under a cloud
now, if other nations sneer at her and point the finger of scorn, and
laugh at her sham professions and infirm actions, at her glorious
flag trailed in the dirt, her honour forfeited, her noblest son
deserted and left to a cruel death, whose name do they connect
with this disgrace ?

Twice Mr. Gladstone has tried to govern the British Empire,
twice he has failed ; and now he is mad with the desire to try a
third time. But the third time may be fatal. Of course, the fault
of failure was not his ; it was the fault of our institutions, and
therefore they must be remodelled to suit his requirements. A bad
workman generally finds fault with his tools. I have no doubt
that if Alexander had failed to ride Bucephalus, he would have
declared he was a brute, and would have sent him to a hack cab, if
there was one in those days.

I often hear it said that political morality is very shady ; but
granting it is as black as it is painted, I suppose there must be
some line beyond which the most licensed may not step. And in
the face of the recent elections it is really interesting to ascertain
where this line is. " Hodge, my boy, here's a cow and three acres
for you, if you only vote for me." " Socialist, my fine fellow, here's
' Ransom ' and ' Restitution ' for you, if you only vote for me."

" Dissenter, my advanced Christian ' chappie,' here's £200,000,000 of Church property for you, if you only vote for me." And now that these offers have fallen short of the expected result, the word has gone forth to the Home Rulers, " Only vote for me, and you shall have anything you ask, even to the half of the kingdom." A man was playing at cards, when he suddenly seized a fork and drove it right through his opponent's hand as it rested on the table, with the remark, " If there is not a card under your hand, I beg your pardon." If I have mistaken Mr. Gladstone's action, if there is no card under his hand, I beg his pardon. All I can say in excuse is that as far as I can hear or read, my impression is the impression of nine out of every ten of those who are spectators of the game. Alexander's courtiers, we are told, considered it criminal to doubt the success of his enterprises ; and so do Mr. Gladstone's. " We will not allow him to be judged by any known standard of political morality," say they ; " his conscience is the only standard that we, or he, recognise. It is very elastic, and answers every possible purpose." Therefore, as far as Mr. Gladstone is concerned, we are evidently out of court. But suppose we make the experiment on someone else. When Lord Salisbury found that England, Ireland, and Scotland had refused him a majority, suppose he had chalked up Home Rule ? and had openly and without disguise said to Mr. Parnell, " Give me your vote and I will give you Home Rule," would there not have been one universal hiss from one end of the empire to the other, and would not the Radicals have hissed loudest of all ? Of course they would ; I hear them now. There have been famous surgeons amongst us who were so proud of their operations that they never thought much of their patients. So long as they cut off arms and legs with more grace, or more speed than their rivals, they were content ; they never inquired whether the patients lived or died ; and so enthusiastic was the admiration of the students for their skill, that they never told them the fate of the patients. And indeed, if they had, the great operators would not have listened —their business was to operate, not to heal.

This is the practice of Mr. Gladstone ; his business is to operate, not to cure. He performs a brilliant operation, makes half a dozen splendid speeches, dismembers his patient with extraordinary skill and celerity, and sends him away, whether to live or die is not his business. That is somebody else's business. If the Irish Land Act has proved an absolute failure, if it has satisfied no one, if the land is far worse cultivated than before, if it has become completely unsaleable, if the judicial rents are unpaid, it does not concern him at all. He performed a brilliant operation, that was his part of the business ; if the patient has since died, that is somebody else's business. He is now turning up his sleeves, and preparing for another tremendous operation that must be attended with great danger, and will probably result in death ; but we are assured he is in excellent spirits. Are the hundreds of thousands of Irish Loyalists who look forward to civil war as the inevitable result of his recklessness, are the landowners who will be ruined, also in excellent spirits ? Somehow or other I think I should feel more confidence in the surgeon if I saw some signs that he realised the tremendous responsibility of what he had undertaken. " What a wonderful man is Mr. Gladstone," say his admirers, "to have settled Home Rule and the Inspiration of Genesis at the same time. He is a whole head and shoulders taller than anyone else!" But suppose he makes as great a mess of Home Rule as he has done of Genesis ; why, he will be a greater prodigy still, as great, perhaps, as the fabled Anthropophagi, who carried their heads beneath their shoulders.

1886.

THE POLITICAL BAR-SINISTER.

WHIGS may protest as they like, but it is a fact that hence-forth two lines drawn from what heralds term the "sinister chief to the dexter base point" will deface many of their political escutcheons. How can it possibly be otherwise? In all morality —turf, social, or political—you must draw a line somewhere, and the political morality that has resulted in this "Cabinet of conver-sion" is altogether *hors ligne*. It is far beyond anything that the most elastic political conscience has ever before conceived possible, and if it becomes general all reliance on the word of public men will cease. No one, of course, is surprised at the sudden conversion of Mr. Gladstone. In such matters he is certainly *hors ligne*, and always has been. All his life he has been courting conversion of some kind or another. We have long since discounted every possible aberration of that phenomenal mind. We know that he always moves more or less in circles, like

> "A fly that turns about
> After his head's cut off to find it out."

If he became a Mussulman or a Protectionist to-morrow, it would not excite any more surprise than his becoming a Home Ruler and Socialist did yesterday. For twenty years his one dominating desire has been to stroke Demos in order to hear him purr. At any cost to the country he must be made to purr, and, moreover, he must purr to him and to nobody else. It is a necessity of his nature. Just now he has got it into his head that Home Rule in Ireland and confiscation of land in England will excite this pleasant murmur. That is the situation. "When the monkey reigns, dance before him," says the Eastern proverb, and now that the reigning Minister "goes in" for Home Rule, the weak-knees who form his court dance before him to that tune; but it is a sad thing to see so many nice fellows rushing violently down this steep place into the sea of Socialism and surrender, in which they must perish. Converts delight to pose as superior persons. Why, I could never make out; certainly most of us prefer consistency to conversion. They enlarge on the shame of their past, and the glory of their present condition

> " I do not shame
> To tell you what I was, seeing my conversion,
> So sweetly tastes, being the thing I am."

But for all that, they know the public is a little suspicious of sudden conversions. "What does he mean by it?" asked Talleyrand when he heard that a distinguished diplomatist was taken suddenly ill. "What does he mean by it?" we naturally ask when we see a politician turn suddenly round on all the principles and pledges of his life. If his conversion means personal sacrifices, we give him credit for honesty of purpose ; but if it means honour, promotion, and money, we don't give him any credit at all. No doubt the conversion of Lord Spencer is as genuine a miracle as the conversion of St. Paul, but it was a long time before even St. Paul overcame the suspicion of honest men. "Is not this he that destroyed those that called on this name in Jerusalem, and came hither with that interest that he might bring them bound unto the chief priests?" So that Lord Spencer and those who have followed his lead must not be surprised if for some time their conduct is viewed with very general suspicion. I should indeed think the country was bewitched if it was not so. St. Paul, moreover, lost everything by his conversion —our recent converts gain a great deal by theirs. I believe this sudden conversion of Lord Spencer to Home Rule is the most complete *volte face* ever performed by any politician in any age or country.

If Alva had put himself at the head of the Dutch Republic, Cromwell led the Cavaliers, or Prince Rupert charged at the head of the Roundheads, it could not have given a greater shock to consistency than Lord Spencer leading the Home Rule party. Six weeks ago every Whig in the country denounced Home Rule and ridiculed the "Cow and Three Acres." May I ask if there is one Whig who in his heart believes in them now? Not one! Is there not, then, something more than suspicion, rather fishy in fact, in these instantaneous conversions? "Oh, it is Mr. Gladstone's influence," they say; "his commanding personality," &c. It is Mr. Gladstone's influence, no doubt, that has worked this miracle ; but not Mr. Gladstone as Mercurius, for he has not made a single convert by his orations in favour of Home Rule, but Mr. Gladstone as Plutus; as the patron of salaries and honours. Where is the Whig who would have called out for Home Rule if he had not got office, or hoped to get it, by doing so? And echo answers, Where? I believe there is scarcely a weak-knee who has joined Mr. Gladstone's Government who is not more or less sorry for himself, and already wishes he was someone else. It may perhaps be a consolation to him to know that this feeling is very general in the country. They were in great haste to take office, but they have gained nothing by their haste. They have paralysed moderate Liberalism in the present House of Commons, they have strengthened the forces of Socialism and disruption, and they are called the "Bread and Butter" party, that's all. The "Bread and Butter" interest, we are told, is more fully represented in this Government than in any former one.

For years the Whigs have been complaining that their leader gave them no lead, and there was some truth in what they said, but now, at least, he has given them a lead, which everyone in the country knows is the only lead that is consistent with honour and duty ; but led astray by the specious arguments of a few hardened old official hands, who cannot conceive that any ridiculous ideas of principles or professions should baulk them of office, they have declined to follow their leader, and have taken office with Mr. Gladstone. Lord Hartington says, "I will not oppose Mr. Gladstone, if I can help it ; but I understand he is pledged to Home Rule, and to the compulsory occupation of land, and this is such an entirely fresh departure for me, so completely opposed to every profession of my faith, that I cannot at once spring to it. If Home Rule and confiscation are necessary, let someone else carry them out; I am not the man." Does not every honest Whig feel that Lord Hartington has selected the path of honour and truth? Why, then, have they not followed him? It is all on account of that infernal bread and butter. "Make your fortune without committing any wrong" was the authorised version of morality; "make your fortune with committing as little wrong as possible" is the revised one. The weak-knees prefer the revised one. I do not blame them. Certainly it is much more convenient. Midshipman Easy's mother was shocked to find the wet nurse was not married. "Please ma'am, it was such a little one," urged the poor girl in extenuation; and now if you are rather shocked at your friend taking office in a Government of surrender and disruption, he replies, "Oh, it doesn't signify, it is such a little one." But the size of it makes no difference. Stealing a lamb is no more excusable than stealing a sheep. If you do sell your conscience to Mephisto it is better to get a good price for the article. Looking at the situation merely from the standpoint of self-interest, those Whigs who against their consciences have been in such a hurry to take the Government shilling have done a very foolish thing. The present Government cannot last; it is impossible. There are even more square men in round holes, more extinct volcanoes, more useless "pumps" in this Government than there were in the last Liberal Government. (I must apologise for the expression "pumps," it is very vulgar, but very expressive.) When Mr. Gladstone left office there was a very general hope that some, at any rate, of the old "pumps" would be put on one side. No such luck. They are all back again; newly painted, it is true, and in new places, but sucking wind as much as ever. It is related that when Mohammed was being lifted up to Paradise some of his attached friends, old official pumps, no doubt, clung unto his cloak as their only chance of ever reaching the Houris. But the prophet was equal to the occasion; finding their company undesirable he whipped out his knife and cut them adrift, and let them down with a run. Human nature is the same in all ages; a certain number of old pumps now cling to Mr. Gladstone's skirts, in the full conviction, and they are quite right, that that is their only chance of regaining office. Why can't he follow the example of Mohammed and cut himself free? It would be an immense relief to the country. This is a Government of guarantees. Mr. Parnell gives guarantees to Mr. Gladstone, Mr. Gladstone gives guarantees to his followers, and his followers give guarantees to their own consciences; but as Mr. Parnell's guarantees to Mr. Gladstone are worth nothing, so Mr. Gladstone's guarantees to his followers are worth less than nothing, and their poor consciences are left out in the cold entirely. But what is the meaning of these guarantees? You don't ask a written guarantee from your host that his wine won't give you the stomach-ache, or from one of Cunard's captains that he won't run his ship ashore. Why, then, should those who take office under Mr. Gladstone ask him for a written guarantee that his policy won't stink in their nostrils? It is absurd. The only object of these guarantees is to protect weak-kneed gentlemen from the consequences of their own acts. They are doing what their consciences tell them is wrong, so they seek to shelter themselves under guarantees that their common sense tells them are nonsense. They want an excuse for taking office, and they find it in a guarantee. It is very simple.

It is the old story, " Fain would I climb, but that I fear to fall." How amazed or how furious the Virgin Queen would have been if Raleigh had asked for a guarantee against accidents! Some day—and that day, apparently, is not very far distant—when the conjuror shows his hand, the weak-knees will bring back their bags of money and cast them at the feet of Messrs. Gladstone and Biggar and Co., and say, " We have sinned." And what answer will they get but the mocking one, " What is that to us? See thou to that." They will have served the purpose for which they were induced to take office. The mischief will be done irremediably. But it will not end. When they see what they have assisted to do—that a free Ireland means a subject England; that the first rumour of war with France, or Russia, or America means 150,000 Irishmen in arms, and every harbour a safe rendezvous for the privateers, and fleets of our enemies, they will perhaps regret that they had not gone and hanged themselves before they put their hand to such a work.

1886.

HAWARDEN SURPRISES.

A MONTH ago you heard everywhere, "Have you read 'The Dawn of Creation?' Mr. Gladstone maintains that Homer shares the inspiration of Moses." "Of course he does," exclaimed the true Gladstonian, "of course he does. I always said so." "Have you read the manifesto from Hawarden?" was in everybody's mouth three weeks later; "Mr. Gladstone has declared for Home Rule." "Indeed!" said the true Gladstonian, a little startled. "Have you read the Proem to Genesis?" was the inquiry everywhere heard last week. "Mr. Gladstone has overthrown Christianity." "Has he though?" gasps the true Gladstonian, as if all the breath was knocked out of his body. In a few days we shall hear—"What do you think? Mr. Gladstone declares the earth is square, and the moon is made of green cheese. "Of course he does; of course he does," will exclaim the true Gladstonian, relieved beyond the mere expression of words to find that Mr. Gladstone has returned to mere speculative studies. Indeed, the kaleidoscope itself cannot compete with that protean mind—even the unforseen cannot keep pace with it. "What is your religion?" asked an inquisitive nobody of a very great somebody. "The religion of all wise men," was the reply. "But what religion is that?" persisted the inquisite nobody. "Ah," replies the great somebody, with a scarcely suppressed chuckle, "that is what the wise men never tell." And so the inquisitive nobody was very properly sold. Now the most inquisitive and most impertinent of mankind would never presume to ask Mr. Gladstone, or anyone else, what his religion was, if, after the habit of wise men, he showed any disposition to keep it to himself; but when he stands up in our midst and preaches to us in Gladstonese, we are excused for asking, indeed we are bound to ask, for a translation. No doubt it is a method of induction especially Gladstonian to exalt the Mosaical inspiration by reducing it to the level of the Homeric inspiration. For if Moses was inspired, why not Hesiod? Why not Anaximander? Why not Keppler? Why not Newton?—

> Nature and all her works lay hid in night:
> God said, "Let Newton be," and all was light.

Why not Darwin? Why not every one the Almighty has in His good time placed on a pinnacle of wisdom, above his fellows, to announce to them the great tidings of eternal truth? Of course everything is possible in this world of ours, and it is quite possible that Moses and Homer received their inspiration from the same source; but it is undoubtedly a thousand to one they did not. It is a fact that they were separated by a period of 700 years, and that through the whole of the Iliad and the Odyssey the name even of the Jews is not mentioned; but this is a chapter of ancient history so obscure and so fanciful, to most of us so childish, that if it amuses Mr. Gladstone to say it is so it is scarcely worth while to contradict him. His reference to Christianity in his " Proem," however, is a totally different affair. It is not ancient history at all—it is present history, a very burning question indeed, so burning that a very few centuries ago it would be a question of a tarred shirt, a few faggots, and a stake. Mr. Gladstone's treatment of Christianity in his " Proem " is certainly one of the most contemptuous assumptions that I should think had ever crossed the lips of responsible man. "It may be," he coolly remarks, "we shall find that Christianity itself is in some sort a scaffolding, and that the final building is a pure and perfect theism." What, then, have we Christians for the last 1,900 years been mistaking the scaffolding for the final building ? For 1,900 years Christianity has been the great beacon light of the world, shining down from the realms above, and now, A.D. 1886, we are told for the first time that what has been the object of adoration and hope to countless millions of mankind is, after all, only a scaffolding, that will be taken down and put away out of sight when the perfect building is completed. What then will become of the souls of those countless millions who, for 19 centuries, have been bowing down to the scaffolding instead of to the perfect building—to the shadow instead of the substance ? And what, after all, is this perfect building to be when it is fully revealed to us ? What is this pure and perfect theism ? It is Deism, or Theism, or Unitarianism, or Buddhism, or Mohammedism, or Gladstonism, or what ? When our scaffolding is removed, who is to explain to us the glories of this brand new building ? Of course it will be indignantly denied that Mr. Gladstone has ever said a word against Christianity, and of course I must allow that he often does speak in language it is impossible to understand ; but if this sentence, " It may be we shall find that Christianity itself is in some sort a scaffolding, and that the final building is a pure and perfect theism," does not mean that, in Mr. Gladstone's views, Christianity is the scaffolding of the past and Theism the perfect building of the future, what does it mean ? Perhaps some student of Gladstonese will translate for us.

1886.

ENGLAND EXPECTS EVERY MAN TO DO HIS DUTY.

" From ship to ship the signal ran,
England expects that every man
This day will do his duty,
For England, home, and beauty."

SO signalled Nelson on the fatal 21st of October, and so wrote
Dibdin, and so sang Braham. It has a very inspiriting ring
about it, and even now gives one rather a choky sensation.
" I have done my duty ; I thank God for it," were his last words,
and none nobler ever issued from the lips of dying man. But is
the spirit dead that made heroes of Englishmen in action, or in the
Senate? I believe not. Just now their minds are so obfuscated
and confused by false doctrines, by sophistry, and hair-splitting,
and Jesuitical refinements, that they cannot distinguish between
black and white, truth and falsehood, honour and dishonour, justice
and injustice, duty and self-interest, conscience and will, blood-
guiltiness and judicial slaughter, rebellion and a " nation justly
struggling to be free," &c. But they are mistaken who assume that
therefore the *pride of race* is dead. It is not. There is life in the
old dog yet. For twenty years the High Priest of Cant has been
educating Englishmen in his pernicious cult, assuring them black
is white and white is black with such an air of candour and conviction that at last they have given up all individual judgment in
the matter, and call black white or white black at his bidding, and,
what is worse, don't care twopence which it is. " Certa sunt
paucis." Truth is contained in a few words, and so is duty ; but
under the present dispensation it is impossible to extricate either
from the cloud of words and sophisms in which they are involved.
It is as difficult to define duty as it is to define beauty. It ought
not to be so, but it is. " Demandez à ce crapaud ce que c'est la
beauté, il vous repondrais que c'est la crapaude." To the hero on
the quarter-deck home and beauty meant Emma or Westminster
Abbey ; to the hero on the forecastle it meant Poll or Sue on the
Common Hard at Portsmouth. Ask one of the weak-kneed just now
what is duty, and probably, after tying himself into many moral or
immoral knots, he will tell you it is Mr. Gladstone. That is his
crapaude. In ordinary days, when black is allowed to be black and
white is allowed to be white, duty is connected with a certain fragile
or elastic article, called conscience ; but now conscience is nowhere, at least it is so hopelessly mixed up with will, with self-
interests, with party, and now with Mr. Gladstone, that it is
valueless even as ballast. It is moved from one thimble to another
with such perplexing rapidity that in a short time the owner himself actually does not know under which thimble to look for it.
Consciences, like horses, go in all shapes. There was a curious
example of this in last night's debate. It is usually accepted as a

fact, not worth contesting, that duty to country precedes duty to party, but a recent convert to Home Rule boldly congratulated himself on always preferring duty to party to duty to country! So, if it amuses him it hurts nobody else, but what I and many others would like to know is, what does he call his party? If he presumes to call that the Liberal Party from which Mr. Bright, Mr. Chamberlain, Mr. Goschen, Sir Henry James, Lord Hartington, the Duke of Argyll, Lord Northbrook, Lord Selborne, are excluded, he is like the "three tailors of Tooley-street" who called themselves the people of England.

However, we won't refine too much on this question of conscience. We won't dispute about the shadow of an ass. "Conscience makes cowards of us all," and no wonder when one actually realises what a costly luxury it is. Supposing a "weak-knee," or, indeed, a "strong-knee" either, by some process of reasoning actually realises what his duty is, is he to do it at any and every cost to himself? Is he not to be allowed to shift the line a little? He may, like the rich man in Scripture, be really anxious to do his duty, and he may hope to effect some convenient compromise. But it won't do. Whittle away as he like, listen to the voice of the charmer—or the tempter—as he will, he must at last come to the line that separates right and wrong. Of course, when he comes to it he can cross it if he pleases; it is entirely his own business. It is only when he insists that he has not crossed it, when everybody sees that he has, that it becomes other people's business. Poor fellow! it is very hard upon him, and he is very much to be pitied. He has just got his seat perhaps, spent a lot of money, spoilt his digestion in eating bad dinners, and cracked his voice in making bad speeches; and now he has got to do it all over again. Really it seems excusable, almost his duty, to save his pocket, his digestion, and his eloquence at the cost of his conscience! The artilleryman gave 50 reasons for not firing a salute, the last being that he had no powder. So the bewildered parliamentarian now gives 50 reasons for not doing his duty, the last being that he has not pluck! It is a very sufficient one.

"I know what my duty is," says he; "but really it is most inconvenient." So he appeals to his leaders for advice and assistance, and immediately he is supplied with 50 reasons, ready cut and dried, for not doing it. Never since England has had a Parliament, never in its most corrupt days, whether they were those of Charles, or James, or William, or Walpole, has there been so much lobbying, so many intrigues and underground influences; so many promises, bribes, and now threats, brought to bear on hesitating parliamentarians. "Do vote against your conscience," was the first *mot d'ordre*, "it will so please the 'old gentleman.' (Why is the 'old gentleman' so often invoked in this crisis?) He is bent on his Home Rule—he does so 'want to see wheels'—do gratify him—he is getting old—he won't trouble you long, and then you can undo it all again, you know," &c. "Don't break up the Liberal party. Duty before decency; party before country; Gladstone before all things" is the next serious admonition. Promises and soft sawder having failed now comes the threats—

" Now listen to me, my weak-kneed friend," says Mr. Schnadhorst,
" if you presume to vote against Mr. Gladstone and my Caucus you
will be a marked man ; we will wrest your seat from you ; we will
brand you as a political Cain, and everywhere you will be ostracised.
More than that, think of your country. If you ' corner ' Mr.
Gladstone, as you flatter yourselves you will, he will turn and rend
you. You do not know him if you think he will go down without
a struggle. Dare to humiliate him, to contradict him too much,
and you will see what manner of a man he is.

> ' His spirit, ranging for revenge.
> With Atè by his side, come hot from Hell.
> Shall in these confines with a monarch's voice,
> Cry havock, and let loose the dogs of war.'

We will loose all the Socialists, Republicans, Separatists, Faddists
at you, and every man Jack of you will be pulled down ; there will
not be one remaining. We will fill our Parliament with men who
hold to the simple and beautiful faith that there is one God, and
Gladstone is his prophet. And with such a Parliament how do you
think your country will fare ? One Parliament—the Schnadhorst-
Gladstone Parliament—will be called together, with the express
purpose of breaking up the Union between England and Ireland ;
but do you suppose it will stop there ? Have not India, Australia,
Canada, equally strong claims for separation, and do you suppose
we shall stop at Ireland ? This is what you may expect if you
drive Mr. Gladstone to dissolution," &c. This is no exaggeration.
This is the fate with which his lieutenants now threaten those who
prefer their duty to his imperious will. Of course it is arrant
nonsense.

Mr. Gladstone may collect together a Parliament composed of
the most extreme men, and they may rush the country on the road
to ruin faster than may suit even him, or he may not. My impression is that he will not, even if the political centre of gravity is so
completely shifted that the Extremists are in the majority. I do
not think they will precipitate the revolution to suit the party
exigencies even of Mr. Gladstone. And, indeed if the handwriting
is really on the wall, if the deluge is inevitable, what does it signify
whether it comes now or six months hence ? One more word to the
" weak-knees," I have done. They think that they can vote against
their conscience and escape detection, but they cannot. The fierce
glare of publicity is upon them. They must run straight, at least
it is plainly their interest to do so. Cicero, once wished that it was
written on every man's brow what he really thought of the affairs
of the State. Well, the kind and searching interest taken by the
party whips in the mental condition of the weak knees has almost
realised Cicero's wish. Virtually it is known what every man
thinks of the present question. It is too late for them to stick their
heads into the sand, and suppose they are invisible. It is a clear case
in which " honesty is the best policy." They are quite right to make
a merit of doing their duty, if they can, but they cannot escape
doing it without incurring disgrace. Under existing circumstances
it has become an act of compulsion. It is only a fool who insists
on finessing when his opponent knows his cards. Taking the most

material view of the question it is better in every way for the weak-knee to vote as all the world knows he thinks, than to vote as all the world knows he does not think. In the former case his constituents may reject, but will respect him ; in the latter they may elect, but will certainly despise him. " I think the Bill will unite England and Ireland more closely, and will do good to both, therefore I have voted for it," says the honest parliamentarian on one side : " I have done my duty. I thank God for it." " I believe the Bill will cause a ,separation between England and Ireland, and do harm to both ; therefore I have voted against it," says the honest parliamentarian on the other side ; " I have done my duty ; I thank God for it." But the poor " weak-knee," what will he say ? " I believe the Bill will cause separation between England and Ireland, and do harm to both, and therefore I have voted for it. I have not done my duty. I thank Mr. Gladstone for it." Poor weak-knees, they are in an awkward fix.

1886.

PLAYING WITH FIRE.

PLAYING with fire is a childish amusement, generally begun in folly, and generally ending in tears; but there seems to be some attraction about it, and certainly children are of all ages, and fire of all kinds, as we see every day. Two men came into the world at the same instant with silver spoons in their mouths. In one the silver spoon represents land, in the other it represents capital. In both cases it is the accident of birth. The fortunate possessor did not make his spoon; he was born so. But his spoon will grow or diminish with good or bad management. It may become either an *ecumoire* or the smallest of salts. Having got their spoons, what do they do with them? They both lend them. The former lends his land, the latter lends his capital. A customer comes to the capitalist and says, I want to borrow £1,000, for which I will pay you £50 a year. "All right," says the capitalist, "where is your security? We don't lend without security." A farmer comes to the landowner and says, " I want to borrow 100 acres of land with its buildings, fences drains, roads, &c., for which I will pay you £100 a year." Now, the 100 acres of land with its buildings, fences, roads, drains, &c., is worth £2,500, so that whilst the capitalist lends his spoon at 5 per cent., the landowner lends his at 4 per cent. We will suppose our friends with the silver spoons are both of them what are called "hard" men of business (and the "hard" man of business is quite as common in the City as in the country), who look upon a contract as an absolutely sacred and inviolable obligation. Well, the trader comes to the capitalist and says, " I invested the £1,000 I borrowed of you in what I supposed was a good business; but it has turned out a bad one, and your £1,000 is lost." "Very well," says the capitalist, " then I will realise your securities, and pay myself." " But," says the trader, "if you realise my securities in a hurry, I may lose half their value." " What do I care?" says the capitalist, " you should have thought of that sooner; a contract is a contract; my money or my bond, or I will make you a bankrupt *sans phrase*." And he does so. " I have farmed the land I borrowed of you to the best of my power," says the farmer; " but prices were so bad I have lost money, and cannot pay the £100 I covenanted to pay you." " Very well, then," says the landowner, " I will take back my land, and distrain for my £100." And he does so. Now, what is the difference between these two men, the capitalist and the landowner? Is there any? There is absolutely none whatever. To each of them the inviolability of contract is the very soul of their business life. But what do we see? We actually see the capitalist, who exacts his pound of flesh as a matter of course, denouncing the landowner for trying to exact his. Such an example of pot calling kettle black is too comical. In Ireland those who have borrowed land from the land-

owner have conspired together not to pay the rent they covenanted
to pay him, and, moreover, not to give him back his land ; and,
marvellous to relate, the capitalist actually pats them on the back
and encourages them in this repudiation. Now, if this is not playing
with fire, I don't know what is. Can anything be more ridiculous,
more completely sham ? Why, every single argument that can be
advanced to excuse repudiation in one case can be advanced with
equal force to excuse repudiation in the other. Suppose the "plan of
campaign" was preached in the City, and landowners urged the
traders to repudiate the contracts they had made with the capitalists,
what would the capitalists say ? They would say it was robbery, and
they would invoke the utmost rigour of the law against the robbers
and against those who abetted them. There can be no doubt about
this. I wonder they do it it is so foolish. It deceives no one ;
everyone knows that when a capitalist denounces the obligations of
contract he is a humbug, neither more or less ; that he is advocating what his business soul abhors, and what he knows is absolutely
fatal to his own commercial existence. Then why do they do it ?
Because they have qualms of concience about contracts and covenants ? Not a bit of it. Try them, and you will soon see how far
their qualms will modify their practice. Why, then, do they advise
the Irish farmers to repudiate their contract with the landowners,
and to keep their land ? Simply because the landowners do not
vote for Mr. Gladstone ! For no other reason in the world. Was
anything ever so comical ? This is combining business with
politics with a vengeance. A nice standard of commercial morality
for the first commercial nation in the world : that you may rob if
you vote for Mr. Gladstone, and you must submit to be robbed if
you vote against him. " I have no land," says the capitalist, "and
whatever happens the Socialists cannot take my Consols." Can't
they ? It is exactly here that the capitalist is metamorphosed into
the golden ass ! It is on his Consols, and not on the dirty acres
of the landowners, that the Socialists have fixed their eyes. They
may eventually break up and partition the land, but their first grab
will be at capital. I am in the fortunate position of having a friend
who is a Socialist, and is thoroughly acquainted with all their views
and aspirations. This is what he tells me. The Socialists hold
that the accumulation of land in a few hands is very injurious to the
community, and they intend to pass a law to make the subdivision
of land compulsory, as it is in France ; but they think the accumulation of capital in a few hands is a hundred times more injurious to a community than the accumulation of land, and they
intend to tax capital very high, and to pass a law making the subdivision of capital also compulsory. They maintain that the
capital of the country has accumulated in fewer hands even than the
land, and that whilst the accumulation of land has entirely ceased
and the tide turned the other way, the accumulation of capital is
increasing more rapidly every day. They maintain that the capitalist creates no wealth and employs no labour, and that therefore his
millions are actually the creation of thousands and tens of thousands
of those who do create and do labour. Socialists look upon capitalists as leeches who suck the blood of those who labour—as a selfish

class who drain capital from'home labour and home industries and invest it in foreign labour and foreign industries. They look upon them as their greatest enimies, and it is their millions they intend first of all to lay under contribution. Their first demand will be for the subdivision of capital, their second for the subdivision of land; but the capital must come first. They intend to subdivide the land, but first of all they intend to subdivide the capital in order to get the means to cultivate the land. And then, moreover, it is so much easier to get at the capital than at the land. It is portable and divisible. Why, one street in the City will yield more money than the land of a dozen counties. The land is all very well, but it requires time, and skill, and industry, and patience, and capital, to make it of any value; and Socialists are rather in a hurry, and have not a superabundance of these things. But capital requires none of them ! Everything about capital is so delightfully simple ! The Socialist mouth waters at the very idea of it ! Now, all this may be very foolish; but, foolish or not, it is positively the programme of the Socialists. Let capitalists ponder. They, at any rate, cannot afford to run with the hare and hunt with the hounds. What constitutes contract and covenant in Ireland constitutes contract and covenant in the city of London. There is no doubt of it, and it is absolutely certain that those who advocate repudiation of contracts and covenants in Ireland will soon hear the cry of repudiation of contracts and covenants taken up in England. What will they say then ? They may excuse their evident insincerity by political sophistry, but that does not alter the facts. It may be amusing to talk nonsense about banishing political economy to Saturn ; but those who venture to reduce this nonsense to practice by preaching the repudiation of contracts are either the vainest or silliest of mortals. As sure as there is a Nemesis that avenges the outrages on common sense they are playing with fire that will consume them.

1886.

AT THE FEET OF GAMALIEL.

THERE is a storm in a tea-cup. Certain sons of Belial have black-balled the anointed, and the elect run about the streets wringing their hands, and crying, Woe to Brooks, to Brooks, the club where the old Whigs dwell! But this is all nonsense. Naturally, the Whigs are not very fond of the Radicals just now, because they call them bad names, and would black-ball them for Parliament if they could ; and it is only natural that when they get an opportunity they should avail themselves of the privilege of doing to others what they know they would do to them. *Do ut des* may always be counted upon as an invariable factor in human affairs. Moreover, there was a club grievance as well. The popular farce of the " Private Secretary " had been, in the opinion of many members, a little over-acted, and some unusual and somewhat provocative incidents had violated *les bienséances* of club etiquette. *Hinc illæ lachrymæ.* Hence these odious black-balls. The Radical Home Rulers insist that all Liberals should at once, *sans phrase*, violate all their former pledges and convictions, pronounce the Home Rule " Shibboleth," and support Mr. Gladstone in his new departure. The Gileadites smote with the sword all who could not pronounce the letter " h." It is to be hoped such an awkward test won't be insisted upon in the House of Commons ! The floor would run with blood ! All the leading Liberals, without exception, decline this preposterous summons. " Stand and deliver ; your principles, or your (political) life," is certainly a new departure in party discipline, and I maintain that, even from a strictly party view, independent Liberals are right in resenting it, and that the country will support them. It is all very well for Mr. Gladstone, and his elect, to cry woe to the sheep who desert the shepherd, but I say rather woe to the shepherd who has deserted the sheep ! Now that force has proved to be no remedy, and that it is evident that slander, and threats, and ridicule will not deter the Liberal Unionists from doing their duty, the *mot d'ordre* has been given to try soft-sawder. " Leave them to me," says the great orator,

> " I'll try once more
> If I can subdue those stubborn principles
> Of faith—of honour."

Somehow, I don't think he will succeed. Fortunately we have amongst us some vertebrate Liberals who are still stubborn in support of the old principles of faith, of honour ; and I believe the country is proud of them.

Moreover, just now Mr. Gladstone's influence with the electors appears to have a somewhat negative value ; his post-cards and certificates of qualification have proved in some cases " Bellerophon's letters " that have brought the bearers more disappoint-

ment than fortune. The fact is, he has not been quite sufficiently
discriminative; the object of his advocacy has been a little too
apparent. Even for a membership of Parliament some conditions
are indispensable, and the engagement to vote on all occasions for
Mr. Gladstone is not quite good enough, if it is associated with
foreign birth, and a defiant advocacy of manhood suffrage and
the Socialistic platform. The assumption that any Radical stick is
good enough to beat a Unionist dog with has its limits, and my
belief is that they are already reached. The position of the Liberal
Party is very simple. "'The fathers have eaten sour grapes, and the
children's teeth are set on edge "—there is no doubt about it. Mr.
Gladstone has taken—God knows why!—such a mouthful of sour
grapes that even some of his most affectionate children find their
teeth on edge, and are seriously alarmed about him. The tag-rag
and bobtail of the Radical party who constitute the Separatist
faction—and I call them so because, with the exception of Mr.
Morley, and he has always been a Separatist, not one single Liberal
of light and leading has joined them—denounce the Liberal Unionists as renegades, turncoats, &c.; but this only shows their ignorance
of the English language. Renegade means apostate, one who
deserts his principles, not one who stands firm to them at any cost.
I think the public understand the meaning of the word better.

But the Liberal Unionists need not be alarmed; they have a very
sufficient answer to these gentlemen. " For twenty years," say
they, " we have sat at the feet of Gamaliel, a Pharisee *des plus fins*,
like he of Jerusalem, as we now discover. We have been as true as
steel to him; we were proud to take him at his own valuation as
one of the *dii adscriptitii*, inspired beings with human bodies,
sacred minds, and celestial souls, born into the world for the good of
mankind. We supported him when he bombarded Alexandria;
when he deserted Gordon; when he caused Arab blood to flow like
water; when he introduced a budget of £100,000,000; when he
coquetted with the three acres and a cow; when he denounced the
cry for repeal of the Union; when he prosecuted the conspirators—
as he called them—with the utmost rigour of the law. But now, in
a moment, without giving us a single reason beyond the usual
" sic volo, sic jubeo,"—for his arguments in favour of Home Rule
are below contempt—all this is absolutely reversed. He commands
us to curse to-day what only yesterday he commanded us to bless,
and to bless what he commanded us to curse; but it is absurd. He
is asking an impossibility. Does he suppose it is more possible
for the Liberal Unionist to change his skin than for the Ethiopian?
What a Colossus he is! and how insolently he asks us petty men
to walk under his huge legs and peep about to find ourselves dishonourable graves. What a man! Who can keep pace with him?
Yesterday, with all the energy and eloquence of his nature, he
proved to us the absolute necessity of always maintaining the
Union; to-day, with still greater energy, he proves to us the
necessity of immediately destroying it." He imprisoned those who
did not agree with him then, and he would, if he could, proscribe
those who don't agree with him now. Is he not a Dictator? If
the conditions were repeated should we not see a repetition of the

proscriptions of Sylla? Is it strange that a good many of the children's teeth are on edge! The modern Canute reverses the *rôle* of our Danish King. The latter compelled his courtiers to acknowledge that he was fallible; Mr. Gladstone encourages them to believe that he is infallible. "Look at me," he says to his courtiers, "watch me, and see how the tide will stop when it approaches me. I am infallible—I am infallible," and the elect all throw up their hands and shout, "Mashallah, Mashallah; he is infallible, he is infallible." But tides are bad respecters of persons, and if rumour is correct he already begins to realise that he must shift his position or get his feet wet. Now, if the truth must be spoken, his position is not exactly a fortunate one. To have your mouth full of sour grapes and your feet in the advancing tide, at this season of the year, cannot be unmixed joy to a human body, even if endowed with a sacred mind and celestial soul. Of course I know, as everyone else does, that it is as completely lost labour to plough the sea shore with a horse and a bull and sow it with salt as to expect any return from turning up Mr. Gladstone's former speeches. He puts a stopper on all inquiry at once; either his mouth did not say what his heart meant, or his heart did not mean what his mouth said—

> "Nul serment n'est gardé, nul accord est sincère,
> Quand la bouche a parlé, le cœur dit le contraire."

It is a dilemma from which no forager in Hansard can possibly escape, but there is a certain speech that he made at Aberdeen, September 26, 1871, that even he, cunning as he is in the art of torturing poor words to reverse their meaning, must find somewhat difficult to explain away. It so absolutely and completely contradicts and reverses everything that he is now so furiously asserting, that it almost reads like the former confession of one who is now trying to fix the offence on some one else! Everyone that reads it must feel that there is a "lying spirit" about somewhere. Where is it? in the Aberdeen speech or in the Hawarden postcards? "Can any sensible man, can any rational man suppose," said Mr. Gladstone at Aberdeen, September 26, 1871, "that at this time of day, in this condition of the world, we are going to disintregate the great capital institutions of this country for the purpose of making ourselves ridiculous in the eyes of all mankind, and crippling any power we possess for bestowing benefits, through legislation, on the country to which we belong?" "You would expect," he went on to say amidst ringing cheers, "when it is said that the Imperial Parliament is to be broken up, that, at the very least, a case should be made out showing there are great subjects of policy, and great demands necessary for the welfare of Ireland, which the representatives of Ireland had united to ask, and which the representatives of England, Scotland, and Wales had united to refuse. There is no such grievance. (Oh, Mr. G., where do you expect to go to?) There is nothing that Ireland has asked, and which this country and this Parliament have refused. Parliament has done for Ireland what it would have scrupled to do for England and Scotland." Remember this ye renegades and turncoats (I use these epithets because I observe they are strictly parliamentary) who have deserted to Home Rule, it is Mr. Gladstone who speaks. Your Gamaliel, who assures you that "there is nothing that Ireland has asked which this country and this Parliament have refused." It is your Gamaliel who tells you that Parliament has done for Ireland what it would have scrupled to do for England and Scotland, or even, I suppose, for gallant little Wales; and since these words were spoken, these assurances given, England has done a great deal more for Ireland, more than anyone then conceived possible she could do or could be asked to do. Since 1871 statesmen have circumnavigated Anticyra, and Parliament has taken a trip to Saturn (or rather to the moon, I suppose, for it is there the Stoics believed the souls of wise men dwelt) in search for the antidote for Irish madness. "We desire to conciliate Ireland," continued Mr. Gladstone, "to attach her to this island in the silken cords of love; but there was a higher and paramount aim in the measures that Parliament has passed, and that is that it should do its duty." And this is the man—it seems absurd on this occasion to call him a statesman—who now denounces the Government for the higher and paramount aim of doing its duty? Now, did Mr. Gladstone say this at Aberdeen, September 26, 1871, or did he not? Did he mean what he said, or did he not? If he did not mean what he said, or say what he meant then, how can we possibly know whether he means what he says or says what he means now?

Is it not a shame to haul in Heaven to attest the truth of a statement to-day, and to haul in Heaven to attest the falsehood of the same statement to-morrow?

> " Du ciel qu'ils attestaient, ils bravaient le courroux
> L'intérêt est le Dieu qui les gouverne tous."

Is it true that self-interest is the politician's god as completely to-day as when Ariosto wrote those lines? I declare—but then I am a man of Belial—that in my opinion the alacrity and cynical indifference with which Mr. Gladstone denies himself, and explains himself away, on all occasions that self-interest, or party interests, require it, has lowered the standard of political honour and political morality to a point it has never before reached. A drunken parson is a much worse example than a drunken soldier, and when we see a man who claims to have a sacred mind and a celestial soul playing the game of politics in a way that makes even the most earthly of politicians stare with amazement, the example is shocking. Up to the last five years there was a certain standard of public morality which public men strove to attain to, with more or less success. Now there is none. The ποῦ στῶ is removed; there is not a foot of firm ground anywhere. Public men no longer allow that they are bound by their public utterances till they have publicly recanted them—they simply pass a wet sponge over all former records, and content themselves with a general *non mi ricordo*. Modern political morality ignores all utterances, and engagements, and pledges that are inconsistent with present interest; proclaims that what is disgraceful in an individual is praiseworthy in a politician—that, in fact, in the game of party politics everything is fair. We are told that Mr. Gladstone has only done about Home Rule what Sir Robert Peel did about Free Trade, but this is a mistake. Sir Robert Peel changed his opinions ; Mr. Gladstone is a renegade to his principles ; and this is not a mere play of words ; the difference is immense. Opinion is a vain, light, crude, imperfect thing—often a child of imagination, and time wears out its fictions ; but when opinions have long been common to all parties and divisions of parties ; when they have received the endorsement of generations of wise men, they become principles ; they correspond to the *lex nata* of the Roman orator ; they are the inheritance of the nation, and are received by the whole community without question and without doubt. The question of Free Trade was a matter of opinion in Sir Robert Peel's time, and so it is now ; and time has worn out some of its fictions. The question of the union of Great Britain and Ireland is no longer a matter of opinion ; it is a principle ; it has received the unquestioned support of every responsible statesman in England during 100 years ; it has become the *lex nata* of the nation. Opinions differ in every age and in every country : even human happiness is only a matter of opinion. In England it is held to consist in Free Trade ; in America, France, Belgium—in fact, in every country but in England—it is held to consist in Protection.

> " Blest be the Princes who have fought
> For pompous names and wide dominion,
> Since by their errors we are taught
> That happiness is but opinion."

Sir Robert Peel never denounced his Free Trade opponents as " men steeped to the lips in treason," as marching through rapine and murder to disruption, as conspirators fed with foreign gold, &c. Sir Robert Peel never prosecuted or imprisoned them ; but all these things, or nearly all, worse almost in some ways, Mr. Gladstone has done to, or threatened, his present allies. Sir Robert Peel turned his back on his economic opinions ; Mr. Gladstone has become a renegade to the *lex nata* of generations of English statesmen, which all his long public life he has maintained was indispensable to the safety of the kingdon and the permanence of the Empire.

Well, what are we to think of this extraordinary transformation ? Is he Proteus himself ? Has he been blind all his life, and are his eyes only just now unsealed ? Has he been miraculously converted, by a *coup de foudre*, like Saul ? Is he swayed by patriotism, or by vanity ; by love of his country, or by love of himself ; or are we driven to the painful conclusion that the " well graced actor " has lingered too long on the stage—that on the verge of fourscore he is beginning to *radoter* ; that his memory is not what it was ; that, in fact, "great men are not always wise, neither do the aged understand judgment."

1886.

TURNCOATS.

WHEN Francis I. scratched on the window at Chambord
"Toute femme varie" he was only telling half the
story. He illustrated the old fable of the lion looking at a
picture of a man killing a lion. "Ah!" said the feline critic,
"the picture is very good, but if a lion had painted it you would
see the lion killing the man." If the lady had scratched her
thoughts on the glass probably the moral would have been reversed.
I think Francis was a sneak, and ought to have been ashamed of
himself. The fact is, he like some others, was beginning to *radoter*.
He was, at last, tasting the dregs of a life of love and war, and he
realised the disappointing fact that—

> " En jeu d'armes et d'amour,
> Pour une joye cent douleurs."

But if this is true of the "Jeu d'armes et d'amour," is it not also
true of the "Jeu de la politique? When a statesman gains a
personal victory, at the cost of his country and his friends, is not
this a case of "pour une joye cent douleurs?" If it isn't, it ought
to be, that is all I can say. Of course, "Tout femme varie;" and
of course, "Tout homme varie" also, only 20 times more. In
fact, the *varie* is so universal a human complaint that, except it
assumes a very exaggerated or aggressive form, it scarcely attracts
even passing notice.

When we read in the morning papers that Mr. Gladstone has
varié, it causes us no more surprise than when we look out of the
window in the morning and see that the wind has chopped round.
We inquire whether it has gone from S. to S.W., or S.E.; or
whether it has gone slap round to N. That's all. That he should
"box" the political compass backwards and forwards in a single
day or night does not now appear to us worth a moment's notice.
It is only when he changes with such furious impetuosity that he
begins blowing a gale from one point almost before he has ceased
blowing a gale from the opposite one, that we begin to realise what
a dangerous Boreas he is. To the nation it is really a matter of
supreme indifference why his changes are so rapid that it is
impossible to keep pace with them. We will assume that the
explanation of his friends and his family, and we believe his own
too, is the real one. "That he is inspired," inspired by a "Higher
Power" *bien entendu*. "Inspired!" it is a word we often use;
what is the meaning of it? It means this—that Almighty God
has thought fit to take some "homunculus" into His confidence,
and impart to him His wishes. In every generation there have
been rogues who have claimed to be inspired in order to assist
them in their *méchancetés*, but certainly Mr. Gladstone is the only
English party leader for whom this Divine right has been claimed;

and, indeed, with the exception of Mahomed, and Voltaire's heroine, La Pucelle, he is the only serious politician who has laid claim to it ; and in both these cases historians have always been in doubt whether their inspiration was the result of self-deception or of voluntary fraud. Now, I maintain, and always shall maintain, that any man who allows his friends to pretend, or who pretends himself, that Almighty God has in His favour broken the everlasting rule that must for ever separate the creature from the Creator, is either a madman or a rogue. There is no other conclusion possible. When one remembers what an essentially ignoble, self-seeking game party politics often is, how often the players are suspected, even if they do not really do so, of having a king or two concealed up their sleeves, it appears to me unspeakably wicked and impious to pretend to Divine inspiration in playing it. If the Almighty confides in one man, why not in another ? Why not in a dozen ?—in a million ? What limit is there ? How many of these uncanny folk are there in the world ? Are they to be found only in England, or are they to be met with in France, or America, or Russia ? How are we to know them ? By their fruits ? M. Delyannis has just now nearly broken up his country. Was he inspired ; or, at any rate, did he think so?

If a belief in Home Rule constitutes inspiration, then, of course, the one who first believed in it was the first inspired. Mr. Herbert Gladstone was inspired before Mr. Gladstone, and Mr. Cowen, Mr. Labouchere, Mr. Bradlaugh, and several others were inspired before Mr. Herbert Gladstone. The process of the inspiration theory is assumed by its supporters to be as follows :—That the Higher Power inspires Mr. Gladstone ; that Mr. Gladstone in turn inspires Lord Blank ; that Lord Blank again inspires Mr. Blank ; and so on and on till the residuum of inspiration descends even to the political little children. The dose becomes small by degrees, and beautifully less.

> " These fleas have other fleas,
>   And smaller fleas to bite them,
> These fleas have lesser fleas,
>   And so ad infinitum."

The position that Mr. Gladstone's incessant changes have placed us in is absolutely bewildering. We are not even allowed the luxury of appealing from Philip drunk to Philip sober—from Mr. Gladstone the irresponsible revolutionary demagogue, to Mr. Gladstone the responsible constructive statesman. He actually denies himself. Never has the plea of *" non mi ricordo "* been advanced with such cynical effrontery. Either what he is reported to have said he now tells us he actually never did say : or what he actually did say he now tells us he did not mean. There is no bringing him to book. He ignores, or forgets, or denies, or explains away everything he has ever said during 50 years, and denounces as turncoats and deserters those who quote his words and recall his arguments. It is astounding. As in the mirage of the Fata Morgana, everything is inverted—traitors are congratulated on their patriotism ; rebels on their loyalty ; dynamiters on their moderation, Those who stand to their principles and pledges are

denounced as turncoats, and those who swallow their principles
and deny their pledges are extolled for their honesty. Six months
ago the resources of civilisation were invoked in favour of the law
abiders, now they are invoked in favour of the law breakers. It is
shocking. But in the name of honesty, of common sense, of
truth, of justice, of national honour, let us a draw a line somewhere. Let us put the saddle on the right horse. Who are the
turncoats? It is not those who stand firm to their pledges and
principles who are the deserters from the Liberal ranks ; not Lord
Hartington, and Mr. Goschen, and Sir Henry James, and Mr.
Chamberlain, who have always opposed an Irish Parliament.
They have no more turned their coats than Mr. Cowen and
Mr. Labouchere, who have always supported it. It is those who,
individually and collectively, have up to this moment opposed
an Irish Parliament and demonstrated its danger and absurdity,
and who now advocate it, who have swallowed their principles,
ignored their arguments, denied their pledges, in order to get—— !
(but it seems impossible, so we will omit the cause). These
are the true turncoats—the most conspicuous, the most dis-
credited England has ever seen, from whom even "courtesy
must turn in disdain." That is the poet's expression, not mine.
Really when one reads of one of these turncoats, the most conspicuous of them indeed, because the most experienced, describing
those men who have not turned their coats, who have stuck to
their principles and their pledges, as " doing the dirty work of the
Tories," one holds one's breath in dismay. The shady discredit-
able incidents of the last few months have, at any rate established,
proved, one moral fact, that there is no gambling, none in the
world, so demoralising as political gambling.

The condition of mind of Mr. Gladstone and his immediate
followers, who pirouette like dancing dervishes, and all the while
imagine they are standing still and everybody else is turning
round, is absolutely without parallel. Again, may I ask with
the historian, " Is it self-deception, or is it voluntary fraud ? "
One thing is certain, that if these pirouetting politicians wish
to prove that they are not turncoats, the sooner they bring an
action against Hansard for defamation of character the better.
Mr. Gladstone now minimises the rights of the Irish landowner
in his land, and we are told forsooth, that he is " inspired." Was
he " inspired," pray, when he exaggerated the rights of the West
Indian slaveowners in their slaves ? If he was not, when did his
inspiration commence ? He now calls to the Irish landowners,
" Stand and deliver ; your money or your life ; " he holds up the
hour-glass to them and says, " The sand is running out, be quick
or you will get nothing." What would he have said 40 years ago
if Lord Howick and Mr. Wilberforce had held up the hour-glass to
Mr. Gladstone, sen., and the other slaveowners, and given them
the same option ?

In looking over the Emancipation debates in " Hansard " it is
absolutely impossible to believe that the former eloquent advocate
of the rights of property in " blood and bone " is the present
eloquent denouncer of the rights of property in land. It is unfor-

tunate for Mr. Gladstone's reputation that he was directly interested to the amount of £70,000 in "blood and bone," and is not interested to the amount of one shilling in Irish land. Mr. Gladstone stands with his hour-glass in his hand, and says to Lord Ormonde and Lord de Vesci, and Lord Fitzwilliam and the Duke of Devonshire, and those who bought land under the national guarantee in the Encumbered Estates Court, and who have just as good a claim to their property as he can possibly have to his, " Sell your land at the price I offer you, or I will deliver you over bound hand and foot to those who will rob you of every acre you have." And this, we are told, is inspiration ! This is the argument of the Prime Minister of Constitutional England ! What is the excuse for this mad haste ? Why is Great Britain to be rushed into revolution ? Why are the rights of property, the obligations of national honour and justice, every canon of public morality, of common sense, of self-preservation, to be torn in shreds in the face of the whole world ? Why does Mr. Gladstone insist on

> " Turning the accomplishment of many years
> Into an hour-glass ? "

Why, does not every one know ? Because he is getting old. Because the golden sands are running through his hour-glass, and whilst a single grain remains he must continue in office, and to continue in office he must secure the Irish vote. Time is the stuff human life is made of, and votes are the stuff that political life is made of, and both time and votes are running short. Of course, it is very sad that

> " His hasty sands are ebbing to the last ; "

that, as many think, his memory is going : that he forgets to-day what he said yesterday ; that he has reached the age when, as Solomon says, " Old men do not understand judgment ; " that he is beginning to *radoter*. It is very sad, but it cannot be helped ; it is the decree of fate—even inspiration does not bestow immortality ; but, in the name of reason and common sense, do great age and failing capacity supply a valid reason for allowing him to "rush " our country into a revolution of which no man living pretends to see the end ? It is no great inducement to a patient to allow his doctor to try some very dangerous experiment on him because he is so old that in all probability he will not live to see whether he recovers or dies. We want a pilot who will stick to the ship and steer her out of danger, not one who will steer her into danger and then slip over the side.

Of course the desire for immortal fame is a very noble one, but still the means by which it is attained must always count for something. One gentleman, with a very long name, sought to attain it by destroying the Great Temple of Ephesus ; and another, with two very short names, sought it by destroying King, Lords, and Commons at one shot. And now Mr. Gladstone seeks to attain it by, as many of us believe, destroying the great British Empire ; and I declare I think this last means is more criminal and more absolutely insane than either of the other two.

1886.

THE LETTER.

I IMAGINE we have nearly heard the last of Mr. Parnell's supposed letter. It has been a godsend to our inventive friend the "Man in the Street." "I happen to know the letter is genuine," says one hardy asserter: "I happen to know it is a malignant forgery," says another; and, strange to say, we all happen to know that neither of these two gentlemen really knows anything whatever about it. Mr. Parnell, of course, knows whether the letter is genuine, and so does the Editor of the *Times*, but probably no one else does, and those who speak with the greatest confidence know least of all about it. But though nobody knows anything about it, every man is at liberty to have his opinion. Well, my opinion is that it is genuine, because I believe that if at the time of the Phœnix-park murders Mr. Parnell had been induced to write a letter, or compelled to write a letter, this is the exact letter he must have written : he could have written no other. It is a question of probabilities. "Is your brother fond of tea?" "I havn't got a brother." "But if you had a brother, would he be fond of tea?" "Is this Mr. Parnell's letter?" "Mr. Parnell didn't write a letter." "But if Mr. Parnell did write a letter, would this be the letter he would write?" "Certainly; he could write no other." If they are not Mr. Parnell's words, I think few can doubt that at the moment when they were written they must have been his sentiments. We are not surprised when we see a man do what we always knew he must do. We are only surprised when we see him do what we never expected him to do. I was not surprised when I read Mr. Parnell's supposed letter, because, under the circumstances, it was the exact letter I should have expected him to write. At the supposed date of this letter Mr. Parnell was playing a perilous, almost a desperate, game. Mr. Gladstone had just denounced him as "steeped in treason to the very lips ;" he had been cast into prison without any form of trial ; and he had declared, in defiance, that neither he nor any of his associates would ever be satisfied "till they had destroyed the last link that keeps Ireland bound to England." Of course, this meant war to the knife on both sides. On Mr. Parnell's side there was no desire to conceal this fact ; it was their daily triumphant boast.

Mr. Parnell maintained that he could destroy this last link by what he considered constitutional and parliamentary methods; but of course nobody doubts that he knew that in America and in Ireland other associations laughed at the idea of making war with rose water, and were seeking to destroy this last link by sharper methods —by terrorism, by dynamite, by assassination, by crime. Of course he knew this—we all knew it. No one doubts—Mr. Parnell himself would not ask us to doubt—that he knew exactly what their practices were, who were the instigators, who were the actors, and who

provided the sinews of war. Probably—I think most probably—
he would have put an end to these murder associations if he had
dared ; but he did not dare. They were stronger than he was : if
he had lifted his little finger against them, they would have killed
him. It was the old story ; he was between the Devil and the
Deep Sea. If he denounced the murder of Mr. Burke, he would
certainly be killed himself. If he did not denounce the murder of
Lord Frederick Cavendish, his Parliamentary career would be ended.
He had no option ; so he did what he was compelled to do—he
condoned the crime of killing Mr. Burke and denounced the mistake
of killing Lord Edward Cavendish. It is easy to say that he ought
to have denounced both. Of course he ought ; but in denouncing
one only he ran the risk of losing his life. Hence, perhaps, his
anxiety to keep his whereabouts secret. The Phœnix-park catastrophe
was both a crime and a mistake. It was a crime to kill Mr. Burke ;
but it was worse than a crime, it was a mistake, to kill Lord Edward
Cavendish. Every one saw this ; even the murder associations
themselves. I have no doubt in my own mind that Mr. Parnell's
sympathies were against the murders. He would have preferred to
hunt with the hounds, but circumstances compelled him also to run
with the hare.

There is no doubt that when the murder associations had tasted
blood, those who opposed the gospel of murder did so at the risk of
their lives. It was stated at the time that a document was drawn
up expressing the detestation of the Home Rule Party in Parliament
at the Phœnix-park murders ; but it was never signed, for a very
good reason—"any one who signs that paper," said a member of
the party, "is a dead man." Now, it appears to me that when he
was in this dilemma, carrying his life in one hand and his
Parliamentary existence in the other, it was perfectly natural, almost
certain, that he would write such a letter, if he wrote any letter
at all. But what does it signify to us whether the letter is genuine
or not ? The question that has such a deadly interest for us is not
whether the individual Mr. Parnell is connected with crime, but
whether the organisation that bears his name, and to which Mr.
Gladstone proposes to hand over a considerable part of the United
Kingdom, is connected with crime. The question that exercises
every one who cares for his country is, whether the extracts from the
Parnellite papers in America, Ireland, and England are genuine.
That is what we want to know. Is Mr. Gladstone asking us to
hand over two millions of our loyal fellow countrymen and a fourth
of the United Kingdom to true men, or to a foreign conspiracy, to
men associated with crime ? Never mind whether what the *Times*
says is true or false—is what the Parnellite papers say true or false ?
That is what we want to know. The revolution, for revolution it is,
is running its inevitable course. In England and Ireland those who
began it are already being put on one side by the more militant
spirits behind them.

Mr. Parnell no more leads the Irish Home Rule Party now than
Mr. Gladstone leads the English Home Rule Party. Their names
remain, but the lead is in the hands of others. Who the actual
leader of the Irish Home Rule party is I don't know, but I think it

is evident to all of us that Mr. Labouchere is the actual leader of
the English Home Rule party. What Mr. Labouchere says to-day,
Mr. Gladstone says to-morrow. Mr. Labouchere inspires, Mr.
Gladstone says ditto; only unfortunately for us his ditto runs into a
volume. And, therefore, when I wish to make a forecast of the
English Home Rule programme, it is Mr. Labouchere's utterances
I consult, not those of Mr. Gladstone—there is nothing like a
quotation. "With fatal and painful precision," said Mr. Gladstone,
"the steps of crime dogged the steps of the Land League."
"with fatal and painful precision," say I, "the steps of Mr.
Gladstone" dog the steps of Mr. Labouchere. It is of no use
shutting our eyes to existing facts. It is Mr. Labouchere who now
"bosses" the English Home Rule party, not Mr. Gladstone. I
believe the country is beginning to realise this at last. Thank heaven!

Mr. Gladstone hopes to return to power; and possibly he will;
—even that is possible in the present state of public opinion; but
when he does it will be on entirely different conditions. "I ask a
renewal of your confidence," he will say to the country, "not for
what I have said or done during the last 50 years, for everything I
have said and done I now acknowledge to have been wrong. For
50 years I have been leading you on the wrong tack, but now I
make a fresh departure. I have thrown overboard all my pledges,
disproved all my former opinions, swallowed all my principles.
I have an absolutely clean slate, and now I ask your confidence for
what I may do. I cannot tell you what that will be, because I
really don't know; it does not depend on me, it depends on
Mr. Labouchere and the extreme Radicals. Ask him, and I have
no doubt he will give you a satisfactory answer." But an entirely
fresh departure at four score is a risky affair both for him who leads
and for us who follow. We already have a forecast of what this
new departure will be. During the last fortnight we have actually
seen the Radical elect invoking the power of Parliament to muzzle
the Press! After this, am I not justified in saying anything is
possible? It is enough to make you "laugh yourself into stitches"
to see the very Esau of journalism, whose hand is against every
man, even when nobody's hand is against him, turning sharp round,
and with sublime audacity denouncing the liberty of the Press!
It is true we have often had reason to wonder at the incongruities of
journalism, and ask ourselves where liberty ends and licence begins?
Why one man may steal a horse with impunity and another
may be hanged for looking over a gate? But though we winced
we never complained; but now the liberty of the Press has been
carried beyond endurance, and the Radical soul is all on fire. The
Times has actually ventured to reproduce, and circulated all over the
country, the sketches of Mr. Gladstone's new allies as drawn by
their own special artists. It is abominable, and, what is worse,
the *Times* defies them to prove that they are not correct likenesses;
and Mr. Bright laughs at the Radical fury, and in a few English
sentences points out that there is still a difference between dignity
and impudence in politics, and the public at once recognise the
distinction. It is very annoying.

But I am really sorry for the Gladstonians; they are so terribly sorry for themselves. I never remember a defeated political party taking their disappointment so much to heart, and they are so terribly angry as—

      " They stand aloof, a noisy crowd,
         Like woman's anger, impudent and loud "—

scolding and vituperating, denouncing and explaining, and getting laughed at in return, like a man who shows a lady's letters to prove he has been ill-used. They are very angry ; but, indeed, they have reason to be so, it was very disappointing ; everything was ready cut and dried, they had swallowed their principles, eaten dirt enough to ballast a coaster, and Humpty Dumpty had only to mount on the shoulders of the Parnellites to ride in triumph into office ; when at the last moment those infernal Liberal-Unionists—Bright, Chamberlain, Hartington, and others—actually took it into their heads to indulge in the damnable sin of consistency. And Humpty got a fall, and his triumph is deferred to the Greek Kalends. Could anything be so annoying ? And now the *Times* has so damaged their new allies in the eyes of the country that they are of very little use to them. Home Rule is no longer a trump card, and they find that they have swallowed their principles and eaten all their dirt for nothing. It is maddening enough to make a saint swear, and the Radical saints can swear like troopers. And to complete their discomfiture the Parnellite juice is getting more and more bitter every day. But there is no escape from it. There they are, and there they must remain, and stew, and stew, and stew till the mess is done ; and a pretty dish to set before the country it promises to be.

                                   1886.

MR. SPEAKER.

THERE is an old proverb that "the Devil knows so much because he is so old." Probably it is true; but if we learn a good deal as we grow old, we certainly unlearn a great deal also. I really believe that when one reaches the critical age of 60, one has had to unlearn almost everything one has learnt. For instance, most of us have been educated in the belief that our parliamentary institutions are the most perfect in the civilised world. Well, now we have to unlearn this flattering tale, and to learn, on the other hand, that to-day, in this year of the Jubilee of our gracious Sovereign, our parliamentary institutions are not only the most imperfect in the whole civilised world, but that they actually stand out as a warning to civilised and uncivilised mankind of what they ought to avoid. I believe it is evident to the whole civilised world that there is not, and never has been, a so-called deliberative assembly so utterly useless for every deliberative purpose as our present House of Commons. Some of us remember an old skit in *Punch* during the Crimean War. One admiral went to the Baltic to do a great deal, and he didn't do it. Another admiral went to the Baltic to do nothing, and he did do it. We have had many Parliaments that have met to do a great deal, and have not done it: and we have had some that have met to do nothing, and have done it; but we have never had a Parliament that did nothing in such a noisy, offensive, and irritating way as the present one. Inasmuch as many of us believe that over-legislation is a *mal du pays*, we ought occasionally perhaps to be thankful for a Parliament that does nothing, if it only does it nicely and pleasantly; but it doesn't. Alas, it is not incapacity that we have to complain of—it is bad manners. Our House of Commons is very very like "the little girl, who had a little curl, right down the middle of her forehead, and when she was good she was very, very good, and when she was bad she was 'orrid." The House of Commons has at times been very, very good, but just now it is simply 'orrid. There is no other expression for it. In other Representative Assemblies—in France, America, Australia, Mexico, everywhere, in fact—members quarrel and call each other bad names, but they incur a certain amount of personal responsibility in indulging in this amusement; they must either apologise or bear the consequences; but in our present House of Commons there is apparently no personal responsibility whatever attached to the use of bad words; members don't apologise; and there are no consequences to bear. They call each other liars, drunkards, cheats, swindlers; but they are never called upon to make good their words; and their apologies are often added insults. I don't believe such license of tongue and gesture has ever been witnessed in any deliberative assembly in the world as may be witnessed every night in the House of Com-

mons. "You are not fit to carry guts to a bear," said Midshipman Easy to the Purser's Steward. "You must apologise, Mr.
Easy," says the captain. "Certainly, sir," replies Jack with his
usual politeness, "I have much pleasure in saying that you are fit
to carry guts to a bear." There is, I believe, no exaggeration in
saying that nine-tenths of the so-called apologies in the House
of Commons are of the Midshipman Easy type. It is a fact that
most of these apologies are even more offensive than the original
insult; they are more deliberate and more studied. I have not the
honour to be in Parliament, but I am assured by those who have,
that the reports in the newspapers give but a very imperfect idea of
the actual manners and gestures of these intentional offenders.
Now I am not a man of blood, and I have no wish to see duelling
re-established; but I swear I believe that very often blood letting is
preferable to insult. Duelling was given up in the belief that
Society would protect its members from insult; but if Society
neglects to do so, or declines to do so, there can be neither reason
nor justice in Society punishing them for protecting themselves.
Society allows a man to defend himself from a blow, but is not
many an insult as cruel as a blow? Often a hundred times more
so. If the House of Commons does not protect its members
from insult, some fine day, or rather, some stormy night, some
honourable member will feel it his duty to protect himself, and a
good thing too. It will clear the atmosphere at any rate. The
House of Commons is composed of 650 individuals, more or less;
all honourable men, of course; though, certainly, some are more
honourable than others. All gentlemen, of course; though it
must allowed some have rather better manners than others.
Amongst this unwieldy number there must always be a certain
percentage of noisy gentlemen, more or less defiant of control—
tant soit peu, rowdy, perhaps. There is nothing new in this;
it has always been the case in every House of Commons—the
rowdy element has always existed in a greater or less degree;
the only difference is that up to this time strict discipline has
always been maintained, and the rowdy element kept in order.
In former Parliaments not only were individual members more
or less protected from gross personal insult, but it was a canon of
Parliamentary faith never ignored—a point of personal honour,
in fact, with the leaders of the different parties in the House at
once to sink all party differences, in order to support the dignity
and authority of the Chair. A few years ago old Parliamentarians
would have thought the end of the world had come if their Speaker
had been yelled at and hooted and defied. Never before, never
once, for one single instant, has a Speaker of the House of Commons been left to the mercy of the rowdy element. Ulysses was
always ready with his club to smite Thersites if he dared to insult
the King of Men, in other words, Mr. Speaker; but alas, this is so
no longer. The Speaker is now nightly insulted, denounced,
threatened, hooted, and Ulysses does not move his club, but
looks on with indifference and his friends with approval. Of
course, the Great Word Splitter has declared that there is an
immense difference between inciting to crime and complicity with

crime, but the ordinary intellect does not appreciate the difference. The man who looks on with indifference or approbation when others are ill-treating an innocent man, is as bad as they are, if not worse—at least that is our ignorant way of reasoning. Again, I ask, why has this great change come over the practice of the House of Commons? Why do not the leaders still unite heart and hand to defend their Speaker? For a simple reason. Because Ulysses for the time has adopted the *rôle* of Thersites! This is absolutely true, as far as I can understand. Mr. Gladstone does not actually tell the Irish members to pitch the Speaker into the horse-pond; but he says "really, after his conduct in imposing the closure on me, I cannot say that he would get more than he deserved." I suppose the fact is becoming evident to everybody that Mr. Gladstone has lost his temper. Inspired persons often do. They are foolish enough to expect the laws of God and man to be altered for their especial convenience, and, unfortunately for them they never are. Of course, it is very annoying to an inspired person to find himself treated like a common man.

Last century a certain Joseph Guillotine, a doctor, invented a machine for shortening human bodies, but the machine was not wanted, and no one thanked him for it, and it did a great deal of harm, and by some circumstances over which, I suppose, he had no control, his own vile body was one of the first to be shortened, and he submitted to the operation with some philosophical remarks about the "irony" of Fate. Well, now, a hundred years later, Mr. Gladstone invented a machine for shortening human verbosity. It was much wanted; everybody thanked him for it, and it has done a great deal of good. But now, unfortunately for him, owing of course to circumstances over which he has no control, he also finds himself one of the first victims of his own invention. But he has not the philosophy of Joseph Guillotine—he will not submit to the operation; he is furious; he expostulates, he denounces, and lifts his arms and eyes to heaven in indignant protest. "How dare you," says he to the Speaker; and to the majority, "how dare you apply the closure to me? Don't you know that it was never meant for me, it was meant for you!" Poor Mr. Gladstone, certainly it is very ridiculous to be hoisted with your own petard, an old Parliamentarian to be choked with his own gag; but there was no help for it; there was a majority of 108 against him, and it was done. Perhaps it would have looked better to submit to the inevitable with dignity or, at any rate, with philosophy. But why were Mr. Gladstone and his followers so furious, so indignant at the imposition of the Cloture? Why? Does not every one know? Because they felt it was deserved! That is what stung them to the quick. "Il n'y a que la verité qui blesse." The Speaker is elected by the members of the House of Commons to preside over their debates, to enforce discipline, to hold the scales of justice between the two parties, and to conduct the business of a deliberative assembly; but unless he is supported firmly, loyally, heartily, *de bon cœur*, by the leading men in the House he cannot perform the duties of his office. It is impossible. His position becomes absolutely untenable. How can the master keep order in the school if the ushers lead the bad boys against him? One would have supposed that honour, chivalry, manhood, self-respect, the first inspirations of common sense would induce every member of Parliament to support to the utmost of his power, the influence, the dignity, the efficiency of the man he had himself selected to preside over the assembly to which he belonged; that he would assist him to make his work as easy as possible, instead of thwarting him in every way, and apparently driving him into his grave. The Liberal party selected the present Speaker, a Liberal, a man of high dignity, of refined manners, of unimpeachable conduct, the pick of the House of Commons; and now the Liberal party, the men who elected him, sit still, see him night after night grossly insulted, and actually pat Thersites on the back! If this is the chivalry of English gentlemen in this year of Grace 1887, then indeed, as far as we are concerned, "the age of chivalry is dead." Note this fact, you English gentlemen who stand forward as representing the English nation: you treat your Speaker, whom you have yourselves elected, who not one of you dare say in your heart is not doing his duty to the very best of his powers and (though he does not parade it so much as some of you do) of his conscience, with less confidence and respect than the very dregs of society treat the judge on a racecourse. The list men, the roughs, the mob do not elect the judge. Sometimes he is wrong, sometimes they disagree with his decisions, and lose their money, but never, never has the judge been hooted, or yelled at, or insulted for a decision he has given on a racecourse as the Speaker has been hooted for a decision he has given in the House of Commons. Imagine Mr. Steel, or the leading bookmakers assembling round the judge's chair after a race and yelling at him, and hooting him, and threatening him, because he gave a verdict against their favourite! But this is actually what the leading political bookmakers, who are now playing double or quits with the integrity of the United Kingdom, are nightly doing to the Speaker of the House of Commons. In the race between Closure and Obstruction, the Speaker has decided in favour of Closure, and the owner and backers of Obstruction denounce and hoot him. But is this the way to get Home Rule? I don't believe it is; on the contrary, I believe it has for the present, at any rate, made it impossible. The British public are not quite such fools as they look; and when they see the advocates of Home Rule insulting the Speaker, turning Parliament into a bear garden, obstructing all legislation, condoning outrages, endorsing the "plan of campaign," denouncing English judges and English juries, appealing for assistance to foreigners and to the bitter and avowed enemies of our country— they may say, "after all, the policy that requires such very impure advocacy as this must be tainted in itself. Perhaps we had better wait till it comes before us in a more respectable shape, and with more responsible sponsors." The position is becoming very critical; there is no doubt of it. The question must soon arise which is to be suspended—the Irish members, or the House of Commons.

1886.

THE OLD COPY BOOK AND THE NEW.

THE Schoolmaster is abroad. Day by day, hour by hour, the morals and ethics of our public schools are being remodelled to meet our changing requirements. Of course the great public school of St. Stephen's has taken the lead. A comparison of the old copy book formerly used in that establishment with the new one lately introduced may prove interesting to your readers.

Manners make the man,
Manners mar the politician.

Honesty is the best policy,
Honesty is no policy at all.

Look before you leap,
Leap before you look.

Call a spade a spade,
Call a spade a shovel.

Sentiment is a dangerous guide,
Sentiment is the only safe guide.

Tell the truth and shame the Devil.
Tell a lie and stick to it.

Union is strength.
Union is weakness.

Reason should control passion.
Passion should control reason.

My country, right or wrong.
My country is always in the wrong.

Do evil that good may come.
Do evil that worse may come.

Virtue nourishes the wise.
Virtue is the pap of fools.

Consistency is admirable.
Consistency is detestable.

Set a thief to catch a thief.
Set a thief to catch an honest man.

The liberty of the Press is the people's right.
The liberty of the Press is the patriot's wrong.

The withy strengthens the bundle.
The withy weakens the bundle.

Who goes slowly goes safely.
Who goes slowly is a fool.

You want a long spoon to eat with the Devil.
You want no spoon at all to eat with the Devil.

Judges are just.
Judges are rogues.

Juries are honest and dull.
Juries are dull and dishonest.

The majority rules.
The minority rules.

Still waters are deep.
Still waters are often shallow.

Silence is golden.
Verbosity is a Bank note.

Don't put off till to-morrow what you can do to-day.
Forget to-day what you did yesterday.

Age brings counsel.
Age defies counsel.

1886.

THE CANDID FRIEND.

M R. GLADSTONE, who can "add colours to the chameleon, change shapes with Proteus," is everything by turns, and nothing long, is now starring it in the character of the Candid Friend.

" But of all plagues, good heaven, thy wrath can send,
Save, save, oh, save me from the Candid Friend."

Wales saw the C. F. in the best possible form. "There is my friend, Lord Lansdowne," he said. (A hiss from a boy in the crowd). "Oh, I see," says the C. F., pricking his ears, "many of you think he is black, very black, and no doubt you have reason. For my part I try to think he is not so black as he is painted—at least, not quite so black ; but I may be mistaken, and pray understand I have not a word to say against Mr. O'Brien, who went to Canada to blackguard him, or against those who paint him blacker than the Author of Evil himself. I respect every man's opinion, especially when it agrees with my own. But I did not come here to defend Lord Lansdowne," continues the Candid Friend, "I came here to denounce England, to denounce Parliamentary England," (the same little boy hisses), "I am not surprised," says the Candid Friend, again pricking his ears, "at that universal shout of execration against that wicked country. For 700 years England has been trampling Ireland under foot. For 700 years mismanagement, ill-treatment, and national crime have been gnawing at the life of that interesting people. The treatment of Lombardy by the Austrians, of Naples by "Bomba," of Bulgaria by Turkey, was benevolent compared to the treatment of Ireland by England. "It is not you alone" (turning passionately to the boy who hissed, who gets rather frightened and tries to bolt) "who denounce her dark, narrow, obstructive, retrogressive" (it sounds like the description of a garret staircase turned upside down) "policy—the whole civilised world, Russia, Turkey, France, Germany, Spain, America execrate it; and not only the civilised but the uncivilised world also—the Red Indian from the great prairie, the fierce Moplas, the timid Tamuls, the chaste Todas of our Indian Empire, the Esquimaux from the regions of perpetual cold, and the Bushmen from the regions of perpetual dirt, each in their different dialects execrate Parliamentary England. But the execrations of England are not restricted to the general denunciations of outraged nationalities. Those noble men of letters, Hervé, Huertas, Ferrand, Flache, Beaumont, Ferry the great French Minister, Casanova the great Venetian moralist, equally execrate its abominations. Is it possible that any nation, however powerful, any people, however proud, can withstand the universal execration of mankind ? Do you mean to tell me that against the authority of these illustrious foreigners the quibbles of such Englishmen as John Bright, Lubbock, Leckie, Hartington,

Chamberlain, Argyll, James, Salisbury, Selborne, Tennyson, Tyndall, Goldwin Smith, can be listened to for one moment? Certainly not. For 60 years France has loved England!" (Ye Gods!) "Are her wishes to be ignored? America, so I am told, has a far greater interest in the Irish Question than England has. Is she not to be listened to? Does any one mean to tell me that these great, these friendly nations are to be put on one side, and that England is to be permitted to manage her domestic affairs against their expressed wishes! No, indeed! Perish England sooner than such an outrage on international duty, such an insult to me should be tolerated.

"But, my friends, be of good cheer. This wretched England, this unclean thing that I am doing my best to hold up to the execration of the world, is, thanks to my unwearied efforts, divided against itself. Not only are Scotland, Wales, and Ireland against England, but England is against 'Parliamentary' England. York-shire is against England, and not only Yorkshire, but the Isle of Man, and Jersey, Guernsey, Alderney, and Sark, and the town of Berwick-on-Tweed. It is impossible that Parliamentary England can be allowed any longer to govern England. England must be disfranchised. You must have a Parliament of Irishmen, Scotch-men and Welshmen; and then indeed I shall be supreme, and everything will go right."

Now, I declare this is scarcely any exaggeration of the tone of Mr. Gladstone's Welsh speeches. Anyone so disposed may find in them authority, ample authority, for everything I have said. It reads like a silly joke; but it isn't. It is the deliberate advice of Eng-land's greatest statesman! If one-hundreth part of what this Candid Friend says of his country is true, dynamite, the knife, vitriol, boiling water, the fate of the Cities of the Plain, would be too good for her. This is the only time I have ever regretted Mr. Gladstone leaving the stump. He was getting on so splendidly. His exaggerations, his misrepresentations, his vindictive incivism were rapidly making his utterances stink in the nostrils of all sen-sible men. He hoped to leave a picture of England that would outrage the world, whereas he has left a picture of himself, with the inscription—"This is the Englishman who has spoken most ill of his country." But even the Candid Friend should be moderately truthful. Truth, the more disagreeable the better, of course, is his keenest weapon. Now, Mr. Gladstone, speaking at Aberdeen on September 26, 1871, said:—"You would expect, when it is said that the Imperial Parliament is to be broken up, that at the very least, a case should be made out showing that there are great subjects of policy, and great demands necessary for the welfare of Ireland which the representatives of Ireland had united to ask, and which the representatives of England, Scotland, and Wales had united to refuse. There is no such grievance. There is nothing that Ireland has asked that this country and this Parliament have refused. Parliament has done for Ireland what it would have scrupled to do for England and Scotland."

On June the 3rd, 1887, 16 years later, Mr. Gladstone, speaking in Wales, said:—"But there is one spot in this Empire where, unfortunately, owing to ill-treatment, mismanagement, and, I must say, national crime, continued through a long series of years, the hearts of the people do not stand in that relation to the rest of the United Kingdom, on which it is desirable it should be placed." Now, ten thousand Mr. Gladstones cannot make both these statements true. One must be false, and is damnably false. If it is true Ireland had no grievance against England in 1871, how can she possibly have a grievance against England in 1887, when for 16 years she had been incessantly doing for her what she would have scrupled to do for England and Scotland? What becomes of his 700 years of tyranny, of national crime continued through a long series of years? There is no use in mincing words. Both statements cannot be true. Either the statement of 1871 or the statement of 1887 is false. "Out of thine own mouth I will condemn thee, thou . . . ." Perhaps I had better not complete the quotation.

Why does Mr. Gladstone tell such contradictory stories in 1871 and in 1887? Why? Is not the reason pretty plain? In 1871 he was speaking to the people of England and Scotland, and asking them to strengthen his hand to maintain the United Kingdom. In 1887 he was speaking over the heads of the English and Scotch people to the dynamite and murder associations of America, to the fierce enemies of England wherever they exist, to strengthen his hands to break up the United Kindom. Of course, as his aims were inverted, so were his arguments. Will Mr. Gladstone name one, only one, to use his own words, "great subject of policy," only one "great demand necessary for the welfare of Ireland, that the representatives of Ireland had united to ask and which the representatives of England had united to refuse?" Has the Parliament of England declined to do for Ireland any one thing that an Irish Parliament ought to do for her? No, it has not. Every one knows that Mr. Gladstone has changed his mind on the question of Home Rule, and now he is swearing by all his gods that he has not changed it one little bit. How silly it is. Why shouldn't the chameleon change his colours, or Proteus his form? Is it their nature to. Three years ago the needle was pointing due south; now it is pointing due north. "Certainly it is," says Mr. Gladstone, "but it is not the needle that has shifted, it is the points of the compass that have gone round. It is not I that have changed, it is Home Rule." But is thy servant a dog, that he should lick up such trash as that? It is rumoured that Mr. Gladstone's passionate appeal to foreign nations is intended to pave the way for a Conference, at which England is to appear at the bar of civilised and uncivilised mankind, to justify her treatment of Ireland. Is this his idea of "peace with honour?" and, alas! can it be true that there are Englishmen ready to support him in it? When Mr. Gladstone invites Americans to come over and strengthen his hand to break up the United Kingdon, I wonder if he realises what would have happened to him if he had gone to America to try and strengthen the hands of the Secessionists to break up the United States? What would they have done with him? Tarred and feathered him, and set him on a rail; nothing more. I was once staying next door to an old gentleman who was subject to attacks of destructiveness, and one day when he was particularly violent I asked the maid what was the matter. Oh, it's only the old gentleman at it again," she said ; " he's a' been and broke almost everything in the house, and now he's smashed his own windows. But I don't think it will last long ; the neighbours are getting sick of it, and will call in the police." Well, this appears to be the case with another old gentleman who is subject to destructive mania. He has made a cockshye of judge, jury, Speakers, Church, Press, the United Kingdom, and now he is actully pelting " Parliamentary England," his own father. But are there not signs that the neighbours are getting sick of it and will soon call in the police ? I think there are.

1886.

WHITE-WASHING.

"THE *Times* letter is an infamous forgery," says Mr. Gladstone to Mr. Parnell. "Your duty to yourself, your duty to the party of which you are such a distinguished leader, your duty to those allies who are now stewing in your juice—above all, your duty to this House—forbids you to take any notice of it." Of course, of course, shout the Tritons of the Radical Party, and the minnows, as usual, bow their heads and murmur—(I am not learned in fish language), "It is the voice of a god, not of a man." But suppose the *Times* had made a similar charge against Colonel Saunderson, or Mr. King-Harman, or even Lord Randolph Churchill, don't we know how the old "Parliamentary hand" would have taken it up? Of course, we do—we can hear his burning words and see his passionate gestures. Of course, he would say, "I know that this charge is a malicious forgery; that it has no foundation in fact; but I am sure I am speaking not only my own convictions, but also the convictions of every member on this side of the House, when I say that the honourable member owes it to himself, owes it to the party of which he is such a distinguished member, owes it to those on this side of the House who exchange with him the courtesies (?) of debate, and, above all owes it to you, sir, to scatter to the winds the vile accusations which he can no doubt immediately disprove and bring to the bar of retributive justice the vile and calumnious slanderers who have published it. Had this been simply the charge of an anonymous correspondent I should have been the first to advise the honourable gentleman to take no notice of it; but I cannot conceal from myself that this accusation comes before us with an authority and a completeness that compels immediate notice. The editor and proprietor, and the entire staff of the most powerful, the most responsible, the most cautious, the widest read, the wealthiest journal in the country, have staked their honour, their property, their very existence, on the truth of this charge. Therefore, I say again," &c., We all know what Mr. Gladstone would have said: and again the minnows would have bowed their heads and murmured, "It is the voice of a god, not of a man." But suppose this letter had appeared when Mr. Gladstone was denouncing Mr. Parnell, as "steeped in treason to the very lips;" when he declared that crime—yes, crime was the word—dogged the steps of the Land League, of which Mr. Parnell was the head; when the Phoenix Park still smelt of blood; when Sir William Harcourt was forcing through Parliament the crushing clauses of his Crimes Act, when Lord Spencer's life was in hourly danger; when Mr. Forster charged Mr. Parnell in the House of Commons, as Cicero charged Catiline in the Senate, with complicity with crime, would the tritons and the minnows have denounced it then as a malicious forgery? Would they then have entreated Mr. Parnell to take no notice of it?

Would they not rather have flung it in his teeth, and said, Disprove
it if you can ? Of course they would. Every human being knows
that. Mr. Parnell's declaration that this letter is a base forgery of
course carries great weight, for he knows the truth ; but I put it to
every man of sense whether Mr. Gladstone's declaration that it is a
forgery is worth more than the declaration of the boy in the street
that it is genuine, unless he has examined the evidence.

Everybody can see that just now Mr. Gladstone has far greater
interest in maintaining the letter to be false than even Mr. Parnell
himself. He and his followers are going through the agreeable
process of what Sir William Harcourt so appropriately described as
" Stewing in the Parnellite juice," and if the juice proves to be
poisoned, if the connection between Parnellism and crime remains
uncontradicted, the pot may boil over, and he will scald his fingers.
Mr. Gladstone is furious with the *Times* for these untimely and
exceedingly inconvenient publications ; but he seems to forget that
nearly all the *Times* statements that connect Parnellism with crime
are collated from the Parnellite prints themselves. It is, indeed,
Mr. Parnell's own familiar friends in whom he trusted, who did eat
of his bread, who have lifted the heel against him. If these
statements are false it is the printers and editors of the Home Rule
papers in Ireland and America who are responsible, not the printer
and editor of the *Times*. The publication of the articles on
" Parnellism and Crime " was, in sporting parlance, a " staggerer"
to the Gladstonians, their ranks were almost threatened with a
stampede. It shocked the public conscience; no one could
disprove it. But—happy thought! Sir William Harcourt and
Lord Spencer—

> " Arcades ambo, et cantare pares, et respondere parati."
> " Arcadians both, and both alike inspired,
> To sing and answer as the song required—"

Suddenly and simultaneously bethought themselves of " official
information." They both declared that their official information
enabled them to state that there never was any connection between
Parnellism and crime. This certainly was a staggerer to the
Unionists, and when one remembers what these Ministers have said
and done about Parnellism and crime during the last five years,
all one can do is to throw up one's arms in astonishment, and, like
Dominie Sampson, exclaim " Prodigious ! " But does not this white-
washing come a little late in the day? does not the " et cantare
pares et respondere parati saute aux yeux " a little too plainly?
It is almost a pity they did not realise Mr. Parnell's state of innocence
before they charged him with being " steeped in treason to the very
lips," and cast him into prison without trial. Such severe chastening
of one they loved was certainly rather contradictory. Well might
he exclaim, who knew the love they bore him :—

> " It's all very well to dissemble your love,
> But why did you kick me down stairs ? "

Mr. Gladstone's unequalled *volte face* on this Irish Question
would be almost comical if it was not so audaciously immoral, and
if it had not completely annihilated all faith and confidence in the

pledges and principles of public men for a generation at least. His former attidude towards Home Rule we remember only too well, but perhaps his present attitude is scarcely yet realised. I hope I shall not over-state it. "Dear bhoys," he says, "Hiberniores Hibernis "—he is now even more Irish than the Irishmen themselves, and the Irish jig comes as natural to him as the Highland Fling— "two years ago we were pulling in different boats. We were then in office, responsible for the public safety, at war with the Land League, and, for some reason or other which you probably understand better than I do, in considerable danger of our lives. Now that is all reversed; we are now in Opposition; we are now in a position of perfect freedom and absolute irresponsibility. We now support the Land League. It is now our political opponents who are in danger of their lives, not we; and naturally our views of crime and outrage have changed very much. Three years ago, owing to some extraordinary combination of circumstances over which I had no control, I found myself pulling in the same boat with the Tories against you. Now, thank heaven, that is reversed. You and I are both pulling in the same boat against the Tories. Things move quickly in these days. I can scarcely believe that only three years ago I was a Unionist, so completely am I now body and soul a Separationist. I have not, indeed, a grain of Unionism left in me. I suppose nobody will ever know what I have suffered; I can scarcely realise it myself. For 15 years I have been a Home Ruler at heart, and for 15 years I have worn the iron mask of Unionism. During the greater part of those 15 years I have been in office, and have done nothing for the cause I have now so much at heart— thank Heaven, this is over, the mask is removed. *Liberari animum meum*, I have emancipated myself, and am now as good a Fenian as Mr. Davitt. There is no longer a pin's head between us. Your views are in every sense my views, your interests are my interests, your ways are my ways. You wish to see Ireland, Scotland and Wales (don't forget gallant little Wales, I have a pecuniary interest in her) freed from the blighting dominance of England; so do I. You wish to see India and the Colonies independent; so do I. You wish to see me in power; so do I. Your 'plan of campaign' is now my 'plan of campaign.' We see no particular harm in shaving a girl's head and covering it with pitch. No doubt it has been done before. We look upon boycotting as a very justifiable expression of the wish of the majority. We see no objection whatever to your appointing agents to collect the landlord's rents. We think, perhaps, for the present shooting in the legs should be avoided as much as possible. Some foolish prejudices still linger with some of us, but we quite agree that a man who takes a farm from which another has been evicted should be treated as a leper. What shocked us three years ago does not shock us now. We have at last realised the important fact that you can't make an omelette without breaking eggs, and that the chapel bell must be kept ringing. Gladstonians and Parnellites are now one, we are bone of your bone and flesh of your flesh, and, what constitutes a much closer bond of interest, we are stewing in the same juice; therefore you must consider our interests as you would your own. You must not, dear bhoys—you must not indeed—let your sensitive natures and your chivalrous sense of honour induce you to fall into the pit that that rascally *Times* has dug for you. ' If my tenants think that by shooting my agents they will frighten me they are very much mistaken,' said an absentee Irish Landlord ; and if the Tories think that by connecting Parnellism with crime they will frighten us from making use of the Parnellite vote they were never more mistaken. Though every statement in the *Times* was proved in a court of law to-morrow, and Mr. Parnell stood on the drop with the rope round his neck, we should still swear he was innocent as the babe unborn, and should make use of his 86 votes. We want the Parnellite vote for other purposes than breaking up the United Kingdom, and having got it and paid for it we shall keep it at any price. Of course during the last five years we have both done many things that were better left undone, and said many things that were better left unsaid ; there were faults on both sides, and as you have not changed your opinions, and as we have entirely changed ours we are compelled to admit that in all probability our faults were greater than yours. In the heat of the Phœnix Park disaster no doubt some of you may have written letters that may bear a doubtful meaning, and these, if published, might prove awkward to you and to us. Don't, I beg of you, try to deny or disprove anything ; content yourself with a simple *non mi ricordo*—it has been my motto through life, and has never failed me—and refer to Sir William Harcourt and Lord Spencer —don't apply to Sir George Trevelyan, he is not yet quite to be trusted—for another coat of ' official white-wash.' "

1886.

TROP DE ZELE.

—

WHAT a nuisance too much zeal is. It is the pit-fall of common sense. Wherever it intrudes in public life it stops the way. It is always mistaken. There is not a case on record of its doing any good, but the list of its victims is as long as Leporello's. It repels the strong and attracts the weak, and unfortunately the weak are the most numerous. No nation in the world has suffered so much in character and pocket from *trop de zele* as we have. It is no exaggeration to say that it has been at the bottom of nine-tenths of our misfortunes. *Trop de zele* is responsible for the folly—crime I consider it—of repealing the Contagious Diseases Act, for the better observance of the Sabbath, for closing museums and picture galleries, and opening public-houses on Sunday. It has given us the Salvation Army. It has converted the temperance movement into a tyranny. It has rammed Free Trade down the throat of common sense, and now too much zeal has induced Mr. Gladstone to coquet with the Clan-na-Gael, and his Radical friends to propose a " Plan of Campaign " in Ireland that, if adopted, must end in chaos. Will no patent medicine mitigate this obstinate complaint ? Are Eno, Beecham, Holloway, and the once renowned Morison helpless to assist us ? The disease *is* curable—it is only wordy flatulence ! The most irritating part of the complaint is that it is simply an hysterical one, entirely on the nerves. We all feel how absurd it is to give way to it ; that with a little determination we could overcome it ; but we don't : knowing perfectly well that *trop de zele* is fatal to truth, honesty, common sense, we go on acclaiming it as a virtue. In 99 cases out of 100 it is mere acting, and the best actor is the most mischievous zealot, because he imposes on the greatest number of the feeble folk. The earnestness, the passion, the intensity that simmers up, and boils over, equally at the greatest events and at the most insignificant. " When now a sparrow falls and now a world " are all acting ; bless your simplicity ! why, that impassioned orator cares no more for the sparrow than you do, and he only cares for the world in so far as it affects himself. Of course it must be so. If a hundredth part of the zeal and passion that we witness was genuine, cases of spontaneous combustion, like that of the lamented Mrs. Faithful, would be quite common. No human clay that ever was kneaded could long bear such fierce internal fires. But now for our English Rochefort and his " Plan of Campaign "— *trop de zele* with a vengeance. Radicals are said to be a kind hearted breed who love to do good by stealth. It may be true. What certainly is true is that some of them don't blush to preach wrong with startling audacity. The Irish people are sick, and the Radical doctors have prescribed a remedy, but, as so often happens, the cure threatens to be worse than the disease. The Irish are in an exceedingly inflammable state, like political tinder, and the cure recommended is to pitch a box of lucifer matches amongst them, with the certainty that some of them will be burnt, probably the wrong ones. This certainly looks like trying to cure disease by death. " You are to treat the scoundrel who profits by your eviction like a loathsome leper," says the Radical Doctor, which to my mind is tantamount to saying, "Shoot the scoundrel who evicts you." Under certain circumstances this advice might be very effective. The aggrieved tenant would treat the interloper like a loathsome leper, shoot the landlord, and keep the farm ; but unfortunately the law in Ireland still holds that shooting a landlord is murder. Of course in the good time coming such a glaring instance of class legislation will be remedied ; but we must deal with things as they are, not as they ought to be, and just now, such is the tyranny and injustice of our Saxon laws, that the tenant who shoots the land-lord has just as good a chance of being hung as the landlord who shoots the tenant. This Radical remedy for Irish discontent is a general one. The doctors make no exception, so of course the more general the application of the remedy the more widespread the benefit.

Well, there are in Ireland about 450,000 tenants, and about 18,000 landowners ; about 25 tenants to each landlord. Now, this discrepancy between landlords and tenants appears to be the only real difficulty in the way of this perfect cure. If there were as many landlords as tenants it would act splendidly ; every landlord would be shot, and every tenant would be hanged for shooting him, and in time the land would get really cleared and return to prairie value. But the landlords are so tiresome—absent or present—they are always in the wrong—confound them. When they are not wanted for any useful purpose we are told there are too many of them ; and now, when they really might be of great use in promot-ing the Radical cure, we are told there are not enough of them. There are not enough landlords to give each evicted tenant a shot ; and the position of the evicted tenant who had not got his landlord to shoot would be as harrowing as that of the poor lion in the picture, that had not got his martyr. In surgery the " radical cure " sometimes means the attempt to escape a natural death by an artificial one. This seems to be the nature of the radical cure offered to Ireland. It requires three conditions to justify it. First the landlord must be a tyrant ; secondly, the evicted tenant must be hardworking and honest ; thirdly, the interloper must be a scoundrel ! But supposing neither of these conditions exist, is the Radical cure still justifiable ? And it is a fact that exactly the opposite conditions do exist. The fierce light of publicity has been blazing on the heads of the landlords and tenants for several years, and I really believe we now know all about them. We know now, as well as we know anything, that the great majority of landlords in Ireland—of course there are wretched exceptions—are as reasonable, as long-suffering, as any class who lend all over the world, and that the tenants are as good as any class who borrow all over the world. Tenants are of all sorts—some are honest, some are dishonest ; some are honest by choice, some are honest by compulsion, and *vice versâ*. The landlord lends his land on contract; the business man lends his money on contract, and we all know the latter will be quite as keen to exact his pound of flesh as the former. What, pray, would the London banker or the man of business say if political agitators went round to his clients, to whom he had lent money, and said, "Don't pay that damned usurer; he is charging you too much interest; pay half of it to me instead, and I will give you a receipt." What would they say, I ask; and there is actually no moral difference whatever between the man who lends his land on contract and the man who lends his money on contract. The distinction that is drawn by political agitators for political purposes is a sham. The strange story is that we actually see men who live by lending money, and who would be mad if the contract on which they lend it was violated, advising and excusing the repudiation of the contract of those who lend their land. The distinction is so sham, so dishonest, so evidently selfish, it makes one sick. Except for the purpose of intensifying class hatred, I don't suppose any one is fool enough to maintain that landlords exist for the pleasure of evicting. We are gravely told that till evictions cease in Ireland no English legislation of any kind can be tolerated. What nonsense! Why, evictions are not confined to Ireland. It is a fact that more evictions take place in London in one month than take place in the whole of Ireland in a year. More bankruptcies are caused by those who lend money in England in a day than by those who lend land in Ireland in a year. On September 20, 1871, Mr. Gladstone said at Aberdeen, "There is nothing that Ireland has asked that this country, and this Parliament, have refused. Parliament has done for Ireland what it would have scrupled to do for England and Scotland." Since those words were spoken, those assurances given, the English Parliament has done a great deal more for Ireland—more, a great deal, than the most sanguine Irishman ever thought it possible an English Parliament would do, or even be asked to do—and if Mr. Gladstone's words are true, and it is a fact that Parliament has done for Ireland what it would have scrupled to do for England and Scotland, it is England and Scotland that are in arrear, not Ireland. Before the Imperial Parliament is asked to do more for Ireland let it overcome what Mr. Gladstone calls "its scruples," and do for England and Scotland what it has already done for Ireland. Why are England and Scotland—London, Glasgow, Manchester, and Birmingham—to be put entirely on one side for Ireland? There is no reason, except that unscrupulous politicians can make capital out of the one and cannot out of the other. In the 4,500,000 who crowd round London there are more evictions, more deaths from starvation, more want, misery, than amongst the 4,500,000 who inhabit Ireland—10 times more, 20 times more. Why has not London as good a right to consideration as Ireland? Let us look at evictions in Ireland and evictions in London, and see where the shoe pinches most. In London a man pays 3s. 6d. a week for a wretched room in a pauper warren, with four bare walls, and if at the end of his week his 3s. 6d. is not paid he and his family are turned into the street, and his stock of furniture is sold. This 3s. 6d. a week gives him shelter, but nothing else. It gives him nothing—no employment, or the means of earning a penny. In Ireland, for 3s. 6d. a week a man gets perhaps three acres of land and a cottage, or a hovel or shelter of some kind, perhaps a patch of garden, perhaps a pig-stye. If he is inclined to work, and be industrious, he can manage to produce a good deal towards the support of his family. For his 3s. 6d. he gets employment. He can work 10 hours a day if he likes at his three acres, and it will pay him well if he does. His rent is not required of him every week, but every six months or 12 months, and he is not turned out, and his pig sold, and his little property seized the instant he is in arrears. He is allowed to go on for a year, or two perhaps, sometimes even five years, before his little holding is required of him. Not only is the land lent him, but the produce of the land, for six or twelve months before he is asked to pay a shilling. Rents in London, in proportion for what you get, are ten, twenty, fifty times more grinding and oppressive than rents in Ireland, and yet we are urged to leave alone the frightful misery that prevails in England in order to advance the comparative prosperity that exists in Ireland! Why is the man who succeeds an evicted tenant in Ireland to be treated as a loathsome leper any more than the man who succeeds an evicted tenant in London? Why is the landlord who for just cause evicts from his 3s. 6d. tenement in Ireland to be shot, any more than the landlord who evicts from his 3s. 6d. room in a pauper warren in London? Is the latter more generous, more considerate? Does he give greater value for his rent? Does he allow the poor wretch who can't pay, who can't get work, to remain on till he can? Not he. No arrears here. No hanging gale. No part payment. Your money or the street. No other option. I repeat, there are more evictions in London in a month, and more miseries attending them, than in the whole of Ireland in a year. What sham. nonsense, hypocrisy the whole cry is! And worse still, that an ex-Prime Minister of England should give his authority to such a shameful deceit. It is a fact, believe it who like, that in not one single point, not one, has Ireland any right or any claim to priority of legislation over England or Scotland. The great gulf between rich and poor is broader and deeper in England than in Ireland; the extremes of wealth and poverty are greater and more emphasised. Parliament has done more for Ireland than for England and Scotland. Is it likely that England and Scotland will long waive their just rights in order that selfish politicians may make more capital? Pauperism, starvation, sickness, drunkenness, vice, these are the subjects that should first command the attention of a civilised or civilising Government. Well, all these, alas, are more grievous, more intensified in England than in Ireland. For several years Ireland has had almost a monopoly of legislation. Do what we can for her she will not be remedied. It is time she should stand on one side for a time and let the other portions of the Empire have their turn. The laws in Ireland are in no degree whatever worse than the laws in England. Ireland is as free and independent as any part of the United Kingdom. Only once has the Habeas Corpus Act been suspended, and that was by Mr. Gladstone. The Irish leave the country not because the laws are unjust, but because there is no work to do. If the mountain won't go to Mahomed, Mahomed must go to the mountain. If employment won't go to the Irish, the Irish must go to the employment; and this is what is happening. It is certain and inevitable, and the effect must continue as long as the cause exists. Give Ireland remunerative industries, give her people remunerative work at home, and they will return to their country, and Ireland will be prosperous ; but without remunerative industries she can never rise above pauperism. Simple agriculture, living from hand to mouth, is a condition of pauperism, unless combined with sale and barter and remunerative industries.

It is not the English laws, it is not the landlords, it is not the Roman Catholic religion, it is not the Protestant religion that has impoverished Ireland—it is Free Trade. There is no more doubt of that than that I am writing this line at this moment. Too much zeal, too much zeal, that is what has brought a deadly sickness on Ireland ; and if continued in the same direction, must cause her death. The obstinate, short-sighted, exaggerated zeal of our political economists, who have forced foreign competition on a patient perfectly unfitted to bear it, has destroyed all the industries of Ireland, and inflicted on her " La plaie la plus devorante "—the curse of chronic and increasing poverty. Free Trade, English and foreign competition, are bleeding Ireland to death, but the Free Trade doctors are inexorable. " My mission is to bleed and purge," said Dr. Sangrado, " if the patient dies so much the worse for him, I have the satisfaction of knowing he has died under the only perfect medical treatment in the world." My mission is to force Free Trade on the Irish, say the Free Trade Sangrados, if the patient dies so much the worse for him, we have the comfort of knowing that he has died under the only perfect system of political economy in the word. Is not this *trop de zele* ?

1886.

CONJURING.

THE Chinese don't believe women have souls. "Dear me," said a mandarin, when he first heard a Christian missionary announce the equality of the sexes in this particular; "I must go home and tell my wife. She will be immensely amused to hear she has got a soul." And so perhaps many of us will be immensely amused to hear that Providence interferes in general elections ; but such it appears is the case. Mr. Gladstone had scarcely advanced thirty miles on his journey to Midlothian when he invoked God's blessing on his approaching efforts to bring a good thumping Radical majority under his umbrella. But supposing Lord Salisbury also invokes Divine support for the Conservative umbrella, it will be very awkward. It will be like the rival Popes at Rome and Avignon, each blessing his own flock and cursing the flock of his opponent one clergyman praying for rain to swell his turnips and his neighbour praying for fine weather to save his crops. Certainly it does appear at first sight rather a *mauvaise plaisanterie* to invoke the support of the Almighty for the disestablishment of the Church and the removal of your neighbour's landmark, which as yet are the only distinct planks in the Radical platform. But I suppose it is all right ? It looks like chaos ; but it is in truth the "dawn of the Radical creation," that is all. We have yet to see what exact form Mr. Gladstone's great *apologia* to the electors of Midlothian for five years of misgovernment, pledges broken, treasure wasted—for blood-guiltiness and red ruin—will take. Will he risk the publican's cry, "God, be merciful to me, a sinner," or will he, with the Pharisee, say, "God, I thank Thee I am not as other men are—that wicked Beaconsfield, that odious Salisbury, that horrid Churchill, or even that good Iddesleigh ! " I think there is little doubt which form of prayer he will adopt—at any rate he has begun well, for he already assumes that Providence is on his side. Of course Mr. Gladstone must be allowed a good deal of licence in this matter. His vanity has been seriously hurt, and he is naturally very sore. He is just now an example of "Les plus rusés sont les premieres pris." He is without any doubt *le plus rusé*, the most cunning party leader this country has ever seen, and he is in the ridiculous position of being the victim of his own ruse. When he threw up the sponge six months ago with a majority of 70, it was a ruse to strengthen his hand. He never for a moment expected that the country would part with him ; he expected the mere thought of resignation would bring the Frondeurs to their marrow bones, and that he would be called back by the unanimous voice of the nation. But he was not ; and now his rival has had an opportunity of showing the public that it is no loser by the change. It is gall and wormwood to the Radicals to see a Conservative Minister so well armed at all points that they cannot pierce a joint in his armour. Anything but this.

Welcome misgovernment under Mr. Gladstone; welcome a revolution under Mr. Parnell; but good government under Lord Salisbury —God forbid !

Leaving Providence alone, what is the position now? The electoral fair is nearly over; and indeed it is time—the performers have swallowed their knives and eaten their balls of fire, produced endless reams of paper from their mouths, the clowns have shouted at each other and grinned through horse collars till both they and their spectators are tired. Even the exciting "twopence more and up goes the donkey" fails to attract. The fun of the fair is over, and the public are only waiting to see the great conjuror perform his well-known trick of turning black into white and white into black before they go home, fatigued if not satisfied. It is his one trick. Nobody can approach him in it; for 50 years he has been performing it in public and private, till practice has made him perfect. It never fails to draw, and indeed it is worth seeing, and when the performer steps into the ring with his conjuring bag and his umbrella (conjurors always have a bag and an umbrella), there is always more or less of a sensation.

Ladies and gentlemen, says the master, if you will allow me, I will now show you my great trick of turning black into white and white into black. Here is a pack of cards. Some, you see, are white, some are black. Now, if you will carefully watch these cards, you will see that as I am addressing you the black cards will gradually assume a paler hue, and the white cards will assume a darker hue, till by degrees the cards that were quite white will actually appear quite black, and the cards that were quite black will actually appear quite white. Here, ladies and gentlemen, are several cards—" Budget of £100,000,000," " Bombardment of Alexandria," " Slaughter of 30,000 Arabs," " Desertion and Death of Gordon," that now appear to you to be quite black. If you will only watch them, and listen to me, you will see them all become as white as snow. And here is one card, " Six months of Conservative Administration," that appears to you now quite white; only keep your eye on it, and you will soon see I will make it appear as black as soot. It is very simple, I assure you—no deception; only the gift of the gab, nothing else. And sure enough the trick will be done before our very eyes, and none of us can tell how.

I don't agree with Sidney Smith that the Scotch are slow at taking a joke. On the contrary, I think their wit is as pungent as their snuff. But even those who have never appreciated a joke before must see something very funny in Mr. Gladstone's coming before them just now to ask for a return of their confidence. Confidence in what? Confidence in his inability to govern—in his inability to keep together the Radical majority? Or is it only renewed expression of confidence in his ability to turn black into white and white into black that he is asking for? But there are signs that the country has had enough of word-painting, and wants a little plain speaking; and this will be very awkward for the Word-Conjurer. His occupation will be gone.

Are not the Liberals rather hard on Mr. Gladstone? He has declared so often, and so persistently, that he wishes to retire from public life, that it is impossible not to believe him. Why, then, do they compel him at the advanced age of 77 to take the field again against his will? Even when he consents it is with the understanding that he is only a "stopgap"—a "stopgap" for whom? For Lord Hartington or Sir William Harcourt? But does the country want a stopgap at all? If the democratic flood gates are really opened, and the revolutionary torrent threatens the land, what is the use of a stopgap? We want a different man; a strong man who can either direct the torrent or arrest it, not a stopgap who would not attempt to do either the one or the other. Never in our history have we had less opening for a stopgap Minister. The issues are before the country—at least they are very rapidly coming before it—and we want rather to make up our minds which side to take than to shirk our responsibility under a stopgap. It is an age of delusions, but the most extraordinary delusion of all is that Mr. Gladstone is the Saviour of the Whig Party! Why, he has destroyed it. Ten years of his rule have reduced it from the most powerful party in the State to a body of from 50 or 60 sulky, expostulating gentlemen, following unwillingly at the tail of the Radicals! A Whig must be a Christian indeed who will now prostrate himself under the umbrella. But what is of far more importance to us than what Mr. Gladstone has done, is what the new electors intend to do. How will they vote? How will they be influenced by the three acres and the cow; by the ransom proposal; by the disestablishment of the Church? It is, I believe, safe to assume this: that the old electorate and the new will not pull together. The bribe of the three acres and the cow is not addressed to the old electors: disestablishment does not tempt them; and the proposed ransom actually comes out of their pockets. They do not forget that ten years ago, when Mr. Gladstone wanted their vote, he offered them the income-tax; but that now he offers them nothing—on the contrary, that he proposes to make them find the bribe to tempt the new electors. How the electorate as a whole will vote nobody can tell, but I think this much is certain—that the old electorate will be far more Conservative than they were at the last election, and that if the decision rested with them they would return a very large Conservative majority. I assume it as absolutely certain that the great mass of moderate Liberals in the country will vote Conservative. How can they help it? They agree more or less cordially with every plank in the Conservative platform, and they detest more or less bitterly every plank in the Radical platform, and the ballot is their ally. The most powerful Conservative agent at the approaching election will be the ballot—for one Conservative who will use the ballot to vote Radical a thousand Radicals will use the ballot to vote Conservative. It is not at all unlikely that the Radicals will be hoist with their own petard. There is one consideration that will exercise very considerable influence in the coming election, and that is the British love of fair play. There are vast numbers who think that if Mr. Gladstone failed to govern with a majority of 70, and threw up the sponge, it is only fair play to give his opponents a chance of governing in his place. One fact, I think, has by degrees come home to the minds of most educated men not in the party swim, and that is, that under no possible

·conditions can Lord Salisbury be as dangerous to the country as Mr. Gladstone, for the very good reason that there is not the same glamour attached to his name, and that he would be turned out, *sans phrase*, before he had had time to do one-hundreth part of the mischief.

1886.

DRIFTING.

WHEN Anarcharsis was asked which was the safest ship, he
answered, "That which has arrived in port." I suppose, therefore, we may assume, that that astute Scythian would have defined as
the most unsafe ship the one that never arrives in port at all, and
such a ship is our Government. Never since God made little fishes
has such an unfortunate, helpless craft been seen on the ocean of
politics. For four long years it has been drifting to and fro, heading
by turns to every point of the compass ; now under a press of sail,
now under no sail at all ; now on one tack, now on the other ;
making sternway and leeway, but never headway ; missing stays,
jibbing, drifting—in fact, doing everything that the most insecure
vessel in the most inefficient hands can by any possibility be made
to do ; a phantom ship, always steering for a port, but doomed
never to enter it ; a warning to all "sailor chaps" to what base
uses a good ship may be brought by want of common sense,
indecision and funk. Joking apart, is it any exaggeration to say
that the Government ship has never once—absolutely not once—
during the last four years been able to enter a single port it
cleared for, or avoid drifting away to some other port it had no
intention of visiting? Has the Government once—even once—
in four years been able to do what it said it would do, or go where
it said it would go ? Has it not, on the other hand, invariably done
what it said it would not do, and gone where it said it would not go ?
What a fortune a betting man might have made during the last four
years by always betting 100 to 8 against the Government programme !
"You say you'll evacuate Egypt in six months—I bet you 100 to 8
you don't ; you say you'll pass the Ilbert Bill—100 to 8 you don't ;
that you'll secure the French alliance—100 to 8 you don't ; 100 to 8
against the Congo Treaty—against the French Commercial Treaty—
against the Suez Canal Treaty—against the pacification of Ireland—
against the pacification of Zululand—100 to 8 against the London
Conference, 100 to 8 against the Mercantile Marine Bill, against
the Half-Sovereign Token Bill, in fact 100 to 8 against anything or
everything suggested or attempted by the Government." This is
no exaggeration ; it is a fact—at least it appears so to me. The
Government appears doomed to the endless task of the Danaides,
filling a sieve with water. This is the price they have paid for
effacing themselves, for placing their actions and their judgments
unreservedly in the hands of a chief who probably has more
quicksilver in his composition than the whole twelve of them
together ; but less of the baser metal—common sense—than the
very noodle of the party. It is because they have pretended to do
what they knew they could not do—rule an empire without an
Imperial policy—because they have attempted to dispense with
experience and common sense—that twelve wise men have been

checkmated at every turn, and that the nation is now sailing round and round the fabled Anticyra, seeking in vain for the charm that shall restore its lost reason. It is said that when Mr. Gladstone succeeded to office he announced that he "intended to rule England according to the inspirations of a Higher Power." Whether he did say so or not I do not venture to decide, but it sounds so like so many things that he undoubtedly has said that I am inclined to believe he did say it. "What instrument is this?" asked Captain Gladstone when he came on board the good ship Empire. "Oh, that's Imperial interests, the compass we steer by," was the reply." "And what is this?" "That's experience, the chart that shows us the shoals, and rocks, and currents." "And what is this?" "Oh, that's common sense, the lead with which we feel our way in fogs and thick weather." "Oh, indeed, and these are what the last captain navigated with, are they? Overboard with them; none of such trash for me." "But," urge the officers, "not only the last captain, but all preceding captains have navigated with them, and, indeed, they have enabled us to weather many a storm, and there is no safety without them." "Safety be——" (I beg your pardon), shouts Captain Gladstone, in a rage; "overboard with them! What do you take me for? Do you suppose I am one of your long-shore captains who requires compass, and charts, and soundings, or the experience of predecessors? Not a bit of it? I am no ordinary skipper, I assure you. I don't trust to compasses, and charts, and the lead. I navigate the ship by the 'inspirations of a Higher Power,' and if that is not good enough for you I should like to know what is." But unfortunately common sense and the "inspirations of a Higher Power" mean very different things—in fact, as explained by results, the latter may be summed up by the monosyllabe "drift." Following this fatal inspiration, we drifted into the bombardment of Alexandria, we drifted into the occupation of Egypt, we drifted into the Conference, we drifted into the Soudan expedition, we drifted into the financial *coup d'état*—we drifted into bad terms with France, Germany, and, indeed, all Europe—we drifted into chaos in Ireland, into chaos at the Cape, and now, if the Radicals are to be believed, we are drifting into revolution at home! I beg their pardon. I forgot; evolution, not revolution, is the word. According to the inspiration of the Higher Power, our case is a very bad one. Poor Britannia is rotten to the core. Evolution alone can save her from annihilation. No longer the model that other nations should imitate, she is a warning of what they should avoid. In the process of evolution, indeed, destruction may come upon all we love and boast of; but what of that? "Il faut souffrir pour être belle!" Out of the impurities of the old Britannia will be evoked a brand-new one—something so smart, so glossy, so spick and span, so Radically symmetrical, that the whole civilized world will exclaim in astonishment and delight, Oh, my!" There are some weak-kneed creatures who tell us that evolution and revolution are very much alike—that we are playing with fire; that we are going so far and so fast, we shall not be able to stop, and we are warned to beware the dangerous maxim that has ruined the honour and virtue of more than one woman and more than one statesman: "that on some conjunctions it is allowable to neglect the outworks of honour, provided they maintain inviolable the fort itself." But what are the maxims of the wise to the inspiration of a Higher Power? But there is no use bewailing our Kismet. Evolution or revolution, chaos or order, we are in for it. Our fate has passed from our own hands into the hands of one who, "unguibus et rostro," by eloquence and by threats, will compel us to do as he wishes. We have elected the bramble to be king over over us, and it is ridiculous now to hesitate in our obedience. "If ye have really anointed me king," says the bramble, "come and put yourselves under my shadow (that is to say, don't presume to thwart me); if not, fire shall come out of the bramble, and consume the cedars of Lebanon." Alas! poor cedars of Lebanon. Alas! poor Lords, in the face of this warning, you have ventured to thwart the bramble. How can you hope, how can you deserve, to escape the fire prepared for you? By all means let us put ourselves under the shadow of the bramble. Let us acclaim Mr. Gladstone for all the great and glorious works he has done for us—the bombardment of Alexandria, the battles of the Soudan, the French and German alliances, the London Conference, the European concert, for our prosperous trade, because he has sent out the fire to consume the cedars of Lebanon. But don't let us go into hysterics over him because he can articulate more words in a shorter space of time than any human being that ever lived, or because he can cut down a tree not nearly so well as a woodman, or read the lessons no better than an ordinary curate! There is nothing grand in these things. It makes our hero-worship vulgar. Let us take warning from the satirist. "Peuple français," said Rousseau, "tu n'est pas peut être le plus esclave, mais tu est bien le plus valet de tous les peuples."

1886.

THE GOSPEL OF MURDER.

T HE History of Religion since the Flood would be funny reading; creditable, perhaps, to the ingenuity of mankind, but
scarcely to their common sense. They have, indeed, in turns
worshipped almost everything, animate and inanimate, clean and
unclean, that the world has produced—bulls, calves, dogs, cats,
alligators, serpents, stocks, stones, and "terminal" figures; and
now, last stage of all, they worship Words. We have had a Stone
Age, an Iron Age, a Bronze Age (the Brass Age, of course, is perpetual), and now we have a Word Age; and the credulous votaries
of this childish superstition

> " Their wings display and altars raise,
> And torture one poor word ten thousand ways."

And a king's ransom is offered to those who can torture a word into
the greatest number of meanings, or, what is better still, into no
meaning at all. Unfortunately for us, the new superstition is fatal
to truth. *Certa sunt paucis.* Truth is contained in few words;
verbosity is fatal to it. Under the demoralising influence of this
new worship a man says and does things that two years ago he
would have sworn by his gods he could never do. The confusion
of tongues is complete; the Tower of Babel was a joke to it.
Even when you know what a man says you do not pretend to
know what he means; and if you talk to your friend in the street
you begin by asking him, What language are we to speak, English
or Gladstonese? A short time ago, I shudder in relating it, it was
whispered that a certain person, who shall be nameless, was writing a dictionary. Imagine a dictionary with a distinct meaning
for every word, for every day in the week, and two for Sundays!
Why the lunatic asylums of the whole world would not have
been large enough to hold half of us. Mercifully, the report was
too bad to be true. It was only a frightful nightmare. As it is,
even without the authority of a dictionary, our mother tongue has
been so altered and disfigured that we don't recognise it—Traitor
now means a loyal man, Renegade, a man who holds to his faith,
Judas means Christ; in fact, every word means the very reverse of
what it has always meant since " Adam was the first man, and
Eve she was the t'other; and Cain he walk the treadmill because
he kill him broder " (rather an awkward incident, of course, in that
age of innocence !) The disintregation of our language goes on at
such at pace that two years are quite sufficient to invert completely
the meaning of any word; take " boycotting," for instance, quite
a recent coinage—we know what it meant when it was first
invented; but I defy the best scholar in the country to define
what it means now. It originally meant "combined intimidation,"
" intolerant tyranny," " moral assassination," the " sanction of

murder," shooting a man in the legs, treating him like a mangy
dog, preventing his going to church, shaving a girl's head, cutting
off a cow's tail, &c.

Well, now it means the very reverse of all this. It is an "Irish
virtue," a "national protest against oppression," the "noble act of
a people struggling, and justly struggling to be free. It is the old
story. "Dat veniam corvis, vexat censura columbis." Two years
ago we thought the ravens were the aggressors ; now we see plainly
that it is the doves. We were indignant with the ravens for attacking the doves ; now we are furious with the doves for resisting the
ravens. We no longer denounce the ruffians who shave the
girl, or shoot the peasant in the legs, or cut off the cow's tail ;
we denounce the girl who owns the hair, the peasant who owns the
legs, and the cow that owns the tail. This mental Fata Morgana
that makes us see things completely upside down is rather comical.
It is no longer the rascal who steals the honest man's watch who
should go to prison, but the honest man whose watch was stolen ;
no longer the man who breaks his contract who is dishonest, but
the wretch who presumes to hold him to his contract. And we
actually see millionaires, whose millions depend entirely on the
sanctity of contracts, advocating their repudiation. "Poor blind
mice," it would indeed be a case of "see how they run" if boycotting and the Plan of Campaign that they advocate in Ireland, were
applied to them in London. They would be ruined. The church-
mouse would be rich in comparison. But is it possible they can be
such fools as to suppose the public do not see the utter absurdity,
if not the absolute dishonesty, of their advocacy ? They may
impose a falsehood on themselves, but they don't impose it on
others. They may shut both eyes, but it does not prevent others
keeping both eyes open. "Grattez le Russe," &c., &c., applies
to everything that is sham—to every man who pretends to be what
he is not. Scratch the sleek millionaire and it is a hundred to one
you find the money-grubber ! Scratch the man who is so liberal,
so generous, so profuse with the property of others, and you find
the miser ! Let but your little finger threaten his wealth and he
will howl as if you stamped on his pet corn. The ostrich sticks
his head in the sand and thinks no one can see him, but the hunter
does, and says, "There's a silly ostrich." And the fool sticks his
head in the fool's cap and thinks his folly invisible ! Not a bit of
it, the public only smile and say, "There's another fool." The
cap of Fortunatus made a man invisible, but a fool's cap does not.
Fools who think they impose on the public by pretending to be what
they are not should take a note of this. And how has all this confusion of tongues come about ? It is very simple. The bell-
wether has a fly in his head, or a bee in his bonnet, or something
wrong somewhere, and tries to say "bah" differently from any
former bell-wether, and all the silly sheep try to imitate him.
Hence the Babel. The public are in despair to see the sheep in
St. Stephens running amuck like the deer in Richmond Park.

Mr. Gladstone is the high priest of the new culte. Like the
wicked magician in Aladdin he is both the master and the slave of
the lamp. He is both the master and slave of words—by turns

they obey him and he obeys them. Notwithstanding the dozen definitions he has himself already given of boycotting, only the other day, with delightful simplicity, he asked the Attorney-General for a new one, as if he had never heard of the word before, and then chid him, in a " superior-person " kind of way, for declining to give it. But the Attorney-General was equal to the occasion ; he fortunately had one of Mr. Gladstone's own definitions in his pocket. " Boycotting," said Mr. Gladstone in 1882, during the debate on the Crimes Bill, is " the combined intimidation made use of for the purpose of destroying the private liberty of choice, by the fear of starvation. The Land League relied upon the combined intimidation of boycotting to enforce its decrees, and the sanction of boycotting, that which stands in the rear of boycotting, and by which alone boycotting can in the long run be made thoroughly effective, is the murder which is not to be denounced." And then he goes on to say, " It is not uncharitable or rash to assume a connection between the words of the speaker (Mr. Parnell in that instance) and the acts that followed. With fatal and painful precision the steps of crime dogged the Land League," &c. At that time, of course, Mr. Gladstone, Sir William Harcourt, and Lord Spencer had satisfied themselves by " their official information " that there was a close connection between Parnellism and crime ; but the revelations of the *Times* have lately dispelled this idea. They have proved to them that their official information was entirely wrong ; that, in fact, the driven snow is not " in it " as regards purity with Parnellism in all its relations. This appears rather odd, because Parnellism is now exactly what it was then ; it has not changed the colour of a single hair.

But I am sick of trying to build an argument on Mr. Gladstone's words. It is like trying to make a rope of sand. His words are no more intended to hold water than a sieve. But still I suppose we may assume that in 1882, at any rate, he believed that boycotting led directly to murder. Does he deny that it leads directly to murder now ? In 1882 those who preached effective boycotting were preaching the gospel of murder. Are they doing so now ? This is interesting, because his most trusted friend and adviser is now directly preaching a system of boycotting infinitely more effective and tending more directly to crime than any preached before. Is he preaching the gospel of murder, I wonder ? Let us, to use Mr. Gladstone's phraseology, when addressing the Nonconformists, "illustrate this matter by what is taking place now."

A short time ago a Radical member of Parliament is reported to have urged the Irish to treat as a " loathsome leper " any man who took a farm from which another had been evicted ; that is to say, he urges the people to treat him worse than a mangy dog, to refuse him food and the necessities of life, to let him starve and die in a ditch. This reads like an exhortation to effective boycotting. At any rate, it is an exhortation to murder. If there is any meaning in the English language, it is certain that only a few years ago Mr. Gladstone denounced much less effective boycotting than this as tending to the promotion of crime, as having murder for its ultimate result. What he thinks of it now God only knows, but he carefully avoids saying anything, and silence is very significant in Mr. Gladstone. Perhaps the member who gave this loathsome advice to the Irish people would demur to the deduction that he was preaching the gospel of murder. He might argue that though treating a man like a loathsome leper is moral murder, it is not inciting to actual murder. To some of us it may appear even worse, because more cowardly; but there is a mental process called reasoning by induction, and it appears to me almost certain that reasoning in this way the exhortations to the moral murder on the interloper would be quite sufficient to cause the actual murder of the landlord. The Radical condemns the man who succeeds an evicted tenant to be treated like a loathsome leper; but the evicted tenant might argue in this way: "You tell me to treat this man like a loathsome leper; but he did not evict me, he had no hand in my eviction: he may profit by my disaster, but he in no degree caused it: the man who evicted me is my landlord, he it is that caused my disaster: but if eviction is such a crime against justice and society that you order me to commit moral murder on this man, who only succeeds me and has done me no bodily harm, in order to avenge it, what am I to do to the man who has turned me out and ruined me?" "Murder him, of course," would be the only logical reply. If I was a tenant animated by a fierce desire of revenge for being evicted, and I was indirectly urged to shoot the landlord who evicted me, I should naturally be very much influenced by the position of the person who gave me the advice. For instance, if "No. 1" or some other professor of the gospel of murder was to say to me Shoot the old—— gentleman—meaning my landlord—I should say Thank you; but if I kill him and I get the rope round my neck you won't be able to take it off. This is not good enough. Shoot him yourself. But if the Radical statesman, sitting at home at ease, urges me between the puffs of his cigarette to commit this murder, he must know that he can see me through it, and save my neck from the rope. This is good enough for me. I'll risk it! When the next landlord is shot shall we be "rash and uncharitable" in assuming a connection between the words of the Radical and the acts which followed? I wonder! I wonder if Mr. Gladstone sticks to his definition of 1882, and still maintains that "the sanction of boycotting, that which stands in the rear of boycotting, and by which alone boycotting can in the long run be made thoroughly effective, is the murder which is not to be denounced." According to my comprehension, Mr. Parnell's supposed letter is an apology for murder. The statesman's speech is an incitement to murder. The former condones past crime, the latter incites to fresh crime. Now, as I would rather condone a hundred murders committed than excite to one fresh one, I would rather a hundred times have written Mr. Parnell's letter than have made the statesman's speech.

1886.

PLAYING WITH FIRE.

REALLY Mr. Gladstone's friends are very unkind to him. They know that he is saying and doing many things that are very foolish, and that, if he was in his right mind, he would never have said or done ; but instead of trying to restrain him, they urge him on to greater excesses. When a spoilt child persists in " showing off," and says and does foolish things, his mamma or his nurse say, " Now, dear, we have had enough of this ; we'll go to bed." It is a curious fact that in second childhood men are even more prone to "show off" than in first childhood. Mr. Gladstone is showing off (and he is a spoilt child, if ever there was one). Won't some of his friends say, " Now, dear, we have had enough of this ; we'll go to bed." What a release it would be to us, and what a kindness to him. It is the only way by which he can save even a rag of reputation. He is tearing it to pieces, as a casual does his workhouse clothes. Say what you will, it is foolish—very foolish indeed, very shocking—for a man who has been Prime Minister of England to pose as a sympathiser with anarchy and public plunder, and to denounce the police for taking steps to prevent it. It is not pleasant to have to say, " Oh ! poor old fellow, he has got *mechant* in his old age : many old men do." But this is actually what hundreds and thousands of his former friends are saying to-day. The case of Mr. Gladstone, although very uncommon, is not unknown. Many men at 8o say and do things that nothing would have induced them to say and do at 40. It is a fact, sad, perhaps, but true, that "the aged do not understand judgment.' But what is uncommon, and has no parallel in the history of civilisation, is to see millionaires, whose only right to their millions is possession, and whose only security in possession is the power of the law to protect property, joining Mr. Gladstone in denouncing the police for trying to protect property. That certainly does "beat all jumps," as they say in the Wild West. What sham men those are who denounce the rights of property in Ireland and stick to it like leeches in England. How they would scream and curse, and hiss with rage, if their Consols or their acres were touched ! How they would yell at the police if they did not protect their property in time of need. When the monkey reigns it is a wise thing to dance before him ; but never, never, did our simian ancestors ever dance to such a tune as this. " What right have you," said Mr. Gladstone to Mr. Balfour, " to support the police at Mitchelstown before you knew they were right ? " " What right have you," we ask of Mr. Gladstone in return, " to denounce the action of the police in London before you knew they were wrong ? " Now, the fact is Mr. Balfour did satisfy himself that the police at Mitchelstown were in the right before he approved of their conduct. Whereas Mr. Gladstone did not satisfy himself that the police in the Lyons case were wrong before he denounced their conduct. The police in Ireland were carrying out the law when they were fiercely attacked by the mob and their lives placed in great danger ; and because they defended their lives Mr. Gladstone would have them hanged. The London Socialists threatened to march through the streets and excite the mob to destroy property, and because the police took steps to prevent them Mr. Gladstone denounces them as inquisitors, and begins babbling about Wat Tyler. What nonsense!

Now, really, is it true that the famous resources of civilisation have brought us to this, that Socialists and Anarchists are to be applauded for planning the destruction of property, and the police are to be denounced for planning its defence ? But this is actually the position Mr. Gladstone has taken up. The Socialists proclaim themselves the enemies of all property, and last year they put their professions into practice by sacking the shops ; and Mr. Gladstone's Government censured the police and removed their chief because they did not repress them with sufficient vigour. To-day the Socialists threaten again to sack and destroy, and Mr. Gladstone and his late Government actually denounce the police because they try to prevent them. It is not only absurd—it is a shame ; it is a disgrace. Both in London and in Ireland the police are denounced by Mr. Gladstone and the Radicals for protecting the very foundation of society and civilisation—the rights of property. " Remember Mitchelstown," cries Mr. Gladstone. Yes, indeed, we shall remember Mitchelstown as long as we live : not, as he supposes, for the misconduct of the police, but for the misconduct of a man who has been Prime Minister of England. Yes, we shall remember Mitchelstown, and South Audley-street, and Bond-street, and Piccadilly. People have not all lost their memories because Mr. Gladstone finds it easy to forget.

Now, what will be the result, what must be the result of Mr. Gladstone's denunciation of the police ? That in a very short time neither the police in Ireland nor the police in England will do their duty. The police are men of like natures to ourselves. Their duties are very often very dangerous and very disagreeable ; if they are to be denounced for doing their duty, they will not long continue to do it. They have the remedy in their own hands. If a policeman is not to defend his life when he considers it in danger, no man will become a policeman. And who knows when his life is in danger so well as the owner of the life himself ? How ridiculous for an outsider 500 miles away to say, " Oh ! your life was not in danger," if the owner of the life thought it was. " I am not going to put myself in the way of being killed if I am to be hanged for defending myself. If I am denounced for defending property, I will no longer do so ; it is no pleasure to me—let the owners protect it themselves." This is what the policeman will say, and who can say he is wrong ? This is the dilemma Mr. Gladstone's last phase of folly has placed us in. I wonder what Mr. Gladstone's City friends think of his denouncing the police because they tried to protect property. Are their sympathies also with the dangerous classes? Where would their property be without the police ? I would ask. Where will it very soon be if they weaken the hands of order and strengthen the hands of anarchy? Before they support Mr. Gladstone in this campaign against order and property, let them realise the situation. It is very simple, a child can understand it. There are in London 40,000 professional thieves, there are 80,000 paupers, there are 300,000 more loafers, Socialists, Anarchists, foreigners, who would rob and pillage, and burn and destroy, if they got a chance. Well, between these 300,000 and 400,000 enemies of property and the owners of property there stand 13,000 police, that is all. If the public give them moral support they will keep the dangerous classes at bay; if the public follow Mr. Gladstone's advice, and deny them moral support, they will shut up, that's all. But is not that all rather a dear price to pay even for Mr. Gladstone's pleasure?

1887.

HORS LIGNE.

WHAT a man is Mr. Gladstone. Man, did I say? What a dozen men rolled into one; an epitome of men, only an epitome of a variety that has never before appeared on earth—*bien entendu*. We must be thankful for small mercies. Nature has never repeated Mr. Gladstone; nothing like him has ever appeared since the ill-omened year 1810. Evidently the mould was broken in which he was made—whether purposely or by accident Nature only knows. Perhaps we scarcely realise the danger we have escaped. If the Gladstone type had been repeated even once only, it is certain that chaos would have come again. With a Gladstone on one side, and a Gladstone on the other, the fate of the Kilkenny cats must inevitably have been ours. If one Mr. Gladstone has so demoralised us that we no longer know black from white, right from wrong, honour from dishonour, patriotism from treason, that we have even lost the meaning of our own language, two Mr. Gladstones would have reduced us to a mental condition in which the cerebral inversion of the famous Major Brown, upside down, would have been an actual object of envy. In all professions—whether soldiers, sailors, tinkers, tailors, gentleman, apothecary, ploughboy, thief, and even politician—there are unwritten rules that ensure a certain uniformity of practice, that restrain the competitors, and keep them within bounds, as it were; and when any one violates these unwritten rules, we say he is *hors ligne*. Without these rules the profession or rather game—for is it not more of a game than a profession?—of party politics would be impossible. Generally speaking, these unwritten rules are very fairly observed because they are a mutual convenience; but there is a constant inducement to break them. The player who breaks them often gets a considerable pull over the player who obeys them. Very often the more license a man allows himself in his words and actions the better chance he has of success. We all know men in society, and especially in Parliament, who owe their success entirely to playing *hors ligne*, giving themselves fuller license of word or deed than their neighbours. Of course, the moral effect of being *hors ligne* depends very much upon the position of the individual so acting. I suppose it would be considered *hors ligne* for a clergyman to play football on Sunday; but certainly we should be more surprised to see a bishop do it than a curate. So an ex-Prime Minister of England, wilfully and incessantly *hors ligne*, defying with fierce recklessness all unwritten rules that have hitherto regulated the game of party politics, is a greater shock to our moral sense than if it were only one of Mr. Schnadhorst's nominees. Now, it is needless to say that Mr. Gladstone is constantly *hors ligne*. He claims to be entirely above the unwritten rules of party politics, and this gives him an immense advantage; but no political opponent must presume to follow his example—if he does his indignation is tremendous. He began very early. It was certainly *hors ligne* for an English Minister to apologise for the heathen Chinee poisoning the wells in time of war. It was certainly *hors ligne* for an ex-Prime Minister to apologise for moonlighters shaving a poor girl's head and covering it with pitch. It was certainly *hors ligne* to assist reckless partisans to drag into disrepute the Speaker of the House of Commons; to insinuate that English judges and English juries are venal; and English justice a farce. It is certainly " *hors ligne* " to denounce a man as a traitor steeped in treason to the very lips, and to cast him into prison without a trial, and two years after-wards to uphold him as a noble patriot. It is certainly " *hors ligne* " for an ex-Prime Minister to take Heaven to witness that for 15 years he has been a Unionist, and then to turn slap round and take Heaven to witness that for 15 years he has been a Separationist. But it is no use enlarging on this subject. Mr. Gladstone is always *hors ligne*, always breaking bounds—that is to say, when it promotes his party objects; it is his normal condition; but during the last fortnight he has eclipsed himself—he has actually out-Heroded Herod. In his Jonah-like anger against his political opponents he has done two things, that, till the contrary is proved, I never will believe England or Scotland, or even gallant little Wales, will condone in silence. He declines to inquire whether the Parnellite party, to whom he proposes to hand over absolutely the lives and property of two millions, more or less, of our loyal and Protestant fellow subjects, are connected with crime or not; and he calls upon the declared enemies of England, the fiercest she has ever had, assassins, dynamiters, and all—for he carefully guards himself from making any exception—to come over and help him to put pressure on Parliament and the national will. Of course, as usual, his followers will make excuses for the dangerous impulses of what Lord Randolph Churchill calls an old man in a hurry, but they cannot shut their eyes to the infamy to which these impulses are dragging the nation.

No man has ever had so much rope given him as Mr. Gladstone. Often and often we have been cheered with the cry—Well! This time, at any rate, he must hang himself. But he never has. He has always managed to riggle out of the noose somehow. But I declare I do believe that now his time is approaching. He has declared his intention to hand over Ireland and 2,000,000, more or less, of loyal and Protestant subjects of the Queen to what Mr. Bright calls—very justly, I believe—a foreign conspiracy, and he calls upon the avowed enemies of England in America and elsewhere to come over and help him to force his policy on the majority of Parliament and of the country. Now, I take it it is *hors ligne* for an ex-Prime Minister of England to apply to the avowed enemies of his country to assist him to coerce the majority of his countrymen, but just at the critical moment the *Times* newspaper reprints from the Parnellite press in Ireland and America some startling statements that appear indisputably to connect Parnellism with crime, and caps them with the now famous letter of

Mr. Parnell, and says to Mr. Gladstone "You must not, you cannot, hand over Ireland and 2,000,000 of our fellow subjects absolutely and entirely to these men till their innocence from these charges is established." "Oh! won't I?" virtually replies Mr. Gladstone. "Guilty or not guilty, I will hand over Ireland to these men, though I have to call on the mob from the streets and the dynamiters and assassins from America to help me." Mr. Gladstone now declares that his official information enables him to state that there is not, and never has been, any connection between Parnellism and crime ; but he forgets apparently that only three years ago he denounced Mr. Parnell as steeped in treason to the very lips; declared that crime dogged the steps of the Land League, of which he was the chief, and cast him into prison without trial. Three years ago, therefore, Mr. Gladstone did see that there was a connection between Parnellism and crime. What has induced him to change his opinion ? Now, whether Mr. Parnell was guilty of treason when Mr. Gladstone put him in prison without trial I don't know ; but this I do know, and all the world knows it, that since that time Mr. Parnell, to his honour be it recorded, has not gone back one inch from the principles he then held and the claims he then advanced, and if these principles and these claims constituted treason then they constitute treason now. Mr. Gladstone himself is the most damaging witness against Mr. Parnell. When the Old Parliamentary Hand appealed to the mob in Hyde Park to coerce the majority in Parliament the appeal fell just a little flat, and he was very angry, and he at once telegraphed to the Home Rule organisation in America to send over addresses and deputations (knives and dynamite as well, I suppose) to enable him to force the hand of Parliament. Was not this a little *hors ligne* for an ex-Prime Minister ? Now Mr. Gladstone knows, like all the rest of the world, that assassination and dynamite societies have been, and there is every reason to suppose are still, connected with the Home Rule movement in America. He knows, as all the world knows, that scores of men in the pay of the American Home Rule associations have for years been going to and fro and up and down the land devising evil against his country, sharpening knives, and preparing bombs ; and, therefore, he knows, as distinctly as he knows anything, that in appealing to the Irish-American Home Rulers to come over to help him to force the hand of the British Government, he is asking the assistance of England's greatest enemies—yes, her greatest enemies—who pray for her destruction, who vow her destruction, who have tried to blow up her Parliament House, her public offices, the Tower of London, her ships, and anything and everything belonging to her—to coerce by threats and actual outrage his own countrymen. Was ever such a foul blow struck by any Englishman at his country? I declare I don't know its parallel in any age or in any country. Certainly we have had to drink deep of the cup of national humiliation. Majuba Hill, the desertion of Gordon, are enough for a generation; but to solicit the assistance of the rowdyism of America, the sworn enemies of our country, to come over and rule us, is a disgrace far, far greater than these. It takes a long time to open the eyes of the masses ; but I

believe they are opening at last, and when they realise the full measure
of the humiliation Mr. Gladstone's appeal is bringing on his country,
I believe the indignation will not be mealy-mouthed. Because Mr.
Gladstone, in his passionate fury against his political opponents,
forgets his duty to his country, forgets himself—swallows himself,
collars and all—are we to do the same? It is absurd. But have
the English and the Scotch and the Welsh fallen so low that they
will tolerate Mr. Gladstone's appeal to the assassins and dynamiters
of America to come over and coerce our Parliament and our Government? Will they haul down the national flag, and say to their
fierce and now triumphant enemies, " Do with us as you will ? "
Will they hand over to a foreign conspiracy, body and soul, two
millions of fellow subjects? I do not believe it. If they do
" actum est de Anglia ; " then, indeed, it is evident that the old
spirit has gone out of the country, that the pride of race is dead;
and we shall then have evidence that cannot lie that Mr. Gladstone
has fulfilled his baneful destiny and ruined his country.

1887.

TOOTH-DRAWING.

THE old French proverb "To lie like a tooth-drawer" (menteur comme un arracheur de dents) is withdrawn from circulation, and is replaced by the modern English one—"to lie like a politician." Recent events have made this change inevitable. It has long been evident that the tooth-drawer is no longer "in it" with the politician ; and it is deceiving the public to continue a pre-eminence that no longer exists. At the same time it is announced that Mr. Gladstone is engaged in compiling a handbook on political morality, for the use of his followers, stating what a Radical, of the pure grit, may and what he may not do to help his party and him-self.

The text of this new gospel of political veracity from the hand of the great master himself is urgently required. Things are too bad to continue as they are. The last figment of the old school of political veracity has disappeared, and as yet there is nothing to replace it. Mr. Gladstone has hoisted his old gingham in the Great Wilderness of Doubt, and offers a complete dispensation, present and retrospective, from pledges and promises to all who will come under its shelter and fall down and worship him. It is astonishing how popular this new gospel is, and with what eager-ness the proselytes throw over the old love and are on with the new ; but it has its inconveniences, and they are considerable ; it establishes distinct and indeed antagonistic codes of veracity for gentlemen and for politicians. What is actually praiseworthy in the latter is actually damnable in the former ! And when a man has constantly to ask himself, Am I speaking and acting as a gentleman or as a politician ? he is apt occasionally to get some-what mixed.

The following is a case in point. " During the fifty years of her Majesty's reign 3,700,000 persons have been evicted in Ireland," says Mr. Gladstone. " During the fifty years of her Majesty's reign 350,000 persons have been evicted in Ireland," says Mr. Bal-four, " and half of this number have returned to their holdings as caretakers or tenants." It appears that Mr. Balfour is right and that Mr. Gladstone is wrong, very wrong ; that in order to strengthen his case against his country he has adopted the very simple process of multiplying the real number of evictions by ten ; but does Mr. Gladstone amend his statement because it has proved to be false ? Oh, dear no ; as a gentleman he would have to do so ; but as a politician, he has not. " A politician should shrink from no state-ment, however false, so long as it gives probability to his story," says Reynard the Fox to his children ; and his advice still holds good with the present generation of politicians—in fact, they have improved upon it. It is very useful to remember that the political morality taught at Malepartus is identical with the political morality

taught under the gingham. "Did you," asks a "put-up" correspondent of Mr. Gladstone, "say that Mr. Parnell was steeped in
treason to the very nails?" "No, I did not," says the Great Man.
"All Wales knows now that I did not;" but I believe all Wales,
and all England, and all Scotland, and all Ireland knows, that he
said that Mr. Parnell was steeped in treason to the very lips. It is
true he said "lips;" it is a shameful falsehood to say he said
"nails." After that it is plain to everyone that the tooth-drawer is no
longer in it. Qualis rex, talis grex. "Who teaches the King of
Macedon teaches all his subjects." Undoubtedly the "nameless
one"—I cannot conceive who it is—who teaches Mr. Gladstone
teaches all his subjects, for his political morality has become almost
immediately the morality of them all. Under the shade of that
deadly upas, the Gladstonian gingham, men say and do things
that only two years ago the most hardened tooth-drawer would
have shuddered at. "The King can do no wrong" may be
a harmless fiction; but it is no longer harmless if his subjects take
it into their heads to imitate him. Philosophers tell us that the
ne plus ultra of human happiness is to have a good digestion and
no conscience. This is all very well for the ordinary tooth-drawer,
but for the higher walks of the profession the possession of a
conscience is nine points of the law. It marks the difference
between the amateur and the professional. The amateur can get
on well enough without a conscience, but a professional is of no
use at all unless his conscience, his motives, his humanity are
are always en évidence ; and besides, nothing is so safe as appealing
to your conscience when you know that it is only another name for
your will. An elastic, very long-suffering conscience is indispensable to the successful politician. "Vellem si liceret," sighed the
Roman Emperor, casting sheep's eyes at forbidden fruit. "Licet
si libet," was the curt reply. But it was enough; and he immediately married his grandmother—no, I think it was his step-
mother; but it does not much matter to us what privileges they
enjoyed in those Imperial days ! "Vellem si liceret," sighed Mr.
Gladstone. "I should so like to go in for Home Rule, secure the
Irish vote, and dish the Tories; but after all I have said about the
unity of the Empire, treason, &c., I really hardly think it would do.
What do you say, conscience?" "Licet si libet," is the prompt
reply, and he does it. "Vellem si liceret," says Mr. Gladstone
again, "I should so like to secure the vote of the fanatics by removing all restraints on the dissemination of disease, but really I am
afraid common sense, humanity, my duty to my neighbours, forbid
me to do it. What do you say, conscience?" "Licet si libet,"
replies the obliging friend, and King Virus reigns supreme. "Vellem si liceret," says Mr. Gladstone, "I should so like to secure the
railway vote by supporting the Channel Tunnel, but I'm afraid it
will hardly do; it is only the other day I gained applause as the
champion of the silver streak. What do you say conscience?"
"Licet si libet" is the reply; and, by Jove, he does it. "Vellem si
liceret," says he once more, "the Established Church has presumed
to cold-shoulder me, and I should so like to smash it up before I
go, and give its emoluments to my staunch friends, the Nonconfor-

mists ; but I declare I think that this is a little too strong even for me. What do you say, conscience ? " " Licet si libet," replies the Demon, and the decree for the Disestablishment is already signed. But these incessant changes of views between Mr. Gladstone and his conscience are rather monotonous. They always end the same way. In fact, such a very highly-trained conscience is merely a copying machine to register its master's will. But if veracity has disappeared from politics, cant has taken its place ; and it is a fact that with the immense majority of mankind it is far more popular and effective.

" One day," said Henning, " Reynard came to the gates dressed like a pilgrim ; he told me he had become a monk, and in obedience to his sacred vow must never touch meat again, so that in future all might feel at their ease so far as he was concerned, and in witness of it all showed me a hair shirt under his coat. Then he said he must hurry away, as he had a great deal of business, and to sing Evensong that day, and away he went reading his prayers most devoutly. Full of joy, I went to my family and told them the news, that since Reynard had turned monk we had nothing to fear. Alas ! the traitor was only shamming ; that very day he captured and carried off the finest of my sons."

Have we not a Holy Fox among us ? Do we not remember how, a few years ago, he told us that he was getting old, that the things of this world no longer interested him, that he was going to devote the rest of his time on earth to singing Evensong and reading his Prayers devoutly ? Did he not show us the hair shirt, &c. ? How we believed him and congratulated each other on the prospect of a little rest. And do we not remember how that very night Evensong and Prayers were pitched to the devil, and he suddenly clutched his unsuspecting opponent by the throat ? Of course, the whole thing was nonsense—only a *coup de maître* in the school of hypocrisy ; our Holy Fox no more intended to become a monk, give up meat, wear a hair shirt, and devote his time to Prayers and Evensong than did Reynard himself. The double transformation was most artistic. It was in the highest degree touching to see the successful orator pitch away his toga and don the hair shirt ; and it was magnificent to see him in a few weeks pitch away the hair shirt and get into his toga again. To retire to the cloister to save your soul, and to return almost immediately to the world to save your country is, indeed, given to but few. The choice between soul and country, did not appear to give him any anxiety. Irish historical parallels were more correct. Charles V. took to the hair shirt, so did Reynard the Fox, so did Mr. Gladstone. The first continued to wear it, the others didn't ; this is a contrast rather than a parallel.

" Oui, je me montrai toute nue
Au Dieu Mars, au bel Adonis,
A Vulcain même, et j'en rougis ?
Mais Praxitèle ! où m'a-t-il vue ? "

said Venus (in good Greek, not in indifferent French), as she stood before the statue of the Venus of Cos ! When we stand before the picture of the Holy Fox we in turn may ask, Where did Heine see our Mr. Gladstone ?

But there is no mystery about it. "This is the story of Reynard the Fox; and as the world was always much the same as it is now, and will remain the same till the crack of doom, his story will last as long, and will be always new, and always full of truth for those who are not afraid of hearing it." Are we afraid of hearing it? Perhaps it is a little too plain to be pleasant.

1887.

WHAT IS REVOLUTION?

CHAPTER ONE.

"WHAT is the most remarkable thing that thas happened to you in your long life?" asked Queen Elizabeth of old Parr. His reply was very interesting, but does not especially affect our subject. "What is the most remarkable thing that has happened to you in your long life?" some one will ask of a distinguished statesman 10 or 15 years hence. (Faust is ever young!) "Getting up a Revolution when I was 78" will be the reply. "What a shame it is," say his friends, "to call our only statesman a Revolutionist. He is, in fact, the only true Conservative out. He only trifles with political sin in order to show how pure he is, how easily he can put it on one side. Read the instructive story of Mocles and Almaïde." Well, I have read the story of Mocles, but it is not encouraging. I am, of course, awfully sorry if he is not a Revolutionist—that is to say, I am awfully sorry if I say he is one when he is not, but "birds of a feather," &c., you know. And when I see all the faddists who have Revolutionary bees in their bonnets flocking to Mr. Gladstone, I naturally suppose he is a collector of revolutionary bees. "See what a lovely bee mine is," says the faddist; "was there ever such a bee?" "Never," replies Mr. Gladstone; but no one will believe it unless I tell them so; it is of no use your telling them; only do exactly as I tell you, and your bee shall become as famous as the bee that settled on the mouth of the infant Plato." Mr. Gladstone is quite right; he is the only man who can make a horse-fly look like a bee or a drone like a Queen. Now, if he doesn't intend to promote the future of these bees, he is dissembling, which in any branch of the confidence-trick is *hors ligne*. If there is no honour amongst honest men it would really save trouble if we were all thieves together. But I don't think he is dissembling; beggars are not choosers, and just now that he is deserted by almost every man of sense in the country, he is entirely dependent on faddists and their bees; they are his only friends. If it was not for them he would be quite alone. "He is quite alone; not even a fly with him," as was said of the Emperor Caligula. Mr. Gladstone knows perfectly well what the extreme politicians in this country want; they show their hands plainly enough, and when he accepts their service he virtually accepts their programme. He has signed articles; and if he thinks he can get their support without paying their price for it, he deserves to be numbered amongst the most credulous of mankind. Will men follow a leader they know does not sympathise with them? And will a leader put himself at the head of men he knows do not sympathise with him? I can't conceive it possible. But what is a Revolutionist? *Cela depend.* No doubt Cassius thought Cæsar was one, and certainly Cæsar thought Cassius was one. Let us see. "A thousand years scarce serve to form a state

—one hour may lay it low." Well, my idea of a Revolutionist is
one who in an hour will lay low the Empire that it has taken a
thousand years to build up ; who will make a clean sweep of every
existing landmark in order to stick up his own sign-post ; who so
undermines men's confidence in the existing order of things that to
live under them any longer becomes impossible ; who cuts the
withy in order to strengthen the bundle ; who burns his bed to kill a
flea ; who invokes chaos to gratify a whim ; who leaps before he
looks ; who appeals to ignorance against knowledge, to sentiment
against sense ; whose vanity is his God ?

> " He wav'd aloft a torch, and, madly vain,
> Sought Godlike worship from a servile train."

Who does this describe ? Anyone in particular, or is it only a fancy
portrait ? I don't know. This, however, is certain, that whether
the portrait is a fancy one or not, it is a very disagreeable one, and
gives one the nightmare. I don't blame the Revolutionist who
risks chaos to gratify a conviction, but I curse the sham friend of
order who risks chaos to gratify a whim. The Revolutionist is of
necessity the very reverse of the Reformer. The trade of the former
is to destroy—the trade of the latter is to amend. " Reform is
impossible," says the former. " How can you reform what is
actually rotten ? " " Down with it, down with it, even to the
ground," shout his admirers, and he smiles approval. Revolution
is relative. What is only a choleric word in the captain is rank
mutiny in the private. Choleric words that are only ridiculous in
the private citizen are positive Revolution in a Prime Minister.
What may be reasonable enough in a new country with new
institutions may easily become Revolution in an old country with
old institutions. There is a considerable difference between building
on vacant ground and clearing away existing buildings in order to
rebuild. The Revolutionist is no good in a new country—he can
construct nothing, it is not his metier, his instinct is to pull down,
to destroy. The ruling passion may continue strong even at the
age of fourscore. To the Revolutionist nothing is sacred that
stands in the way of his will ; he knows no hard and fast line
beyond which he will not go. Judge, jury. Speaker, House of
Lords, Church, property, political economy, Habeas Corpus,
Empire, all go down like ninepins if they thwart his will. When
he wants support he will pay any price for it—take it on any terms,
in any form, from anyone. He does not hesitate one moment to
cut the withy and scatter the bundle if he thinks it will enable him
to break up one or two of the sticks. How the bundle can be tied
together does not concern him. As a rule, Revolutionists do not
indulge much in the outward show of religion. They laugh at lip
service, at humanitarian platitudes, at familiar invocations of the
Almighty, but they worship cunning. The Holy Fox is their
"totem." They know very well that cant is the hook with which to
draw out Leviathan, and that cant is always a trump card.

" Put your trust in God," said Cromwell to his men before crossing a river ; " but mind you keep your powder dry." " Put your
trust in God," says Mr. Gladstone to the Hawarden fruit growers,

but there he stops. If he had added, " But mind you use plenty of manure," it would have added immensely to the sense of his advice; but it would have spoilt the sentiment. But, nevertheless, it is a fact, if anything is, that God helps those who help themselves. He will give those fruit growers most fruit who use most manure, and I do not see why they should not be told it. " We have gauged our leader," say the Revolutionists, " we know him down to the ground, his strength and his weakness; we hold him in the hollow of our hand. We know that we must pay him personal homage, that we must fall down and worship him ; but why shouldn't we ? It amuses him and doesn't hurt us. But we know that if we do wor-ship him he will in his turn give our somewhat shady principles the seal of piety, and Leviathan is very fond of piety ! We may some-times have doubts of his pious efficiency ; we have none at all of his destructive efficiency. We know that he can destroy more in one year than any other ten public men can destroy in a generation. That is good enough for us, and now that he has accepted our pay, it is quite certain we shall not allow him to remain idle."

1887.

WHAT IS REVOLUTION?

CHAPTER TWO.

THE last Reform Bill suddenly gave an immense preponderance of political power to what are called the masses, and when it was passed, every one, Tory and Radical alike—every one who could understand that two and two made four, proclaimed openly that if any statesman, who had influence with the masses, was unscrupulous enough to excite them to combine against the classes, Revolution was inevitable. Well, the hour came, and so did the man. The unscrupulous leader sprang to the front, and has excited the masses against the classes in language so bitter, so fierce, so uncomprising, so suggestive, that Mr. Goldwin Smith, a Radical of the old grit, declares that the most envenomed period of the American wars offers no parallel to it. Deliberately, carefully, with great pains, Mr. Gladstone has sown the wind; do we suppose he is so far wanting in common sense that he would have taken all this trouble if he had not expected to reap the whirl-wind? Of course he did—of course the storm will burst. Like the thousand and one fanatics who have in turn convulsed society, he believes that he is inspired, that his will is God's will,

> " And pleased the Almighty's orders to perform.
> Rides on the whirlwind and directs the storm."

But he doesn't. Phæton thought he drove the horses of the sun, but he didn't. It is as certain as anything that he who raises the storm will perish by the storm. The first victim of Revolution is invariably the reckless man who opens the flood-gates. Of course the mere advocacy of Home Rule for Ireland need not mean Revolution ; but the way it is advocated very easily may. Home Rule is advocated as the right of the masses against the classes—of the rich against the poor, of " les nouvelles couches sociales." It is a demand that the Imperial Parliament be suppressed, that the Empire be broken up, and return to its primordial atoms. There is no use being mealy-mouthed about it, it is too late. If it is granted on the ground on which Mr. Gladstone advocates it, the Imperial system under which we live and have become powerful is at an end. Now, this is what I call Revolution. Others may call it what they like, but that is what it actually is. The man, whoever he is, who tells the masses that poverty and wealth result from misgovernment, makes government responsible for a condition of things that he knows no government can prevent; he tells the patient that he can cure him when he knows that the disease is incurable. I suppose it does not require a conjuror to prove that there always have been, and always will be, rich and poor, workers and loungers, masses and classes. So long as one half of mankind continues to accumulate, and the other half continues to disperse, it must be so. If all the wealth of the world were equally divided to-morrow morning, it would be very unequally divided to-morrow night ; the process of accumulating and dispersing would already have begun. How can you prevent those who accumulate from leaving their accumulations to their children, or to those they love best ? Hence comes the silver spoon—the privileged class who lounge and don't work.

Job was a rich man with his 10,coo sheep, and his lambs and his oxen and his camels and his she-asses, and a very great household— he was very rich and probably his servants were very poor ; and we may be sure the poor envied the rich, the workers the loungers, those born with a horn spoon in their mouths envied those born with a silver spoon, and those with a silver spoon envied those with a golden spoon just as much then as they do now. This will always be so—as long as one man accumulates and another disperses. And, indeed, it would be very disagreeable if it were not so. I don't know how the world would get on if everybody accumulated, or if every one dispersed : it would be very inconvenient; everybody would be in everybody else's way. There is no novelty in this inevitable antagonism of mankind, neither is there any novelty in vain and mischievous men seeking to turn it to their advantage. The friction between the masses and the classes is universal, unceasing. Both the States- man and the Revolutionist know this ; the only difference is in the way they treat it. The former tries to minimise, the latter to intensify it. I think this is all very plain, and can be read without magnifiers. " Nothing is so easy as to govern by bribery," said Mr. Gladstone to Mr. Parnell when the latter offered the land to the Irish people. Mr. Parnell might now with perfect politeness return the compliment. Nothing is so easy as to excite the masses against the classes—the raw is always there, any child can irritate it, if he likes ; but once irritated the wisest of mankind has never been able to calm it down. The means of exciting class irritation are so simple, the results so certain, that to some minds the desire to do it is irrepressible. Those who do so invariably claim to be in- fluenced solely by a desire to help others ; but, unfortunately for them, in every case history proves to a demonstration that the moving cause is a desire to help themselves.

The Revolutinary mania is a distinct disease, as distinct as dipsomania or kleptomania, or any other mania. It has been diagnosed scores of times. It generally attacks young men between the ages of 20 and 30—after 40 its attacks are less frequent, and its symptoms less acute. Its invariable course is to moderate as age advances. At 50 few men are revolutionists ; at 60 scarcely any ; at 70, none. Of course Mr. Gladstone is an exception, and a very remarkable one certainly ; but his is the only case that occurs in the history of the disease. There is absolutely no other instance on record of a man over 75 being attacked with the most acute form of the disease. As the doctors have never seen such a case before, of course they do not know how to treat it. They watch it with intense anxiety, and, in the interest of mankind, pray that it may not be repeated. On one point they are agreed—that it is incurable.

Mr. Gladstone has his quiver full of them. He is not afraid to speak to his enemy in the gate. " Look at the masses who support me," says the modern Sempronia, triumphantly. "These are my jewels—Earls Granville, Spencer, Rosebery, Aberdeen, Kimberley, Barons Wolverton, Kensington, and, last not least, the great connecting link of the classes, Sir William Harcourt. Blue blood, all of them ; blue blood and millions combined ! And then look at these miserable specimens of the classes opposed to me—Bright, Chamberlain, Caine, Henry James, Robert Phillips, Jessie Collins, Tyndal, &c., not an earl or a millionaire amongst them; quite common people." Curiously enough, Mr. Gladstone's specimens of the " masses " are the sons of men who wiped their noses with cambric ; whilst the specimens of the " classes " who oppose him are the sons of men, who, as Nadir Shah said of himself, " wiped their noses with their elbows."

Now, whether he likes it or whether he does not—whether he cares or whether he does not—it is a fact, without any doubt whatever, that in the eyes of the masses, in the eyes of the classes, and in the eyes of that Flying Dutchman " civilised mankind," Mr. Gladstone now stands before the world as the apostle of the English Revolution. He knows perfectly well that his inflammatory appeals to the masses to exercise their newly-acquired power to push aside the classes, and take the government of the country into their own hands, means Revolution. Our Golden Image may be broken up, and become as chaff on the summer threshing floors— or it may not—at any rate he does not know, and apparently does not care. And why should he care ? At four-score his sands are running out. He may have time to sow the whirlwind ; but it is almost impossible he shall live to reap the storm. He leaves that to others. Vain in his own conceit, confident in his inspiration, dissatisfied with the past, angry with the present, reckless of the future, he pretends to do, what no mortal man has ever yet been able to do, to turn on the tap of Revolution, and turn it off when he likes ; but he can't. Vanity is his Lethe ; it makes him forget.

1887

THE PRODIGAL'S RETURN.

THE "weak-knee" has knuckled down, the jelly-fish has collapsed, the Prodigal has returned, and the fatted calves are having a bad time of it. The rejoicing over the one sham Unionist that has repented has taken the form of fierce denunciation of the ninety-and-nine just Unionists who need no repentance. Yes, Sir George Trevelyan has returned to the bosom of his afflicted family, and all is forgotten. But oh, aimless Prodigal, "quæ te dementia cepit?" What madness impelled you to go; and, more wonderful still, what madness has induced you to come back again? Surely the game was not worth the candle. "Tout comprendre c'est tout pardonner." If we only knew the secret motives that have prompted this astonishing double shuffle we might not only pardon it, but we might actually find it our agreeable duty to class it with the noblest acts of responsible man. This is supposing we could understand Sir George Trevelyan's motives; but we cannot; nobody yet that I have heard of attempts either to explain or to excuse it. It is true he has given us his own explanation; but as Dangle says in the "Critic," "Egad, I think the explanation is the harder to be understood of the two." His explanation of why he went makes it absolutely impossible to understand the explanation of why he came back again. Of course he declares that since he left Mr. Gladstone, everything has changed; but this is just what Mr. Gladstone declares has not happened. He swears that nothing is changed, and this is rather awkward for Sir George Trevelyan; it takes the only puff of wind he had out of his sails. He is, in fact, exactly in the position of Louis XVIII. when he re-entered Paris; nothing is changed, only there is one Separationist the more! *Quelle mouche l' à piqué.* What devil has impelled him to an act that has literally set on edge the teeth of the most audacious of political free lances. Only the other day he was amongst politicians quite a superior person, very superior indeed; now he is a sort of nondescript, "one of the middle sort, betwixt hawk and buzzard." His conduct is useful in one way. It shows how nearly extremes meet, and how even clever men sometimes illustrate the old proverb, "He went out a donkey, and came home a jackass." No one in this world is infallible, not even the youngest, or the oldest; and, of course, the wisest of mankind sometimes change their minds; the wiser they are the oftener they change them, it appears to me. Only what the wisest of mankind never do is to give their reasons for changing. Not only is it unpardonable for a public man to give reasons, but it is bound to use such indefinite words and phrases that no traces of former statements and opinions can ever be brought home to him. "Then as I went away," says Reynard the Fox, Author of the "Modern Statesman Handbook," "I whisked my brush over every footstep, so as to destroy all traces of my visit. I learnt the art from my father, and have put it into practice many a time with perfect success." No doubt Reynard the Fox was a master of all cunning, but I believe the Old Parliamentary Hand could have given him a 14 lb. beating over any course in the world. The Scripture Prodigal left his father's house because it was apparently too respectable for him—he had a taste for low company. The Unionist Prodigal, on the contrary, has never shown any taste for low company, except politically. He did not leave his paternal roof because it was too respectable, but, on the contrary, because the goings on there were so disgraceful that he could not stand them any longer. The fact is that he discovered that his "Awful Dad" was playing old Harry with everything about the place, making ducks and drakes of property of which he was only trustee. Even when he found out what his unscrupulous relative was doing, he did not go willingly ; he hesitated, he employed every argument an accomplished sophist could invent to excuse his remaining. He expostulated with him, he argued with him, he pointed out that honour, consistency, recent pledges, patriotism, forbade the policy he was pursuing; but in vain. It was only after he satisfied himself, and satisfied everyone who listened to him, that it was impossible, actually impossible, for him to remain any longer in such company, that he reluctantly went away, telling an admiring world he left his party because he preferred political annihilation to the ruin of his country; and now he has returned, almost immediately, because he prefers the ruin of his country to political annihilation. At least, this is how we are compelled to understand him. Sir George Trevelyan's double conversion, his double confession, " I have sinned before Radicalism and before the G. O. M.," has more than a double political value. No man ever gave so many distinct and final reasons for a political act as he did for leaving Mr. Gladstone. When, therefore, in a few months he can come humbly back, hat in hand, and say, " Although every one of my distinct and final reasons for leaving you still exists, and, indeed, have become more distinct and conclusive every day, yet my faith in you is so strong that I have swallowed them all, and come back to you, asking only to be taken again to your bosom," well may the " Holy Fox " exclaim with justifiable vanity, " Verily, I have not seen such faith, no, not in Israel ;" and neither has anyone else. Whether Sir George Trevelyan's return is an act of faith or an act of folly I don't know, but this I do know, that all the reasons he gave for leaving a year ago have been intensified twenty times since he left. His "Awful Dad" has not repented of one single act that drove him out of the house. He has not changed one item of his programme ; on the contrary, he is more determined, more audacious, and more reckless than ever. Every day has added proofs of the folly, the wickedness, the impossibility, the actual treason of his proposals. However, everything is a matter of opinion in this world. " Hungry dogs will eat dirty pudding," as the Scripture Prodigal realised when he ate the husks ; but I swear that under the circumstances I should prefer the husks of the Scripture Prodigal to the humble pie of the Unionist one. In politics, as in other professions, sometimes the shortest road to

dignities lies through indignities; but I do think I would rather
sweep a crossing than commit such an act of political *auto da fe*.
When political minnows are caught by such baits people say, "Oh,
it is only another minnow!" But here is a Triton, a very big fish
indeed, no less than the modern Aristides—the man who has
probably taken more trouble to be called "The Just" than did
Aristides himself. "Why do you wish to ostracise Aristides?"
asked Aristides of the voter who asked him to write his name on
the oyster-shell. "Because he takes so much trouble to be called
'The Just,'" was the reply. Landing him is indeed something to be
proud of. Sir George Trevelyan was so laborious in marshalling
his facts and arguments, and in proving, *coram populo*, that it was
impossible—yes, actually impossible—that he could agree to Mr.
Gladstone's policy, and the world so thoroughly agreed with him
that it was impossible that he should remain, that his sudden return
has made them look like fools. He has, in vulgar parlance,
deliberately put them in a hole. The credulous public has been
more completely sold than it has ever been by any previous statesman. "Look at me," said Aristides II.; "look at me. Mark me
well. I am no ordinary man—I am Aristides II.! What other
men do for various reasons—good, bad, or indifferent—I do for one
reason alone, because I am 'The Just.' I am a born statesman;
politics are the breath of my nostrils, without them I die; but
sooner than do this thing that my soul abhors, that my conscience
and my experience both tell me is disgraceful to myself and ruinous
to my country, I will lay down my political life. Am I not a
martyr? Am I not worthily called 'The Just?' Was Cincinnatus
a patch on me?" How incredulous folk believed and exclaimed,
"A Daniel come to judgment!" At last we had discovered the
fabled Phœnix, a Radical who preferred his country to his party.
It is true some ill-conditioned persons shook their heads, and
hummed,

> " No truth in plaids, no faith in tartan trews,
> Chameleon like, they change a thousand hues."

This chosen of Scotch constituencies professes over much, and
alas, these ill-conditioned persons were right. He did profess too
much, a very great deal too much. Sir George Trevelyan was not
only the most remarkable figure in the Unionist secession because
of his exceptional claim to the character of Aristides, but because it
was understood that he knew more about Ireland than the author of
the Dawn of Creation. Mr. Gladstone did not know, because he did
not wish to know, anything about the Clan-na-Gael, the connection of
Parnellism and Crime, &c.; but Sir George Trevelyan did know.
His life had been in danger; he had hunted down and hung the
Phœnix-park murderers. He knew all about them, and the
organisation that employed them. He carried out with remarkable
vigour the most severe and comprehensive Crimes Act ever
known. He was held up to obloquy, and indirectly charged with
complicity with murder, with odious vices. He was lampooned
in company with disgusting criminals, and therefore he knew
whom he had to deal with, and he is reported to have spoken out

with no hesitating tongue. "The law must be enforced," said he; "Home Rule means separation, and separation means reconquest," &c.

It was speaking with this full knowledge of Irishmen and Irish affairs that Sir George Trevelyan, after long and anxious doubt, decided that he could not support Mr. Gladstone; at least, he thought he so decided, and so did we; but it appears we were both mistaken; he had actually decided the very reverse. Radicals generally appear to be cut to one pattern, but there is a difference even in them. Mr. Chamberlain, for instance, is a Radical of Radicals, but when he was taunted with voting with the Tories he replied, "At any rate I am voting with English gentlemen in support of the interests of my country." But such an alliance is gall and wormwood to Sir George Trevelyan, more than his pure Radicalism can stand. "I know that my country is in danger," he said, "I have proclaimed it from the housetops. I know that if I support the Government I may aid in its defence. I know that if I vote with Mr. Gladstone I shall assist in its ruin; but, sooner than soil the spotless ermine of my Radicalism by voting with the accursed Tories to defend my country, I will vote with the blessed Radicals to destroy it." But this is strange. When Sir George Trevelyan was in office, when he was nightly insulted, outraged, denounced in the House of Commons, who did he look to for support, for sympathy, for encouragement against traducers? Why, to this same Tory party with whom contact now appears to him a disgrace. No doubt that charity is splendid that induces a man to prefer his traducers to his defenders. Hawk and buzzard again. Individually, I prefer the terrier that bites the hand that punishes, to the spaniel that licks it. But again, of course, tastes differ.

"When Mr. Gladstone runs down a steep place," said Lord Shaftesbury (*vide* his Life, vol. iii., page 451), "his immense majority, like the pigs in Scripture, but hoping for a better issue, will go with him, roaring in grunts of satisfaction." Well, Mr. Gladstone did run down the steep place, and his immense majority did go with him, roaring in grunts of satisfaction; but Sir George Trevelyan was the one piggy who refused to go. When he saw what they were doing he turned tail and bolted in the opposite direction; but blood was thicker than water. He did not run very far, and no sooner did he see the last of his friends disappear in the waters than away he scampered after them roaring with quite a peculiar grunt of his own. Now, of course, such devotion was very touching, and attracted great attention to piggy; but the *pas seul* was rather comical, his end would have been more dignified if he had gone down the steep place with the rest of the herd. And now what is the result of it all? It is this—that of all the turncoats that have startled us with the rapidity of their political toilets, of all the men who have sworn black was black one day, and have taken God and all His saints to witness that black was white the next, Aristides II. is the most remarkable. It is sad—that is to say, it is sad to those who believe that "droiture" is the proudest motto of English statesmen. "No man ever lost himself in a straight road," said the Emperor Akbar. Sir George Trevelyan has lost himself—at least many of us think so, though probably he does not—because he has left the straight road of the English statesman and taken in preference the most tortuous and deceitful of all roads, that of the "sophistical rhetorician."

1887.

BLUSTER, LOGIC, & AUDACITY.

IT is, I believe, generally allowed that every one, from the duke to the dustman, in some shape or another possesses a faculty by which he can judge of the goodness or wickedness of his actions. This faculty we call conscience. We all have it, even party politicians, and, stranger still, even Gladstonian-Parnellites claim to have it also. Certainly in their case it is so very small that, like the baby of Midshipman Easy's wet nurse, it don't count. " Please mum, it was such a little one." It is possible to have too much of a good thing. Some of us actually have too much conscience. "We wear it on our sleeves," as Iago says. But not for daws to peck at, but for goody-goodies to admire. We air it on all occasions; we take the public into our confidence about it, as other people do about their poor souls. But it is a mistake to profess overmuch about souls and consciences ; least said soonest mended. When a man parades his soul, or his conscience, it is always a hundred to one he is going to take in someone, or try to do so. Poets tell us of "those rods of scorpions and those whips of steel which conscience shakes at us ;" but, as a fact, conscience is not a hard master at all, but a very kind one. It troubles most of us mighty little. Indeed, if it were not for the honour of the thing we should almost be as well without it. Very often we do leave it at home, and never even miss it, and become wonderfully brave and audacious in its absence. Politicians are very independent of this troublesome faculty, for, as a rule, they hand it over to somebody else to take care of. When a man keeps his own conscience there is a certain personal responsibility attached to it ; but when it is in another man's keeping the owner is no more responsible for it than Faust was for his soul when he had handed it over to the Devil. He has a lovely time of it till the reckoning comes. Kindly matrons advertise for babies to take in to nurse, and promise to treat them as their own ; but they don't. And so our political leaders advertise for consciences to take in to nurse, and promise to treat them as their own, and it is possible they do, for they treat their own shamefully. Consciences that have been lent generally return in such a state of shame and depression, and so shrunk up, that even their owners hardly recognise them. I suppose it may be taken for granted that if a man does not take care of his own conscience nobody else will take care of it for him. In China it is held that women have no souls, and a mandarin, hearing a Christian missionary preaching about women's souls, rushed out, saying, "I must go and tell my wife ; she will be so amused to hear she has got a soul." Now, wouldn't it raise a grim smile on the face of many a party politician if he was gravely assured he had a conscience ? I declare I think it would ; but for the sake of argument we will allow that politicians have consciences—very,

very small ones, weenie, sickly little things—lent or let for a
consideration to some hard-hearted leader, who snubs and scolds
and starves them till actually they have lost all the qualities of
consciences. Now, as a matter of fact, it is of no use lending your
conscience ; if you could get rid of it altogether well and good, but
you can't. Consciences have a disagreeable habit of every now
and then coming home to roost. This is very awkward sometimes
for the owner, and places him for the moment in really a very
painful position. What is he to say to a conscience he has lent to
someone else ? Suppose, by way of illustration, that in the lobby
or the smoking-room a Gladstonian-Parnellite is boarded by his
conscience. "My friend," says the conscience, "I am very glad
to have a word with you. I am very unhappy ; you must try and
do something for me ; you really must. You remember you lent
me to Mr. Gladstone, and I have had a very hard time of it, a very
'unconscientious' time of it indeed, if you will forgive a bad pun
(above the average of the locality, however, I assure you). Now
this is not fair—it isn't indeed. I get all the kicks and you get all
the halfpence. Mr. Gladstone, I speak it with great regret—but of
course there can be no secrets between us—is very hard on
consciences ; he has no bowels of compassion for them whatever ;
he is incessantly boxing the political compass himself with a
rapidity that is appalling, and he expects us to scamper round with
him without a question asked or reason given ; he is always deceiving
us. 'You have deceived my master twice,' said the Ambassador
of Louis XII. to Frederick, the Catholic. 'Twice,' exclaimed he,
with an oath : 'I have deceived him more than ten times.' Well,
of course Mr. Gladstone does'nt swear, but I do ; and I swear he
has deceived me ten times ; and I declare I believe that, like
Frederick the Catholic, he is proud of having done it. I wish you
to realise, dear friend, what I suffer day and night on your account ;
it is wearing me to a shadow ; I am not half the conscience I was ;
soon there will be nothing left of me whatever. Believe me,
consciences do not lie on beds of roses in St. Stephen's. 'Leave
all hope behind' greets them as they pass the portal of this Inferno
of Consciences. But I see that you are in a hurry to get to your
club, and can't spare much time to discuss matters with me. I
would accompany you if I could, if only to see how consciences
are treated at clubs and in society ; but of course you have paired
me or handed me over to the affectionate care of your Party Whip,
and so I must remain here, but I daresay you will be quite as happy
without me, only I conjure you not to hand me over again to Mr.
Gladstone—the life of a conscience with him is awful. But before
you go I wish you would to some extent explain to me your true
position ; it would be an immense relief to me ; in fact, if I am to
remain your conscience, it is necessary you should do so. Ever
since I have known you you have been a strong out-and-out
Unionist ; in season and out of season you have always paraded
your love of the Union, and your determination to stand by it at all
costs. Not content with speaking for yourself, you have dragged
me in by the ears to corroborate you ; you have constantly had Mr.
Gladstone's speeches on your lips, proving the absolute necessity of

the Union, denouncing those men who were marching through
anarchy and murder to destroy it, proving how nobly and generously
the English Parliament had acted towards Ireland, how it had done
far more for that country than it had ever done for England or
Scotland, or even gallant little Wales. Well, I have stuck to you
like a man, and every time you have appealed to me before your
constituents I have placed my hand on my heart and made them a
low bow as a proof of my assent. Well, now I find that, without
consulting me in the slightest degree, without giving me a chance
of "getting out," you have gone slap round and left me what is
is vulgarly called in a hole. Now, God knows we poor consciences
are elastic enough; we are accustomed to being stretched and
strained a good deal; we are not by any means particular, and can
shut our eyes and hold our tongues, at times, with praiseworthy
discretion—our unfortunate position compels us to do so—but on
my honour as a conscience, with still some figment of self-respect
left, I swear I cannot understand your shaking hands, and patting
on the back, and cheering to the echo, the very men who only a
year ago you denounced as anarchists, traitors, and even worse.
I cannot understand you denouncing the tyranny of the Parliament
you have only just been extolling for its generosity; shouting
'Turncoat,' 'Judas,' at your late colleagues because they still
repeat the very same Constitutional formula you repeated with such
pride and complacency only a few months ago. Of course nothing
is so easy as to quote Mr. Gladstone against himself, only when you
do so it is necessary to ascertain in what direction the Great
Weathercock was pointing at the moment. But you beat me when
I hear you passionately declare that all your carefully rehearsed
perorations in favour of the Union were false, and all your
denunciations of the Separatists were libellous. I declare I begin
actually to doubt my existence. I feel as if my very identity was
destroyed. Do I belong to you, or to some one else? You must
relieve my anxiety a little; you must indeed, or I shall strike work.
I can bear most things, as you well know; but, by thunder, to use
a strong expression, you are asking too much, even of your
conscience."

"Dear Conscience," replies the Separatist, yawning, "keep your
shirt on. Don't get in a passion; it won't mend matters, and it
bores me. Lend me your ears—the longer the better—and I will
explain. But I am rather in a hurry; this atmosphere is very
depressing. You see I am the victim of circumstances. That's a
good expression, isn't it? It means a great deal, but defines
nothing. Well, I know I lent you to Mr. Gladstone, and to tell you
the truth, I wish to goodness you had stayed with him. Just now
I really don't want you; in fact, I don't know what to do with you.
You stop the way, and that is very awkward. Conscience, like
fire, you know, dear friend, is a good servant, but a bad master.
Now, which do you wish to be? If the former, all well and good;
if the latter, we shall quarrel. When Mr. Gladstone made his
inspired *volte face*—I call it inspired, for nothing short of inspiration
could have enabled a man to get round half so quick as he did—
I was taken a little aback. It was some time before I could make

up my mind what to do. There was a time, as you remember, dear friend, when we first began our limited partnership, when the interests of country came before the interests of party, and when consistency had an actual parliamentary value. Well, that is all past now; the interest of party comes first, the interest of country is nowhere; and as for consistency, 'Oh, no, we never mention it,' 'its name is never heard.' It has actually no market value whatever; in fact, it is withdrawn from circulation. Well, of course, all this will seem to you an entirely fresh departure, but it is all right. You must not be old-fashioned, dear friend. If you are a Gladstonian, you must do as the Gladstonians do. Times change, and we change with them. I have changed, and so, my friend, must you, if you intend to remain with me. Of course, dear Mentor, you know better than any one that I am quite an ordinary sort of a man—average as to brains, rather below average as to knees. There is no suspicion of inspiration about me; and, except tobacco smoke, I evoke very little out of my 'inward consciousness,' as the phrase expresses it. Now that the old-fangled notion of duty to country is pigeon-holed—for the time, at any rate—my position is considerably simplified. I have only to decide between two courses instead of three. Formerly I had country, self, and party to think of; now country is gone, and there is only self and party. I have to decide how I shall stand best with my party, and how I shall stand best with my constituents. Shall I stand firm to the principles of the Union that Mr. Gladstone has taught me, or shall I join Mr. Gladstone in denouncing these principles as the teaching of the Devil?—that is, of course, of the Tory party. I have to ask myself on which side of my political bread is there more butter? 'Under which King, Bezonian? Speak, or die.' Which leader will add most to my popularity amongst my constituents? Can I afford the luxury of consistency? Can I afford to tell the truth and shame the Devil—that is, vote against Mr. Gladstone, or shall I act a—— and stick to it? This is rather an awkward predicament for both of us, dear Mentor, is'nt it? Awkward for me, but doubly awkward for you; but you know, 'Needs must when "somebody" drives,' and if 'somebody' is not driving now, I'm a Dutchman. I did not long hesitate. There was no doubt on which side the butter was thickest. Mr. Gladstone, with octogenarian impatience, has so excited the masses against the classes, so impressed the people with a conviction of the tyranny and injustice of the present order of things, so excited the several nationalities against Imperial rule, that revolution appears inevitable. Things can never again settle down on the old lines. He has sown the whirlwind with a fierceness that even I must allow takes one's breath away. I must whirl away with it or face the storm, and that, of course, I cannot do. How can a weak-knee contend against a strong wind? I should be swept to Jericho or Jehoram, or some place out of sight. Lord Hartington promises law, order; Mr. Gladstone promises Revolution. The former says, Respect your neighbour's landmark; the latter says, Remove it. There cannot be much doubt on which side the numbers who have no landmarks will be. "Le bon Dieu est toujours avec les gros bataillons," whether composed of soldiers or voters; and so, dear conscience, will I. I also will go with *les gros bataillons*. Don't you think I am right? Of course, consistency and your approbation, dear Mentor, go for something; but not for much when the majority of my constituents go the other way. So the die is cast. I am sorry for you; I feel it is rather rough on you, but what am I to do? I must save my political life; and, after all, *Suum cuique* is not a bad motto to go through the world with. Is it? Mr. Gladstone is Generalissimo of the Liberal Party, but no longer their leader in the field. He is, in truth, too costly to wear every day; we want another for working days. He is nearly 80, and has too much to do. What with Hittites, the Greater Gods of Olympus, the Dawn of Creation, Proems, reviews, post-cards, &c., he has only some spare moments to give to the affairs of the kingdom. So, dear Mentor, I have had to look out for another leader to whom I may entrust you. I have found one, and I hope you will like him. The Gladstonian-Parnellites had the choice of three militant leaders—Bluster, Logic, and Audacity. Now, Bluster is a great man, very powerful, very clever, very ready, very experienced, with a soft corner in his nature somewhere, it is said, but somewhat unscrupulous (in politics only, *bien entendu*). Bluster would do very well. He can gyrate almost as quickly as the Great Dervish himself; but he suffers from two disadvantages. He, like me, is pledged up to the eyes to maintain the Union; and he, like me, has to swallow all his principles and professions every time he opens his mouth. And, moreover, he has not the courage of his opinions, or rather, of his professions, for what his opinions are I don't pretend to know. Now, the fact of Bluster being a very big man, specially fashioned hollow to swallow his principles without even a wry face, does not help me, who am small, and not built hollow; and besides, when I am urged to do what I know—even without your prompting, dear Mentor—is altogether wrong, I want a leader who will give me the necessary courage to do it—who will lead me on, not merely point out the road I am to go. The Bombastes Furioso Plan of Campaign that says to us, weak-knees, 'Lead on, brave army: and when you've won the battle let me know,' reverses my requirements. It is not good enough when my leader urges me with violent speed to illogical and illegal action; I expect him to back me up, to vote straight himself, not to send me to the lobby and walk out of the House without voting. So Bluster won't do. Then comes Logic. Here is quite another man, no bluster about him--cool, collected, logical, consistent, nothing to recant, nothing to explain away, no phrases, no denunciations, no principles or professions to swallow. I should have liked to followed Logic as my leader. There is a consistency and conviction about him that by the side of Bluster and Audacity, is very attractive, and give one almost a feeling of self-respect: but it is impossible. I have already learnt the whole logic of the Irish question from Mr. Gladstone himself—he proved to me step by step, with a fulness of argument and illustration and satire that no one else can equal, the absolute necessity of the Union, and the absolute absurdity of breaking it up; and I know that if I begin to talk Logic now, I should talk the logic of Union as taught me by

Mr. Gladstone, not the logic of Separation as taught by Mr. Morley.
I should be quoting the orders of my Generalissimo against the
orders of his Lieutenant, and that would be sheer mutiny. Logic
is of no use to a Gladstonian-Parnellite. It is like the sword
Hector gave to Ajax: when used in a bad cause it turns against the
user. So Bluster and Logic are put on one side, and by the process
of elimination Audacity becomes the leader. Audacity—again
audacity—always audacity—that's the quality to help you on in life
—especially public life. With some poor soulless plodders industry
and perseverance produce fair results ; but without audacity they
are of very slow growth. Audacity, like Jack's bean-stalk, will grow
enough in one night to form a ladder to fortune ; and, besides,
audacity has such irresistible attraction to the weaker sort of men.
It seems 'to bind and mate them,' as Bacon says, even against
their will ; and you know, dear Mentor, we have often agreed that I
have always been a little weak about the knees ; and this courage
that audacity gives me, even though it is a little Dutch, is very
agreeable. Audacity alone is good enough for most things, but
when it is combined with talent, energy, quickness, wit, cynicism,
journalism, good manners, a kind heart, and a not over-sensitive
epidermis, it is powerful indeed. Audacity has nothing to recant,
no professions, or principles to explain away. He does not
condescend to anything so tame as logic. ' Don't be a fool,' says
Audacity, ' don't bother yourself to explain your change of front.
Deny boldly that you have changed at all. Swear that in your
heart you have always been a Home Ruler : that you only dissembled
for a season till the fruit was ripe for plucking, and that even that
delay nearly broke your heart. Denounce the Unionists as the real
turncoats, and renegades, and traitors. Yell at them. Call them
Judas, Barabbas, and murderers, anything you can think of. Don't
stick at trifles. Disgrace Parliament. Insult the Speaker. Paralyse
the Government. That is the way to get the masses on your side.
That is the way to score.' Audacity does not meander about the
wrongs of Ireland, &c. He says nothing about that. The question
of the Union, says he, is only indirectly a question of Ireland. It
is a question of democracy, of *les nouvelles couches sociales*. It is
the chapel bell that is ringing out the old order of things, ringing in
the new. Not only in Ireland, but in England, Scotland, and
Wales also. The confiscation and nationalisation of land and the
expulsion of the landowners in Ireland means the confiscation and
nationalisation of land and the expulsion of landowners in England
and Scotland and Wales also. The cry of ' No rent, no taxes ' in Ireland
means the cry of ' No rent, no taxes,' in the rest of the kingdom.
Audacity does not advocate separation in the interest of Ireland
at all, but in the interest of the democracy, in the interest of
the revolution. Now, dear conscience, you can see how all this
suits me down to the ground. It is a perfectly fresh departure for
me. I leave the past alone, nothing that I have hitherto said about
the Union bothers me any longer. The case has entered an entirely
new stage. My brief is no longer marked ' Ireland,' but ' Democracy.'
It is not that I love the Union less, but that I love Democracy
more ; what I said about the Union was quite true, but it belongs

to the past order of things. That is finished. Mr. Gladstone has closed that page, and has opened another, and taken a fresh departure. The new page he has opened is Confiscation ; the fresh departure is Revolution."

1887.

IN AND OUT—ORDER AND DISORDER.

THERE are two Mr. Gladstones, the counterfeit presentment of two brothers ; here they are as like as chalk is to cheese. Mr. Gladstone In Office, and Mr. Gladstone Out of Office.

IN—Supports the police on every occasion.

OUT—Denounces the police on every occasion.

IN—Avenges the brutal murder of Mr. Burke.

OUT—Condones the equally brutal murder of Constable Whelehan.

IN—Employs informers to suppress crime.

OUT—Denounces informers as inciting to crime.

IN—Declines to receive a deputation of London Socialists.

OUT—Overflows with gush for London Socialists.

IN—Pays £8,000 to London shopkeepers for the damage done by the mob in 1886.

OUT—Telegraphs his opinion that the mob are incapable of doing mischief in 1887.

IN—Denounces Mr. Parnell as a traitor.

OUT—Applauds Mr. Parnell as a patriot.

IN—Imprisons Mr. Parnell without trial for using language inciting to rebellion.

OUT—Denounces the imprisonment of Mr. O'Brien for using language ten times as strong.

IN—Declares Ireland has no complaint against England.

OUT—Declares Ireland has 700 years of English oppression to avenge.

IN—Declares that Parliament has done more for Ireland than it has ventured to do for England and Scotland.

OUT—Declares that Parliament has done nothing for Ireland but oppress her.

IN—Calls on all loyal men to strengthen his hand against the Home Rulers.

OUT—Denounces as tyrants and turncoats those who oppose the Home Rulers.

IN—Proclaims 200 meetings in Ireland.

OUT—Declares it is illegal to proclaim a meeting in Ireland.

IN—Appeals daily to the Conservatives to support him in preserving law and order in Ireland.

OUT—Denounces the Conservatives for trying to preserve law and order in Ireland.

IN—Declares that crime dogged the steps of the Land League.

OUT—Declares it is illegal to interfere with the Land League.

IN—Denounces obstruction in Parliament in every shape.

OUT—Supports obstruction in Parliament in every shape.

IN—Declares the majority in Parliament shall govern.

OUT—Declares the majority in Parliament shall not govern.

IN—Denounces the " no rent " agitation.
OUT—Supports the " plan of campaign."
IN—Denounces the Channel Tunnel.
OUT—Supports the Channel Tunnel.
IN—Ridicules the right of "civilized mankind " to coerce the Egyptian policy of England.
OUT—Appeals frantically to " civilized mankind " to coerce the Irish policy of England.
IN—Destroys Alexandria ; commits untold Egyptian atrocities.
OUT—Denounces Bulgarian atrocities.
IN—Slaughters noble Arabs for defending their country.
OUT—Defends treacherous Boers for slaughtering our troops.
IN—In the the name of England blesses Turkish rule in Egypt.
OUT—In the name of England curses Turkish rule in Bulgaria.
IN—Dismisses Colonel Henderson for too little energy.
OUT—Denounces Sir Charles Warren for too much energy.
IN—Declares President Lincoln had saved an empire.
OUT—Declares President Davis had made a nation.

But what is the use of going on ? It is sufficient to say that in Opposition he denounces everything he supported in office, and that in office he supported everything he denounces in Opposition. How are you to treat such a weathercock ? As a responsible person, or as a curiosity ? It is difficult to say. If our familiar friend acted in this way, we should say, " My dear fellow, you can't know what you are talking about ; either you must be a fool to talk such nonsense, or you must think us fools for listening to it. Evidently you don't know your own mind ; you are as unstable as water. You change your opinion as easily as you do your button-hole, and as often—red camelia to-day, white camelia to-morrow. Your judgment is as unsteady as the feather that dances in your mistress's bonnet. What you swore was black yesterday you swear is white to-day. What you swear is white to-day you swore was black yesterday. You may be colour-blind, but we are not, and our eyes and all our senses tell us that what was black yesterday is black to-day, and that what is white to-day was white yesterday. We know, therefore, that you are wrong— absolutely, entirely wrong. What we do not quite know is whether you are trying wilfully to deceive us, or whether you are actually incapable of judgment."

" When the devil was sick, the devil a saint would be :
When the devil was well, the devil a saint was he."

In office Mr. Gladstone is as jolly as a sand boy, goes to the play, gives dramatic breakfasts, reads the lessons in church, and intones the Psalms like any other man. In Opposition he is " like a mildew'd ear blasting his wholesome brothers." It is astonishing. In Opposition he plays exclusively to the pit and to the gallery. In office he plays exclusively to the stalls and the boxes. He can't play to the masses and the classes at the same time ; it is not in his nature. He must set them by the ears or he can't act. But what is the use of making a fuss ? Gab is King ; Verbosity is his Prophet. Honesty, Veracity, Consistency are voted slow. " I have only one political faith," says Mr. Ruskin, " and that is, that Mr.

Gladstone is a windbag." Well, I have another, but it is a very strong one ; and that is, that Mr. Gladstone is only an agitator, without the smallest leaven of statesmanship. Here is my reason. Thirteen thousand policemen keep guard night and day on the neutral ground between order and disorder, between the respectable and the predatory classes. The predatory classes outnumber the police by hundreds to one. It is only the strong conviction that the law will support them, and public opinion back them up, that enables the police to face these tremendous odds. Remove this confidence in the support of the law and public opinion, and the police will be unable to make head against the promoters of disorder, and we shall have a repetition of the Gordon riots.

Order is in possession, and all the powers of the law and of public opinion are on its side. Before Order yields to Anarchy all these powers will be employed to protect it; it must be so, it always has been so. In all large communities there are four elements—the predatory classes, the police, the soldiers, the owners of property. If the police are strong enough to hold in check the predatory classes, the soldiers are unnecessary ; if the police are not strong enough to hold them in check, the soldiers become necessary at once. When the police are weak, the predatory classes advance, and so do the soldiers (they have been already confined to barracks). When the police are strong, the predatory classes fall back, and so do the soldiers. Well, in the face of this certain danger, Mr. Gladstone is working night and day, by insinuations, by misrepresentations, by exaggerations, by inventions, to weaken the police in every possible way, to deprive them of the support of public opinion and of the law, and to rally against them all the forces of anarchy and disorder. Is this the act of the statesman or of the agitator ? Can there be any doubt ? It is the work of the agitator, the most reckless, the most unscrupulous, the most unpatriotic this country has ever seen. If his efforts are only partially successful, there will be fighting in the streets. Is this what he wants. Does he wish to see the streets in the hands of the mob, or does he wish to see them in the hands of the soldiers ? He must wish one or the other, or he would not do as he is doing. Perhaps he wishes both. Who knows? He is very old, and of course he knows a great many things ; but there are some things we know as well as he does—or better even. We have a mentor he apparently never consults—Common Sense ; and Common Sense tells us some things about him that are not very complimentary. Well, Common Sense tells us as follows :—That in his present temper Mr. Gladstone would rather ride into office on the back of King Mob than not ride in at all. That we should employ every means in our power to prevent his doing so. That Remember Mitchelstown ; Remember Lyons the Socialist; telegram to the Bermondsey processionists, mean simply down with the police. That if it was not for the police the predatory classes would sack London. That if public opinion and the law do not support the police they cannot make head against the predatory classes. That if they fail to do so it will become a question of anarchy or martial law. That the police under Lord Salisbury have no more to do with politics than they had under Mr. Gladstone. That the police did their duty at Mitchelstown, and in the Lyons case. That the times are very critical. That this is the first time in our history that distinct, deliberate, avowed defiance of the law has found an advocate in an ex-Prime Minister of England. That the more Mr. Gladstone tries to weaken the police and loosen the bonds of order, the more we should try to strengthen them, to "serrer les rangs," and stand shoulder to shoulder in the cause of order. That if Mr. Gladstone took office to-morrow he would be obliged to support the police, employ informers, and carry on the war against lawlessness, just as it is being carried on now.

But Common Sense suggests something else—something that in the ears of some persons will sound almost like blasphemy. But, then, Common Sense is no respecter of persons. It is said that Mr. Gladstone is never allowed to read anything that can do him harm. Would it not be as well if this useful censorship was applied to what he writes? It does not signify to us twopence what entereth into him, but it does signify to us very much indeed what cometh out of him; and certainly some of his recent utterances, oral and written, have been so audacious, so seditious, so absolutely certain to provoke breaches of the law in England and Ireland, that some of his greatest friends have expressed doubts as to whether he was perfectly responsible for what he says and writes. Really they ought to look after him. Mr. Allman, ex-trouser-presser, and Mr. Gladstone, Ex-Prime Minister, both use seditious language likely to provoke a breach of the peace; but one sentence from the ex-P.M. is more likely to provoke a breach of the peace than columns from the ex-T.P. Why, then, should the latter be imprisoned and the former not even warned? Why should the disciple be punished and the apostle go scot free? This is not common sense, neither is it justice. In China, when a crime is committed, punishment is inflicted on the person who causes the crime, not on the person who commits it. If the law is defied in Ireland and bloodshed follows, or if the law is defied in England and bloodshed follows, it is not the poor dupes who shed the blood who should be punished, but those whose wicked utterances encouraged them to shed the blood. No doubt the most powerful and the most prominent instigator of defiance to the law at this present moment is Mr. Gladstone, and it appears absolutely certain that bloodshed will follow his teachings, if it has not already done so. If he was in China, he would, without any doubt whatever, be in prison in the place of his humble imitator, the ex-trouser-presser; but then in some matters the heathen Chinee has more common sense than we have.

1887.

UNCLE SAM TO JOHN BULL.

"HOW long will your institutions last?" asked an American lately of me. "Who knows?" I answered, "Do you?" "Yes, friend John, I do. Lend me your ears (they are long enough for us both—*aside*) and I will tell you. I will tell you, moreover, what we think of you over the water. Not quite so much as you think of yourselves perhaps, but still it may be of service to you. You have lately taken to the 'one-man' principle of Government, and, as you always do, you have carried it to a ridiculous extreme. You have got your 'one-man,' and you have given him absolute control over everything you possess. You place him above the Constitution. You give him *carte blanche* to do what he likes. If anythings offends him he cuts it off, and you applaud him. Your institutions will last just as long as they don't interfere with his will; the moment they do down they go, Lords, Church, and Crown. How can it be otherwise? You are a funny people. You seem to prize your public man as you do your wine—for age. You get quite hysterical over them as they approach 100. You apparently like the old bottled flavour in your statesmen. We, on the other hand, prefer a younger and sounder wine. Age commands our respect; but does not, as with you, command increased confidence; on the contrary, 'great men are not always wise,' says Solomon, 'neither do the aged understand judgment.' In fact, we find that age has its disadvantages in public men. They are more vain, more opinionated, more intolerant of opposition: and they lose their memories, and do not 'understand judgement.' Moreover, some are destructives by nature, and in these the instinct of destruction intensifies with age. With us no man ever presumes to active political life after seventy. I know you say your 'one man' is 'inspired,' and is, therefore, an exception to every general rule, but we don't care much for inspired men even 'in the wood.' In the Senate we laugh at them. And how is your 'one man' inspired? Has he the inspiration of 'Celestial grace,' or is he only 'inspired by the spleen?' Both are possible you know. Which is it? It is important to know. Whichever it is, I think my experience of inspired men in many countries and in many walks of life will safely warrant me in betting 100 to 1 that this inspiration is all gas—that your 'one-man' is only an ordinary mortal after all. Hear the truth. We sometimes think you have gone mad. You are so foolish, whether through the inspiration of spleen or the inspiration of 'Celestial grace,' we do not know; but so it is. If you cannot pull yourselves together very quickly you are done. Sentimental Radicalism, which is your present fancy, may be excellent in theory, though we think it nonsense, but practically it is absolutely incompatible with the institutions you possess. They cannot exist together. One must go. Which is it to be? Which will you stick to, your institutions or your sentiment? Just now you are like the dog in the fable—you have a very fine piece of meat in your mouth, but you are inclined to drop it in order to snap at the shadow in the water. This is literally true. You have, or had, a Constitution and institutions that have, in the opinion of civilised mankind, answered admirably, and some of which even we have envied. What do you think of that? And you seem inclined to drop them, in order to snatch at an impalpable nothing. As professional Republicans we are aghast to hear your amateurs advocating theories of socialism, of ransom, of spoliation and division, that were laughed out of court in this country twenty years ago, and that would now, in all probability, bring the professor of them in close proximity to a barrel of tar and a bag of feathers.

" Positively we talked out, and dismissed as nonsense, proved to demonstration, theories of equality and of government that you are seriously discussing to this day. Do you know that your sentimental Radicalism, your profession of higher motives than your neighbours, and of much higher motives than really influence you, are very irritating to us? We don't make a parade of our humanity, or bemoan our blood-guiltiness; but neither do we slaughter men like sheep, as you did in the Soudan, nor destroy commercial cities as you did Alexandria. What a hypocrite you are, John. I really am ashamed of you, and what on earth do you expect to gain by all this pretence of goodness and unselfishness. What is the use of parading your motives, when everybody knows that your motives are the same as other nations' motives—your own interest? With all your loud professions of superior political morality, we in America do not for one moment allow that there is a pin's head to choose between your public men and ours. In fact, during the last ten years you have rather startled us; your political consciences must have had a bad time of it; we doubt if any have survived. Your public men have swallowed more principles and denied more promises than ours have done in half a century. I cannot tell you how many pegs you have gone down in our estimation since Majuba Hill, and the desertion of General Gordon. We hardly recognise you as the same breed; the bull dog seems transformed into the spaniel. Instead of showing your teeth when you are struck, you fawn on the hand that chastises you.

" My dear John, we are sorry for you; we are indeed. We are not very fond of you, but we like you next to ourselves; and what we liked best in you was the bull-dog grip that made your Empire, not the spaniel whine that is losing it. Actually, when we look at you we feel inclined to exclaim, ' Ichabod, thy glory is departed!' If we want to be reminded how Englishmen spoke and thought and acted thirty years ago, we have to look for him in Australia or Canada, or New Zealand, or America. It is a fact that we have a great deal more of your old spirit than you have yourselves. Friend John, you are in a bad way; if you cannot retrace your steps from the debilitating atmosphere of sentimental Radicalism that now surrounds you, and return to the more bracing atmosphere of common sense, you are done, done to a moral. You have very little time. You are literally approaching the brink of Imperial and

Constitutional convulsion. Have you lost all pride in your Empire, in your race, in your grand history—in the mighty dead whose deeds have made the name of England ring throughout the world ? We in America have had our trial, and a crucial one it was ; but the bull-dog spirit of the old breed saved us. We, too, had vain sophists, and sentimentalists, and men incapable of national pride, and men of jaw, as you have now ; but we soon put them on one side, and declared that our kingdom should not be broken up. But there were 'men' in those days. We had 'men' amongst us ? Have you, excuse the enquiry, have you any ' men ' amongst you ? And if they come to the front will you stand by them ? The great difference between us, dear friend, is that when our great trial came we were guided by ' law.' Now yours has come on you, you are guided entirely by ' jaw.' What strikes your friends in this country as the worst symptom in your case is the universal apathy that seems to have overtaken you. Nothing much seems to rouse you ; you seem prepared for anything. Your Constitution, your institutions, the unity of your kingdom, your vast Empire, seem to have lost their interest for you. You do not seem to look to the past or to the present, but to some indefinite future—some great impending change. You seem to think that your institutions, of which a few years ago you were so proud, are now not worth the trouble of defending. Of course institutions that are violently attacked, and which nobody thinks in their interest to defend, are doomed ; they must go by the board, and that very quickly. Your case is a very simple one—we have diagnosed it long ago. All classes are doing badly ; there is a general shrinkage all round. With the exception of a few bankers and brewers, and dealers in money, everybody is losing money. You are apathetic, indifferent,. and will soon be discontented, because you feel that goodness is going out of you ; because you are getting poorer. We in this country see all this very plainly, but you are so infatuated you will not see it. It is not that your institutions have suddenly failed, it is because your ridiculous theories of Free Trade have imposed conditions on you that make profitable labour impossible—conditions under which your land must go out of cultivation, and your factories give up producing.

"Time was, forty years ago, my poor friend, when you had a complete monopoly of every manufacturing industry, and you laughed at the possibility of any nation competing with you. Forty years have changed all that. We see it ; all the world sees it except yourself, and you won't see it. None so blind, you know, dear John, as those who won't see. The French, the Belgians, the Germans, the Austrians, we ourselves, can produce almost every thing cheaper, and, in many cases, better than you can, and as you admit our goods to your markets, of course we simply swamp you. Friend John, it is time for you to reconsider your position. You are no longer the first industrial nation in the world ; you are not, indeed, even the second. You will soon be out of the industrial race altogether, if you do not take steps to save yourselves. Let me give you a little advice. Mistrust inspired statemen, stick to common sense. Prefer the man who insists that white is white and black is black, to him who proves to you that black is white and white is black. Beware the 'glittering eye' that 'holds' you against your better judgment. It more often means madness than wisdom. Remember that ' great men are not always wise ; neither do the aged understand judgment.' Consider the requirements of your industries as they are now and as they were forty years ago. Don't suppose that you will do yourself much good by shifting political power into the hands of the least educated. Above all things, remember that the majority is nearly always wrong, and that in nineteen cases out of twenty the *vox populi* is only the voice of .the interested agitator." This is the warning given me by my American friend. I leave your readers to judge whether there is anything in it.

1887.

A REMARKABLE SPEECH.

O F course the opinions of Mr. Burke or Mr. Fox on the Act of Union 100 years ago no more affect the question of Home Rule to-day than their opinions on the vexed question of dry or sweet affects the present taste for champagne. They gave their opinions according to their lights as to the probable result of a great experiment. One said to John Bull, "The Act of Union will give you the stomach-ache;" the other said, "It won't." But neither of them could possibly tell; they could only speculate. But the Union of Great Britain and Ireland is no longer an experiment ; we have now had 80 years' experience of its actual working, and what, in most cases, is the deliberate, unprejudiced opinion of men of light and leading as to the result ? What has the experience of 80 years taught us ? That is the question. Shall we insist on maintaining the Act of Union, even by force, or shall we cut the painter and let our erring sister drift away ? Public reason and the public conscience have been so dazed and staggered by Mr. Gladstone's fierce and unexpected denunciations of alien rule, of foreign tyranny, of 700 years of oppression, of nationalities suppressed, of " savage laws savagely administered ; " his appeals to justice, to public opinion, to lawbreakers, to dynamiters, to the proclaimed enemies of England all over the world, have been so passionate and indiscriminate that many amongst us have got mixed up and confused, and exclaim with trepidation *où suis-je* ? Therefore it is a national relief to come across a carefully-worded and elaborate *résumé* of the whole case—a plain unexaggerated statement of the points at issue between the two countries ; that treats of the past, present, and future of the question, by a leading statesman now living, with a completeness that leaves actually nothing to be desired. It is, indeed, an unspeakable relief; it gives one breathing time, and actually offers us a chance of regaining the straight road. The vigorous and inspiriting words that claim for the unity of the Empire the very first rank amongst national duties ; that declares boldly, and in the face of the world, that, good as is the law of conciliation, there is yet a higher and a permanent law, and that is national duty; that declares that though England desired to attach Ireland to her by the silken cords of love, yet that force may be necessary to prevent national disruption, and to put Parliament right with the national conscience, with the opinion of the world, and with the principles of justice, is, word for word, the language and the arguments of Lord Hartington and the Liberal Unionists. The indignant terms in which this remarkable speech denies that the Imperial Parliament has ever refused to remedy the grievances of Ireland, that insists that there is not a single question that the Imperial Parliament is unequal to deal with ; the crushing statement that there is nothing that Ireland has asked that the Imperial Parliament has refused — that, in fact, the Imperial Parliament has actually done for Ireland what it would have scrupled to do for England and for Scotland, raises this speech to the level of a State Paper, that, as far as argument is concerned, has disposed of Home Rule for all time. There is no mistaking the contemptuous banter that sums up Irish grievances in their inability to catch fish, and describes the only inequalities between the two countries as the levying of certain taxes on Englishmen and Scotchmen that are not levied on Irishmen, and the free grants of public money in Ireland for purposes for which it is not granted in England and Scotland. It ridicules the idea of Home Rule by the example of Scotland and Wales, and denounces as absurd the policy that would disintegrate the great capital institutions of this country for the purpose of making ourselves ridiculous in the sight of all mankind, and destroying our power of doing good. In the endless flood of useless utterances, this remarkable speech has been very much overlooked ; but it is not yet too late. The matter is treated in so calm, argumentative, exhaustive, and reasonable a manner that every one who reads it must feel that at length this burning question is presented to him in an intelligible form. It is to my mind almost a national duty to have the speech reprinted and put into the hands of every voter in the three kingdoms.

" This United Kingdom, which we have endeavoured to make a United Kingdom in heart as well as in law, we trust will remain a United Kingdom ; and although, as human beings, the issues of great events are not in our hands, but are directed by a higher Power, yet we intend and mean, every one of us, high and low, not those merely who meet within this hall, but those who crowd the streets of your city, and of every city from the north to the south of this island—we intend that it shall remain a United Kingdom. We are told that it is necessary for Ireland to close her relations with the Parliament of this country and to have a Parliament of her own. Well, now, why is Parliament to be broken up ? Has Ireland great grievances ? What is it that Ireland has demanded from the Imperial Parliament and that the Imperial Parliament has refused ? It will not do to deal with this matter in vague and shadowy assertions. I have looked in vain for the setting forth of any practical scheme of policy which the Imperial Parliament is not equal to deal with, or which it refuses to deal with, and which is to be brought about by Home Rule. So far as my research has gone, I have seen nothing except that it is stated that there is a vast quantity of fish in the seas that surround Ireland, and if they had Home Rule they would catch a great deal of that fish. But there are fish in the seas that surround England and Scotland. England has no Home Rule, and Scotland has no Home Rule ; but we manage to catch the fish. You would expect when it is said that the Imperial Parliament is to be broken up that, at the very least, a case should be made out showing there were great subjects of policy and great demands necessary for the welfare of Ireland, which representatives of Ireland had united to ask, and which the representatives of England, Scotland, and

Wales had united to refuse. There is no such grievance; there is nothing that Ireland has asked and which this Parliament and this country has refused. This Parliament has done for Ireland what it would have scrupled to do for England and for Scotland. What are the inequalities of England and Ireland? I declare that I know none, except that there are certain taxes still remaining which are levied on Englishmen and Scotchmen, and which are not levied over Irishmen; and likewise there are certain purposes for which public money is freely and largely granted in Ireland, and for which it is not given in England and Scotland. This seems to me to be a very feeble case indeed for the argument that has been made, by means of which we are told that the fabric of the united Parliament of this kingdom is to be broken up. But if the doctrines of Home Rule are to be established in Ireland, I protest, on your behalf, that you will be just as well entitled to it in Scotland, and, moreover, I protest on behalf of Wales that they are entitled to Home Rule there. Can any sensible man, can any rational man suppose that, at this time of day, in this condition of the world, we are going to disintegrate the great capital institutions of this country for the purpose of making ourselves ridiculous in the sight of all mankind, and destroying any power we possess for bestowing benefits through legislation on the country to which they belong? One word more on this subject, and it is this. People say we have tried to conciliate Ireland, and that we have failed. I do not admit that Ireland is not going to be conciliated; but I say this, that we must always keep in mind that there is a higher law to govern the actions of Parliament and of politicians than the law of conciliation, good as that law may be. We desire to conciliate Ireland, and we desire to soothe her people—the wounded feelings and painful recollections of her people. We desire to attach her to this country in the silken cords of love; but there was a higher and paramount aim in the measures that Parliament has passed, and that was that it should do its duty. It was to set itself right with the national conscience, with the opinion of the world, and with the principles of justice; and when that is done, I say fearlessly, that, whether conciliation be at once reached or not the position of this country is firm and invulnerable."

This remarkable speech, remarkable, indeed, in every way, was delivered by the Prime Minister of England, Mr. William Ewart Gladstone, at Aberdeen, on the 26th of September, 1871. I am told that this is the same Mr. Gladstone who now denounces as traitors, turncoats, tyrants, &c., those who still act up to the noble truths he then enunciated. I decline to believe it; it appears to me impossible. There is a limit to all things, even to the gyrations of Jim Crow. Oh, fie, fie, fie! Thy sin's not accidental. It's a trade.

1887.

INSPIRATION.

" M R. GLADSTONE is inspired on the Home Rule question," says Hysteria. "Nonsense," says Common Sense ; "he's no more inspired than you or I are." "But he tells us he is," urges Hysteria. "Well, then, he is making a fool of you," replies Common Sense. "He is inspired just as much as Mr. Parnell or Dr. Tanner is inspired, not a bit more nor less." But Hysteria won't be undeceived. Inspiration is too good a card to throw away without a struggle. "The work in which I am now engaged," says Mr. Gladstone, " is one of the noblest causes that ever wakened up the energies of mankind, or ever asked and won the favour of the Most High." "A work," he goes on to say, "which it is not profane and irreverent to say the Prince of Peace would recognise and bless." Now, wooing and winning are very different things. It is only in the very extreme cases of religious hysteria that the poor patient ever ventures to assert that he has won the favour of the Most High. No wonder such audacious nonsense was received with shouts of "He's a jolly good fellow." Nothing fetches the many-headed like audacity. Now, according to Mr. Bright, Lord Selborne, and 19 out of every 20 thoughtful and educated men in this country, the work that Mr. Gladstone has at present set himself to do with his whole heart is to assist a foreign conspiracy to break up the British Empire. Of course, love of country, pride of race, and all that sort of thing is a matter of taste, a question of degree. In England just now it is at zero ; but still, low as it is, it does seem comical to ask Englishmen to assent to the proposition that a foreign conspiracy to destroy their Empire is the noblest cause that ever wakened up the energies of mankind ! What an awful community of scoundrels we must be if this is true. It may be possible that Home Rule has won the favour of the Most High —nobody knows ; it is quite certain that Mr. Gladstone does not know, and it seems to me very profane of him to say he does. I do really believe this dragging the awful name of the Most High into a mere political discussion is probably as profane and irreverent an act as can be conceived. So utterly profane is it that you cannot even discuss it without profanity ; without saying and hinting at things that you feel it is profane to say and hint at. Familiarity with sacred subjects is far more certain to induce contempt for them than the most openly expressed contempt. To ignore the Most High altogether is not so profane as to presume to bring him down to your own level, and to claim His confidence. It is disgusting— there is no other word for it.

Of course many people think there is a certain amount of profanity in praying to the Most High for special objects, without considering whether your good may not mean somebody else's harm. I think it is only silly. If, unfortunately, each person got what he prayed for, the world would be in a nice pickle. Prayer would soon be at a discount. It certainly seems somewhat ridiculous for one farmer to pray for rain to make his roots grow, whilst his neighbour is praying for dry weather to get in his crops. But though thousands pray every day for the furtherance of the object they have for the moment at heart, I never remember one who ventured to declare that he had secured the blessing of the Prince of Peace and had won the favour of the Most High. What a silly jargon of words, meaning absolutely nothing. Certainly Mr. Gladstone is unlike any man that ever breathed. He is a phenomenon, perhaps, not a man. But he is not a god ; he has no divine attributes about him whatever. Positively he knows no more of the will of the Most High than the very humblest of us all. What does he mean, then, when he talks about having won the favour of the Most High ? Does he mean that he, Mr. William Ewart Gladstone, has been in communication with the Most High and the Prince of Peace on the subject of Home Rule, and that they have expressed approval of his scheme ? Now, every man, woman, and child knows absolutely that Mr. Gladstone has had, and can have, no communication from the Most High on the question of Home Rule or any other ; and that when he says, or implies, that he has, he is saying and implying what is simple nonsense. " It is very childish," say his friends, " it is a way he has ; he has always done it ; it amuses him, and it does not hurt us—on the contrary, it has an immense effect with the masses." It may be so ; but, nevertheless, it is a most offensive way of taking the name of the Most High in vain. Fortunately, it is not catching. No one out of the pulpit, in any country in the world, practises the *sanctam insaniam* of Mr. Gladstone.

Three years ago he described this same work, identically the same work, carried on by identically the same men, and by identically the same means, as treason, rapine, crime, &c., and imprisoned 2,000 persons, more or less, for supporting it. Had the Prince of Peace recognised and blessed it at that time ? Had Home Rule then asked and won the favour of the Most High ? Was it then one of the noblest causes that ever wakened the energies of mankind ? Now this is really very important for Mr. Gladstone. It affects his favourite pose as the confidant of the Most High. Three years ago he led us to believe he was inspired ; but on that occasion his inspiration took the form of preserving the Empire, now it takes the form of destroying it. The contradiction is rather startling. It is not startling to see Mr. Gladstone spin round like a dancing dervish. We are accustomed to that, but it is startling to see his sources of inspiration spin round with him. We must conclude that three years ago, when he denounced Parnellism and crime, and cast Mr. Parnell into prison, Parnellism and crime had not then asked and won the favour of the Most High. It would be most interesting to know when this extraordinary incident took place, and how. Mr. Gladstone, I suppose, knows. Ought he not to make a clean breast of it. Did he follow the commands of the Prince of Peace to become a Home Ruler ? Or did he persuade the Most High that Home Rule was the right thing ? Did Mr. Gladstone follow or lead ? He must have done one or the other. Which does he wish us to believe? Cromwell, perhaps, claimed a certain amount of inspiration, and he was always consistent; he did not one day say God was on the side of the Parliament, and the next day He was on the side of the King, And then Cromwell was a great Englishman. I don't think a foreign conspiracy to break up his country would have been described by him as one of the noblest causes that ever wakened up the energies of mankind. I wonder what spectacles Mr. Gladstone wears, evidently they magnify too much. When Mr. Gladstone is a Unionist he assures us that the Most High is in favour of the Union. When he is a Separatist he assures us that the Most High is in favour of separation. But when he becomes a Unionist again, as he certainly will when the cat jumps round, what will he tell us then? Not content with dragging in the opinions of dead men, of which he can know nothing, he now drags in the opinion of the Almighty. Undoubtedly, it is profane to discuss such a subject, but then the odium of profanity does not rest on those who ridicule the preposterous assumption of Divine inspiration, but on those who have the audacity to assume it.

If Sir William Harcourt, or Lord Rosebery, or Mr. Morley, or Mr. Parnell, or Doctor Tanner were to assure us the Prince of Peace was on their side, we should laugh at them, but they could not condescend to such nonsense; but every one of these gentlemen knows exactly as much about the opinion of the Most High on this matter as Mr. Gladstone. The Great God of the Christians, the *Ens Entium* of eternity, cannot be brought down to the level of the greater gods of Olympus, who walked and talked with mortals in the shady groves of Mount Ida. Yes; Mr. Gladstone is inspired—I grant it; but it is by the *vox populi*, not, as he would have us believe, by the *vox Dei*.

1887.

THE RAIL-SPLITTER AND THE WORD-SPLITTER.

TWENTY-SIX years ago our American cousins had their constitutional crisis. The Southern States wanted to cut the painter and drift away from the Northern States; but fortunately for them, their leading statesman thought otherwise. He was a rail-splitter by trade; a strong man, of few words; accustomed to use the Scythian phrase, to call a spade a spade, a horse a horse; a man who never went back from his word. And he said, " No; though the South can boast as noble sons as the North, as good lawyers, orators, soldiers, and honourable gentlemen; though the people demand separation to a man, they shall not have it. They shall not, so long as I can wag a finger, break up the United States." So spake America's "Grand Old Man;" and he was right. And he was a strong man, and succeeded, and saved the Union. Well, now England has her constitutional crisis. Ireland wishes to cut the painter and drift away from the United Kingdom; but unfortunately for her her leading statesman is a " word-splitter" by trade, not a "rail-splitter." A man of words—"a word-catcher that lives on syllables;" words are to him what the mist was to his friends, the Greater Gods of Olympus, to conceal his flight when worsted in the battle. He scorns the Scythian phrase. Plain language is unknown to him. He calls a spade a shovel, and a horse a quadruped, in order that at some future time he may swear he meant a cow, or a jackass, or an elephant, or a camelopard—anything, in fact, but a horse. The man of few words saved the United States. The man of many words threatens to ruin the United Kingdom. When the Southern States demanded separation the Grand Old Rail-Splitter said, No, you shall not go; I will strain the resources and the constitution of my country till they break. I will call out my last man, and stake my last bottom dollar before you shall mutilate that glorious tree whose branches overshadow the earth: and I know that future generations of Americans will say that I was right and that I have done my duty. And the G.O.R.S. was right; Americans already say, and will always say, that he was right, and that he did his duty. Well, our Grand Old Word-Splitter takes the very opposite view of national duty. When Ireland demands separation he says Yes, by all means, you shall go. It is true the party who demand separation number amongst them no distinguished men, and is chiefly supported by foreign conspiracy; it is true that those who are loudest in their demand for this separation are the sworn and boastful enemies of England; but still you have 86 votes; and if you continue to support me I will strain the Constitution till it breaks. I will fan into flames if I can the revolutionary spirit of the country; I will set class against class—the masses against the classes; I will invoke the assistance of the mob in the streets, of your enemies over sea. I will make Constitutional Government impossible, Parliamentary Government a farce, in order that I may break up the United Kingdom, and let you go. I myself will lay the axe to the root of this cursed upas tree of English domination, and hew it branch from branch till not one remains to poison the earth; and, of course, future generations of my countrymen will say that I was right; that I was a Grand Old Man; and that I did my duty. So says the G.O.W.S. But he is wrong. Already his countrymen are beginning to say, You have not done your duty; you have betrayed your country. The "rail-splitter" will be for ever remembered by the Americans as the man who staked everything to keep America a great country. The "word-splitter" will, if I am not much mistaken, be for ever remembered by the English people as the man who did his best to make England a small country. I will do anything—everything—to preserve the unity of my country, said Mr. Lincoln; I will do anything and everything to destroy the unity of my country, says Mr. Gladstone. Both God and man stand aghast at such destructive fury in a man of fourscore. Mankind has never before seen anything like it. Elephants occasionally become destructive in their old age, and are called rogues, and the ignorant natives worship them, believing they represent the power of evil; but those who are entrusted with the public safety put them in restraint. Well, the ignorant in England, when they see the destructive fury of Mr. Gladstone also believe him to be inspired, and so do I, by the power of evil. Oh, for the Scythian phrase? Shall we never hear it again? Is it dead as far as the English language is concerned? Shall we never more hear a spade called a spade — a traitor a traitor? How much longer are we to be bamboozled with the ridiculous "Pidgeon English" that inverts and obscures our mother tongue; that splits up words till they have no meaning to them whatever, that distinguishes between war and military operations, between inciting to crime and complicity with crime?

How much longer are we to listen to the shameful morality that teaches that it is an honourable thing for a statesman to go back on his word, to deny his pledges, to swallow his principles; that teaches that there is only one sin a party man may not commit, only one sin that shall not be forgiven him, and that is the damnable sin of consistency? If, during the agony of the American crisis, the "word-splitter" had appealed to the American people to break up the Union, and let their erring sister go, what reply would they have given him? And what reply ought he to get now from Englishmen when he appeals to their sworn and bitter enemies to come over to help him to compel them to let their erring sister go? What answer? I think every true Englishman knows in his heart what his answer should be. It is possible that before very long the world may know it too. Talk of American opinion! Does not every lisping child know that there is not a man of light and leading in America, who is not bidding for the Irish vote, who does not regard with disgust the shameless appeal to the worst elements of their nation to come and range themselves under Mr. Gladstone's umbrella? Once before Mr. Gladstone got us into collision with

THE RAIL-SPLITTER AND THE WORD-SPLITTER.

TWENTY-SIX years ago our American cousins had their constitutional crisis. The Southern States wanted to cut the painter and drift away from the Northern States; but fortunately for them, their leading statesman thought otherwise. He was a rail-splitter by trade; a strong man, of few words; accustomed to use the Scythian phrase, to call a spade a spade, a horse a horse; a man who never went back from his word. And he said, "No; though the South can boast as noble sons as the North, as good lawyers, orators, soldiers, and honourable gentlemen; though the people demand separation to a man, they shall not have it. They shall not, so long as I can wag a finger, break up the United States." So spake America's "Grand Old Man;" and he was right. And he was a strong man, and succeeded, and saved the Union. Well, now England has her constitutional crisis. Ireland wishes to cut the painter and drift away from the United Kingdom; but unfortunately for her her leading statesman is a "word-splitter" by trade, not a "rail-splitter." A man of words—"a word-catcher that lives on syllables;" words are to him what the mist was to his friends, the Greater Gods of Olympus, to conceal his flight when worsted in the battle. He scorns the Scythian phrase. Plain language is unknown to him. He calls a spade a shovel, and a horse a quadruped, in order that at some future time he may swear he meant a cow, or a jackass, or an elephant, or a camelo-pard—anything, in fact, but a horse. The man of few words saved the United States. The man of many words threatens to ruin the United Kingdom. When the Southern States demanded separation the Grand Old Rail-Splitter said, No, you shall not go; I will strain the resources and the constitution of my country till they break. I will call out my last man, and stake my last bottom dollar before you shall mutilate that glorious tree whose branches overshadow the earth: and I know that future generations of Americans will say that I was right and that I have done my duty. And the G.O.R.S. was right; Americans already say, and will always say, that he was right, and that he did his duty. Well, our Grand Old Word-Splitter takes the very opposite view of national duty. When Ireland demands separation he says Yes, by all means, you shall go. It is true the party who demand separation number amongst them no distinguished men, and is chiefly supported by foreign conspiracy; it is true that those who are loudest in their demand for this separation are the sworn and boastful enemies of England; but still you have 86 votes; and if you continue to support me I will strain the Constitution till it breaks. I will fan into flames if I can the revolutionary spirit of the country; I will set class against class—the masses against the classes; I will invoke the assistance of the mob in the streets, of your enemies over sea. I will make Constitutional Government impossible, Parliamentary Government a farce, in order that I may break up the United Kingdom, and let you go. I myself will lay the axe to the root of this cursed upas tree of English domination, and hew it branch from branch till not one remains to poison the earth ; and, of course, future generations of my countrymen will say that I was right; that I was a Grand Old Man ; and that I did my duty. So says the G.O.W.S. But he is wrong. Already his countrymen are beginning to say, You have not done your duty; you have betrayed your country. The " rail-splitter " will be for ever remembered by the Americans as the man who staked every-thing to keep America a great country. The " word-splitter " will, if I am not much mistaken, be for ever remembered by the English people as the man who did his best to make England a small country. I will do anything—everything—to preserve the unity of my country, said Mr. Lincoln ; I will do anything and everything to destroy the unity of my country, says Mr. Gladstone. Both God and man stand aghast at such destructive fury in a man of four-score. Mankind has never before seen anything like it. Elephants occasionally become destructive in their old age, and are called rogues, and the ignorant natives worship them, believing they represent the power of evil; but those who are entrusted with the public safety put them in restraint. Well, the ignorant in England, when they see the destructive fury of Mr. Gladstone also believe him to be inspired, and so do I, by the power of evil. Oh, for the Scythian phrase? Shall we never hear it again? Is it dead as far as the English language is concerned? Shall we never more hear a spade called a spade — a traitor a traitor? How much longer are we to be bamboozled with the ridiculous " Pidgeon English " that inverts and obscures our mother tongue ; that splits up words till they have no meaning to them whatever, that dis-tinguishes between war and military operations, between inciting to crime and complicity with crime?

How much longer are we to listen to the shameful morality that teaches that it is an honourable thing for a statesman to go back on his word, to deny his pledges, to swallow his principles ; that teaches that there is only one sin a party man may not commit, only one sin that shall not be forgiven him, and that is the dam-nable sin of consistency? If, during the agony of the American crisis, the " word-splitter " had appealed to the American people to break up the Union, and let their erring sister go, what reply would they have given him? And what reply ought he to get now from Englishmen when he appeals to their sworn and bitter enemies to come over to help him to compel them to let their erring sister go? What answer? I think every true Englishman knows in his heart what his answer should be. It is possible that before very long the world may know it too. Talk of American opinion! Does not every lisping child know that there is not a man of light and lead-ing in America, who is not bidding for the Irish vote, who does not regard with disgust the shameless appeal to the worst elements of their nation to come and range themselves under Mr. Gladstone's umbrella? Once before Mr. Gladstone got us into collision with

American public opinion, and he got the snub direct. May we hope that he may get the snub final! In the American war Mr. Gladstone espoused the cause of the South, said Mr. Davis had made a nation, and, it was said at the time, speculated in Confederate Bonds. Now, it was the Confederate Bonds that enabled the Confederate States to build the Alabama; and, therefore, every holder of Confederate Bonds, more or less directly, assisted to create the Alabama claims. Mr. Gladstone, therefore, if report was true, assisted the Confederate States to build the Alabama, and then compelled us to pay for the ravages she committed. And now, again, he is bringing us into collision with American feeling. He is appealing to every one in America who hates England, to those associations who openly boast of the damage they have done her, and of the damage they will do to her, to come over, assassins, dynamiters, and all to range themselves under his umbrella, and strengthen his hand. "These infernal fellow - countrymen of mine," says he, "won't do as I wish; come over and help me to compel them." He may be absolutely certain that not one true American will listen to this shameful appeal. It is astounding; and I ask again what answer should Mr. Gladstone get from his countrymen for such a craven blow? Mr. Gladstone just now seems to have got America on the brain; the Chief "Big Collars" visits the Chief "Red Shirt," and asks him—a savage from the Far West, who did not speak a word of English, who had scarcely seen an Englishman—what he thought of the *entente cordiale* between America and England. But this, of course, was dotage; he might as well have asked him what he thought of the Decalogue or the Dawn of Creation.

With astounding assurance Mr. Gladstone tells us that Ireland stops the way; but any one can see with half an eye that it is Mr. Gladstone himself, and Mr. Gladstone alone who stops the way. It is he who is the lion in the path, and will let no one pass till his rage is pacified. Let us exactly realise the position. It is Mr. Gladstone, the Old Parliamentary Hand, ex-Prime Minister of England, who is utilising the experince of 50 years to make Constitutional Government and Parliamentary Government impossible; who is doing his utmost to smash up the ladder by which he has mounted to fame; who, like the old Border cattle lifters says to his enemies, "Thou shalt want ere I want." If I do not rule no one else shall! Has it become a fiction that the Queen's Government must be carried on? Does Constitutional opposition mean Parliamentary paralysis? Lord Salisbury has a majority of 100 in the House of Commons, and an overwhelming majority in the House of Lords. And yet Mr. Gladstone says, "You shall not carry on the Queen's Government. You shall not govern. I and my minority will prevent it." What does it mean? Does it mean that the part is greater than the whole? That the minority in Parliament is more powerful than the majority? That a majority of a 100 is not sufficient to enable a Government to govern? If so, then representative institutions have broken down, and Parliamentary Government is proved to be a sham. But will the majority permit this ridiculous imposition—for it is nothing else—to continue? Has not a majority its duties as well as a minority? Is it not the duty of the majority in Parliament to carry out the legislation that the majority in the country demand? The present Parliament was elected to save the Union. Are they not to do it? They have a clear majority of 100 in the House of Commons. Is not that enough? Are they to hold their hand because a vain, disappointed politician bids them? The Government say, the country desires that the Union should be maintained; our official experience enables us to state that this Bill is absolutely necessary to maintain the Union; we are responsible to the English people for the necessity of this Bill, and we accept that responsibility.

But Mr. Gladstone, who has no present responsibility, who has no present official information, says " this Bill is not necessary, and in spite of the wishes of the people and your Parliamentary majority you shall not pass it;" but every Englishman, Scotchman, and Irishman knows that the opposition to this Bill is a sham, that it is not the Bill that the minority oppose, but the Government. Every one knows that the Bill is to restrain lawlessness, not to repress liberty to protect the minority, not to coerce majority; to enable honest men to do their duty, and fulfil their obligations in peace and safety; and men are actually beginning to ask themselves whether honest men do not require help to do their duty and fulfil their obligations in peace and safety in Parliament quite as much as in Ireland.

1887.

AN IMPOSSIBILITY.

SOME things that appear impossible at first sight become possible when examined closely; other things that appear possible at first sight become more impossible the more you examine them. This is one of the latter. The more we examine it, the more impossible it appears that Mr. Gladstone, or 500 Mr. Gladstones, can put off all useful legislation for England, Scotland, India, and the Colonies till the Irish question is settled. " My own years," says Mr. Gladstone, "make the settlement of the Irish Question a preliminary to all useful legislation." It may be very sad that Mr. Gladstone is nearly 80 years old; but it is not our fault. Why are we to be punished for what we cannot help? What has Mr. Gladstone's age got to do with the progress of useful legislation? Indeed, I wish he was 40 instead of 80; we should not then see him the idol of anarchists and the champion of disorder ! Joshua commanded the sun to stand still that he might continue to slay his enemies. Jupiter put Phœbus to sleep for three days for a more agreeable purpose. More strange still, after the death of St. Patrick the sun continued to shine for 12 days ! And now Mr. Gladstone coolly proposes to stop the parliamentary sun *sine die*, because he is old ! How very comical ! " I am getting old," says Doctor Gladstone to Britannia; " before I retire from practice I wish to cut your leg off." " Thank you so much," says Britannia ; "it's awfully nice of you to think of it, but I would rather not. I hope that under proper treatment it will get all right without an operation." " But it shan't get all right ; I will cut it off," screams the doctor ; " I will let you see if I am to be disappointed of an operation when I have set my heart upon it. We will soon see whose will is the strongest. You shall have nothing to eat or drink, no sleep, not a moment's rest, till you let me cut it off. I will make your life a burden to you ; I will raise every man's hand against his neighbour's ; I will denounce law, judges, jury, the police ; I will put myself at the head of disorder, of anarchy, of revolution ; I will invoke the plagues of Egypt upon you ; I will hold you up to the obloquy of civilised mankind ; I will invoke the aid of your enemies all over the world ; there is nothing, absolutely nothing, I will not do sooner than be baulked of my whim." Now, this is no exaggeration—not in the very slightest degree. Mr. Gladstone has already made good his words. He is at this moment at the head of anarchy and revolution. He has publicly denounced order and acclaimed disorder. " Remember Michelstown " has no other meaning than down with the police. The roughs in Trafalgar Square cheer his name before they proceed to sack the shops. He has held us up to the obloquy of civilised mankind ; he has invoked the aid of our enemies all over the world ; and at this very moment he is working night and day, *unguibus et rostro*, by coaxing some and kicking others, to make the Queen's Government impossible. And all because he is in a hurry and that nasty Parliament won't let him "see wheels go round."

Let us count noses. "It is very vulgar, I am afraid," as the masher said when he eat mutton ; but it is occasionally very useful. The population of Great Britain and Ireland is about 34,000,000. Of this 34,000,000 about 5,000,000 are Irish. Of this 5,000,000, again, about 3,000,000 are Home Rulers ; that is to say, 3,000,000 out of 34,000,000 demand separation from England and Scotland ; and Mr. Gladstone stands forward and says, till these 3,000,000 have all they want to the very uttermost the 31,000,000 shall have nothing at all. This is rather a peculiar view to take of the situation certainly. It remains to be seen whether the 31,000,000 will see it in the same light. If Mr. Gladstone came into power to-morrow, with a majority of 100 in the House of Commons, he would in his first Session only touch the fringe of the Irish Question. Another appeal to the country would be required. The House of Lords would have to be abolished, the prerogative of the Crown to be curtailed, before the settlement of the Irish Question could even commence. How many sessions will that take ? If the 31,000,000 are to wait for all useful legislation till the Irish Question is settled, they will literally have to wait till the Greek Kalends, and this they are beginning to realise. But will 31,000,000 of people suffer themselves to be fooled with such nonsense as this ? It may be right to let Ireland go ; but it cannot be right to do so because Mr. Gladstone is nearly 80 years old. When he urges his great age as a reason for at once allowing him to cut off a great limb from the Empire, he is, in fact, urging the very strongest reason why he should not be allowed to do so. His memory and his judgment are terribly impaired by age and hard work, and he sees things in an exaggerated and false light that is quite astounding. The arguments and opinions of Mr. Gladstone at 80 are to the arguments and opinions of Mr. Gladstone at 40 exactly what Turner's pictures at 80 are to Turner's pictures at 40—wild, confused, unintelligible, pitiable. What sense is there in entrusting important work to a man who in the course of nature cannot see it completed, and whose judgment has gone astray ?

Mr. Gladstone tells us plainly that he is in a hurry, but unfortunately it is not he alone who is in a hurry. There are others who are in a hurry too—a still greater hurry. He is afraid the Irish Question should slip through his fingers, and those who hang on to his political skirts are afraid that he should slip through their fingers. His is the name they conjure with, and they are in a hurry to utilise to the utmost the present hysterical emotion in his favour. It may not last. The tension is getting rather strained. He has gone too far. " Depasser le but c'est manquer la chose." There may be a reaction, and that would be awkward. The position is now supremely ridiculous—31,000,000 people in England and Scotland, 200,000,000 in India, and our Colonies are condemned to stew in their own juice because one man is 80 years old and must not be contradicted ! It is absurd. England and Scotland have far more need of useful legislation than Ireland—a hundred times more.

During the last few years Parliament has actually *epuiséd* itself in removing the material grievances of Ireland. There are none left—at least nobody knows what they are. " It is our turn now," say the English and Scotch ; "you have removed the material grievances of the Irish, now remove ours." Oh, dear no, says Mr. Gladstone, your turn has not nearly come yet. It is true the Irish have no material grievances to complain of, but they still have their sentimental grievances. Until these are quite removed nothing can be done for you ; absolutely nothing. Sentiment before sense, my friends, or justice either.

But the material interests of England and Scotland are very urgent, and cannot wait. Six millions of English and Scotch agriculturists—law-abiding citizens—are on the verge of ruin ; the wolf is at the door. Drink is impoverishing the country and deteriorating the British breed. The frightful increase of drink amongst women almost excludes us from the pale of civilisation. Our fiscal absurdities are ruining our industries, and driving our workpeople abroad. These are some of our material interests ; are they to receive no attention till the sentimental interests of the Irish are satisfied ? Our boasted parliamentary system and our boasted Free Trade have both broken down, and yet we are to stand still till Mr. Gladstone gives us leave to move on ! Again, I say, it is absurd. And why, pray, should the sentimental interests of 3,000,000 in Ireland take precedence of the material interests of the rest of the Empire ? Has Ireland any grievance against England ? Have her interests been neglected in favour of the interests of England and Scotland ? Hear what Mr. Gladstone said at Aberdeen in 1871 :—" Ireland has no grievance against England. The English Parliament has not scrupled to do for Ireland what it has not ventured to do for England and Scotland." This was 16 years ago. Since then the Imperial Parliament has actually stultified itself in removing the material grievances of the Irish. In their interests political economy has been banished to Saturn, and the farmers have got such a hold on the land that they can actually sell their tenant-right for more than the fee simple ! Mr. Gladstone, failing in judgment and in his estimate of things, has taken it into his head that the sentimental interests of 3,000,000 of Irishmen, subsidised and directed by a foreign conspiracy, should take precedence of the material interests of 31,000,000 of English and Scotch law-abiding citizens. But he is wrong. English and Scotch farmers and labourers are beginning to see clearly that Irish farmers and labourers are in every respect better off than they are ; that whilst in Ireland they have got the three F's and three acres and a cow, in England and Scotland they have none of these things.

"It is all very well to say stand on one side, and make way for Irish legislation," they will say, when they realise what fools they are being made of. " Be just before you are generous ; you have done much more for the Irish than you have for us. It is our turn now. Our case is far harder than theirs, and our needs more pressing, and we have a much stronger claim on the attention of Parliament. Put us at least in as good a position as you have put them before you call upon us to make more sacrifices in their favour." The urgent needs of 31,000,000 can no longer be put on one side in order to gratify the sentimental interests of 3,000,000, or even to accommodate Mr. Gladstone's advancing years. Legislation for the Empire must go on, and, for some time at any rate, legislation for England and Scotland must take precedence of legislation for Ireland. Let us take a common-sense view of the situation. When Parliament is sitting we have 5½ working days a week. Let us so divide them that each division of the Empire shall get its fair share of needful legislation. Let us allot one day to Ireland, one day to Scotland, two days to England and Wales, one day to India and the Colonies, and half a day to the foreign affairs of the country, limit all speeches to 10 minutes, and then a Parliament of Common-sense actually appears possible, and the Parliament of Gab will remain only as a horrible nightmare.

1888.

THE "MARQUIS" BLUE-BOTTLE.

I SEE one of the morning journals compares landowners to blue-bottle flies—they are very large, very noisy, and very useless. I don't see the force of the comparison, but let that pass. Well, Mr. Morley is going to Ireland in a few days to assist the agitation against Blue-bottles in that country, and, like an experienced showman, he takes with him the most enormous specimen of the genus blue-bottle that the three kingdoms can produce. At Hampton Court is still found the largest of English spiders, called the " Cardinal ; " and at Studley Royal is found the " Marquis " Blue-bottle. Well, Mr. Morley has captured a " Marquis " and takes it with him to Ireland. The " Marquis " represents at least a dozen ordinary Blue-bottles rolled into one, and he can buzz—oh, yes, he can buzz. I will back him to buzz against any Blue-bottle in the world. The " Marquis " that Mr. Morley will exhibit in Ireland is one of the largest landowners in the country. Three or four immense properties are centred in him. He presents to dozens of livings, he counts his tenants by scores, and therefore to see him leading an attack on landowners as a class, denouncing the payment of rent, advocating the Plan of Campaign, and advising the tenants to keep the land, takes the breath out of one.

God only knows what madness has seized on our Blue-bottle that he is now seeking to devour his own species.

> " Say, sire of insects, mighty Sol,
> A fly upon the chariot-pole
> Cries out, ' What blue-bottle alive
> Did ever with such fury drive ? ' "

There are only two explanations—either he has buzzed himself silly, or what is equally probable, he is an arrant humbug. I have known many startling reformations in my life—a distiller denouncing drink, but that was when he had retired from business ; the wife of Bath taking to tea and hassocks, but that was when she was old, &c. But to see a large landowner denouncing land-owning beats anything. I should as soon have expected to see the Pope denounce the cardinals. But, somehow, fouling one's own nest does not always answer ; some people don't like it ; the deserter is always regarded with suspicion. When the record was left open for the public to inscribe their names, yes or no, to the question whether Louis XVI. should have his head cut off or not, a working man, seeing that Philippe Egalité, who had preceded him, had written, " Oui," immediately wrote " Non," saying, " Puisque Egalité dit oui; moi, je dis non." He, at any rate, did not think much of birds that fouled their own nests ; and it is quite possible that the sight of one of the largest landowners in the country

denouncing land-owning may have a directly opposite effect to what
is expected. It will show the utter unreality of the agitation.
Egalité, no doubt, thought that by cutting off his cousin's head he
would save his own ; but he did not. And probably our Blue-bottle
thinks that by attacking bluebottledom in Ireland he may save it in
England ; but he won't. If he succeeds in pulling down landlordism
in Ireland, he is quite certain to be buried under the ruins. I do
not defend landowning ; it may be very wrong for all I know, and so
some who don't own land think, apparently. Certainly it has its
inconveniences. There are duties connected with the ownership of
land, but none at all with the ownership of Consols. In the one
case a man is obliged to do his duty *coram populo ;* in the other, he
need do no duty at all unless he likes it. Land has its duties ;
Consols have none. Consols have their sweets ; land, alas ! has none.
If landowning is wrong, of course it is a noble act of self-sacrifice
for a landowner to denounce it ; but, then, of course, he ought not
to continue to hold it. Let a thief become a thief-catcher by all
means, but in that case it is generally understood that he no longer
picks pockets—at least I imagine so. By all means let landowners
denounce land-owning ; only it is absurd for them to continue to
hold land. Mr. Morley will have an easy task of it. He is honest
and consistent. He will say, " I represent the Revolution wherever
it raises its head. I am against all landowners, whether in England,
Scotland, or Ireland. ' The land for the people ; down with all
Blue-bottles,' that is my cry, and that is why I have brought over
this gigantic specimen, this " Marquis," to show you. Indeed, he
is very interesting ; he shows what training will do even for a
Blue-bottle. He is a real monster ; he represents at least 20 of
your Irish Blue-bottles, and oh, he can buzz. You will hear him
soon. He has just been perverted from the heresy of landowning,
and I have brought him over, regardless of expense, that you may
hear him make his public profession of faith. A landowner himself,
he advises you to pay no rent, and to keep the land, and directly he
returns home he is going to put his professions into practice—give
up all rent, and hand his land over to his tenants. He, at any rate,
is an honest man ; he would scorn to ask others to do what he
would not care to do himself. Is he not a noble Blue-bottle ? Look at
him again. Shake him by the hand. Hear him buzz, buzz, buzz-z-z !
Isn't he delightful," &c. I think Mr. Morley is quite justified in
assuming that Lord Ripon is going to give up his land, otherwise
he dare not surely venture to lead a crusade against other landowners.
It would be too monstrous.

But do let us ask Lord Ripon a few questions, He is a gigantic
landowner in Yorkshire, where he collects rents and exercises the
rights of property, and his neighbours—Lord Fitzwilliam and the
Duke of Devonshire—are also large landowners in Yorkshire, where
they also collect rents and exercise the rights of property. But they
are also landed proprietors in Ireland, and Lord Ripon denounces
them for collecting rents and exercising the rights of property in
Ireland, but does not say a word against their collecting rents and
exercising the rights of property in Yorkshire. Why is this ?
Because if he denounces them for exercising the rights of property

in Yorkshire, he would have to denounce himself, and that would be
inconvenient. Vain man ! Can't he see that if it is disgraceful to
exercise the rights of property in Ireland, it is equally disgraceful to
exercise them in Yorkshire—that a Blue-bottle is a Blue-bottle still
whatever side of the Irish Channel he hails from ? He thinks it
easy to denounce landowners in Ireland, where he has got no land,
but finds it a serious thing to attack them in Yorkshire, where he
has got so much. But if Lord Ripon cannot attack the Duke of
Devonshire, or Lord Fitzwilliam, in Yorkshire, with what reason
does he attack them in Ireland? Does he mean to say they are
worse landlords in Ireland than they are in Yorkshire? For many
years neither of them have drawn a shilling out of Ireland ; they
have spent all they have received from their Irish estates on the
estates themselves. Will Lord Ripon say that he has done more
in Yorkshire ; and if he has not, how comes it that he is now
throwing stones at those who have ? If it is wrong for the Duke of
Devonshire and Lord Fitzwilliam to hold land in Ireland it is wrong
for them to hold land in Yorkshire ; and if it is wrong for them to
hold land in Yorkshire, it is wrong for his brother-in-law to
hold land in Yorkshire, for any one, in fact, to hold land in
Yorkshire. What nonsense. I never remember such a bungling act
of folly. Why, it wouldn't impose on a suckling. Lord Ripon is going
to Ireland to denounce Lord Fitzwilliam, the Duke of Devonshire, and
other Irish landowners, and to exhort their tenants to pay them no
rent, and to hold the land. But suppose an Irish landowner was to
come over to Studley Royal and call Lord Ripon's tenants together
and say :—" Gentlemen, at great personal inconvenience to myself,
but impelled by an overpowering sense of duty, I have come over
to denounce—yes, to denounce—the conditions under which you
hold land from Lord Ripon. Compared with the universal practice
in Ireland, the conditions are so hard that I am satisfied that, when
the public realise the difference, he will be compelled to treat you
with more justice. Generosity, gentlemen, I do not ask from him
—but justice, simple justice. My advice to you is to demand from
him exactly the same conditions that I and all other landowners
grant—and, indeed, are compelled to grant—to our tenants. If he
denies you this justice, then I distinctly advise you to pay no rent ;
hold the land, and he will soon come to reason. That there may be
no mistake, I will tell you what are the conditions on which I let
my land, and you will see by comparison what sort of a landlord
Lord Ripon is. All my tenants have the three F's—Fair rent, fixed
by the Government ; Fixity of tenure ; Free sale. My tenants can
sell their lease to anyone they like ; often they sell it for more than
the fee simple of the land. Now, have any of you these privileges ?
Many of my tenants have paid no rent for three years. Is your
landlord more considerate than I am ? My tenants can crop the
land exactly as they like. Can you ? For 3s. a week I let a
cottage and three acres of land, sometimes more. Does Lord
Ripon do this ? I preserve no game, no foxes, employ no game-
keepers. Poaching, therefore, that fills your gaols, is unknown on
my estate. Finally, I present to no Church livings." Now, any
Irish landowners who stated this to Lord Ripon's tenants would be

telling the truth, the whole truth, and nothing but the truth, and I think it would be rather awkward for Lord Ripon.

> " Now, elderly gentlemen, let me advise,
> If you're married and haven't got very good eyes,
> Don't go poking about after blue-bottle flies,
> Don't wear green specs with a tortoise-shell rim,
> And don't go near the river unless you can swim."

Our elderly gentleman has gone poking about after blue-bottle flies, and he has tumbled into the river of Revolution. He can't swim— Blue-bottles never can ; all he can do is to float with the stream till some lusty trout or dainty grayling, attracted by his struggles, sucks him under and makes a meal of him. He won't have to float far.

1888.

AFFAIRES DE FEMMES.

W HEN we see a cock strutting about with his hens, we think, of course, he is leading the hens—not a bit of it, the hens are leading him ; they wander where curiosity or pleasure attracts them, and he struts after them, and if he lags behind, a cackle and a flutter will immediately recall him to a sense of his duty. So it is all over the world, and so it ever has been since the days of Adam. Everywhere men fancy they lead the women, but everywhere women know they lead the men. " Women are fools," said Rousseau ; "they have no wit, no genius, they don't even know how to describe love ; I only know one exception." " Oh, but you do know one exception," replied a young lady with ready wit, " and if every man knows one exception, our total won't be so bad after all "—and that is the whole Law and the Prophets. Women total up better than men—ever so much better. Women lead men, because they are the cleverer animal — infinitely more clever. Amongst a hundred men, we are told you will find two *spirituel* ; amongst a hundred women you will find one fool. In wit, in intelligence, in resource, in persistence, in patience, in endurance, in the highest kind of courage, women have the best of it. We do not believe that there is a single case of heroism, endurance, excellence, endowment in man that you cannot find its equal in woman. Men reason about the human heart, women simply read it. The former preach, the latter practice ; and, of course, it is always 100 to 1 on the latter. All the reasoning of men will not stand a moment before the instinct of women. "If lions could paint," as the lion said in the fable, " you would see the lion killing the man instead of the man killing the lion." If women wrote history and painted men, perhaps we should see another illustration of the fable. Talk of the martyrdom of man ; the martyrdom of women may yet be written. Woman was bad from the beginning, say men ; she caused the Fall—" bon pour meisseurs les hommes "— but the fact is that it was Adam who received the injunction about the apple, not Eve. " It was in Adam all sinned," not Eve. Which of them started the unfortunate idea we shall never know ; but Adam was a sneak to say it was Eve, and it is ridiculous to be angry with Eve for eating of the Tree of Life. What should we be now if she had never learnt the difference between good and evil ? Why, our Simian progenitors would have had the best of us. It is very amusing to speculate on a state of society in which for 40,000 years women had made all the laws for their own benefit. What would be the position of men then ? But, alas for theories, there is a " Royaume des Femmes " in our midst where for several years female influence has been paramount, and which we regret to say has become a public nuisance. The history of Bulgaria is not a long one, but, such as it is, it may be written in three words,

"Affaires de femmes." "Affaires de Femmes" suggested the election of the handsome Prince Alexander of Battenberg to the Throne of Bulgaria; "Affaires de Femmes" brought about the election of Prince Ferdinand of Coburg; "Affaires de Femmes" inspired the forged Bulgarian despatches; and now, worse than all, "Affaires de femmes" is responsible for this Battenberg marriage. Evidently the ladies have made an awful mess of Bulgarian affairs. It is very disappointing. This Battenberg marriage is absolutely and entirely an "affaire de femmes." We don't suppose there are a dozen men from one end of Europe to the other who care a snap of their fingers about it.

"It is a case of true love," we are told; "and Prince Bismarck has set all the kind-hearted women in the world against him by opposing a love match." And so, I suppose, was the elopement of Paris and Helen a love match; but all the same for 10 long years it kept the world in arms; and as for "all the kind-hearted women in the world," we don't believe they are such fools as to wish to make one bride at the cost of making 10,000 widows. If lighting the torch of Hymen in this case in reality means lighting the torch of Mars, kind-hearted women would probably prefer having the operation postponed to a more convenient season.

True love is apt to be unfortunate. There is nearly always a lion in the path. It is very sad to read of poor Pyramus and Thisbe under the mulberry tree; but it is a fact that in this world there is a better chance for a *mariage de convenance* than for a *mariage de cœur*. In this particular case the lion *haute politique* stands in the path, and a very awkward customer he is, to say the least of it.

> "Grave authors say, and witty poets sing,
> That honest wedlock is a glorious thing."

And so no doubt it is; but there are exceptions, and this appears to be one of them.

We don't believe history affords such another instance of the influence of the unforeseen on human affairs as the present crisis in Germany. The gates of Janus were opening wider every day; every day the prospects of peace were getting brighter, when suddenly these ominous portals begin to close again, and every day the prospects of peace become less. And why? Because a cloud no bigger than a man's hand has suddenly developed into a blizzard. Only the other day, when the Emperor died, the universal remark over the whole civilised world was, "What would happen to Germany if she lost Prince von Bismarck?" Well, if what we read is true, she has lost Prince von Bismarck. He is not, it is true, dismissed; but his power is broken, and his removal is now a matter of no importance. It is said that the reign of the great Chancellor, of the one man who can compel peace in Europe, is gone. That he has gone down, not on any great principle of national interest, but before a Court intrigue. Bismarck is weighed against Battenberg, and Bismarck strikes the beam. "Je jeu ma tête," said De Broglie when he played revolution. "Je jeu mon Battenberg," say the German Court party when they play a similar stake. It is absurd. "Woe to the vanquished," cried stern Brennus, as he cast his massive sword into the scale against

Rome's ransom. "Woe to the war-maker," are the words of Bismarck as he casts his great name into the scale of peace. And will not Germany hear him? Will not Europe hear him. We think they will. The great German Chancellor has a European value far beyond any value he may have as the Minister of Germany. He is at this present moment, and has been for 15 years, the Prince of Peace. His enemies hate him, of course, and of course his enemies are numerous at home and abroad; but the most bitter of them allow in their hearts that for 15 years every act of his public service has been directed to the maintenance of peace. He, indeed, is the lion that has stood in the path of war.

We do not think that any event in this century would cause such danger to Europe as the fall of Prince von Bismarck. Other events, of course, have caused war, but such a war as now threatens Europe has never before been suggested to civilised mankind. Germany, with two or three millions of armed men, stands face to face with France and Russia with four or five millions of armed men. At a word five or six millions of men are ready to fly at each other's throats. What keeps them back? One thing only— the unity of Germany. By immense efforts, by immense sacrifices, she has carried to its very utmost limits, the old principle, " Si vis pacem, para bellum." She is so thoroughly prepared for war that her enemies dare not break the peace. But it is not only military power that has given her the security of peace—it is unity, unity of Government, unity of force, unity in military and foreign policy. It is unity alone—one head, one heart, one hand—that has given Germany 15 years' peace. Well, if that unity goes, what will happen? The agitation amongst all classes in Germany is not surprising. For 15 years the policy of Germany has been as open as the day; every child knows it as he does his alphabet. The people know that this policy has succeeded, that it has given Germany wealth and peace. The Emperor who for 28 years directed this policy has just died, almost with his last breath impressing its maintenance on his successor; but almost before he is cold in his grave—" But two months dead—nay, not so much " there is a talk of reversing his policy; and dismissing the pilot with whom he had weathered so many storms. There are circumstances about this reversal of the policy of the Great Emperor and the Great Chancellor that make it especially distasteful to the German people. Not only is the haste indecent, but the apparent subservience of national to family interests at such a critical moment is maddening. If family interests destroy the national policy, what is there to take its place? All Germany knows that the noble Prince from whom they hoped so much is stricken by the hand of God. His reign is an interregnum; and that an interregnum should be made the occasion of destroying the bulwark of German unity, and exposing her to the awful calamities of war with Russia and France, is too much. There can be no doubt of the result. Germany will not part with her great Minister till the clouds roll by. The more foreign intrigue assails him the more national feeling will rally round him.

The last words of the old Emperor were "the dying hero's call "

for German unity; and when the clouds gather round the Father-
land, as they are gathering now, and the sounds of "Le Revanche"
become ominously distinct, her sons will again stand in spirit by
the simple camp bed, and again swear allegiance to the exhortations of the honest old soldier—again in spirit they will hear—

> "The sound of that wild horn,
> On Pommeranian echoes borne,
> The dying hero's call."

The idea is general throughout Europe that the intrigue against
the German Chancellor is supported by England. It is most unfor-
tunate. It is absurd; but it does not gain less credence on that
account. "The resignation of Prince Bismarck," says a Russian
paper, "would signify the triumph of the English party at Berlin."
"The English party at Berlin!" What does it mean? What
English party is there at Berlin? What German party is there in
London? Of course it has no meaning, and it is an insult to the
English people to suggest that it is possible. The fall of the
Great Chancellor means the triumph of the English party at Berlin.
Ye gods! It is, indeed, enough to make the old Emperor turn in
his grave. What should we say if the fall of Lord Salisbury
or Mr. Gladstone were proclaimed through Europe as the triumph
of the German party in London? The feeling of Germany is very
strong on this subject—the temper of the public almost dangerous.
Already painful rumours are in the air; demission is not the only
subject that is discussed.

Before all things the German people desire peace; their statesmen tell them that in the present crisis of Europe the proposed
marriage constitutes a danger to peace, and they are determined it
shall not take place, and they fiercely resent as an impertinence,
and as an unfriendly act any foreign interference with their national
interests. "This is entirely a German question," say they; "you
foreigners have nothing to do with it. It is we who have to pay
the piper, not you; dance to any tune you like, but don't presume to dictate to us what tune we are to dance to."

"Courage! Messieurs et mesdames, prenez, demandez, n'ayez
pas honte," said an indignant steward who saw that the guests
were abusing his master's hospitality, "on voit bien que vous
n'êtes pas chez vous;" and that is what Germany says to the
impertinents who interfere in their affairs. You are abusing your
opportunity, "On voit bien que vous n'etes pas chez vous."

1888.

PANIC.

ENGLAND, we are told, is in a panic; in other words, England is in a funk. Now, of course, it is not very dignified to be in a funk, but it is not an uncommon complaint; nations suffer from it as well as individuals. It is an hysterical affection, but none the less distressing on that account. It is not at all necessary that danger should be real to cause a funk. A cloud passing over a hill side has been mistaken for an impi and caused men to run like hares. A man may fancy a mad dog is after him, and though it may turn out to be only a friendly cur, he may, nevertheless, have passed a very bad quarter of an hour whilst he supposed it was a mad dog. Of course, it is better never to be in a funk, but it is certainly better to run from a friendly cur than to remain and be bitten by a mad dog. During what is called the coal famine of 1871-2 there was never actually a scarcity of coal, but the mere apprehension of it was sufficient to send up the price of coal 300 and 400 per cent.! If we were at war with France, or Russia, or America, it is not at all certain that we should be actually short of corn; but it is quite certain the mere apprehension of being short of it would send up the price of corn 300 or 400 per cent. Panic is fear; but caution is not panic, it is often common sense; shoring up your house when you see signs of the foundation giving way is not panic. Vaccinating your household when small-pox is prevalent is not panic. Increasing insurance to meet increased risks is not panic, it is common sense.

Lord Salisbury falls foul of Lord Wolseley for having let the cat out of the bag. "It was a very mean trick of you," he says, "to bolt the cat at a City dinner; you ought to have brought the bag here and bolted the cat on the floor of this House, and then we should have had rare sport." But, with all due deference to Lord Salisbury, he labours under a mistake. There was no cat in the bag at all; it was bolted long ago; and if Lord Wolseley had brought the bag to the House of Lords, it would have proved as empty as some of their Lordships' heads! What is the use of pretending the cat is still in the bag, when everyone knows it is all over the place? Does anyone in his senses doubt that the naval and military attachés of France, Germany, and Russia know as much, or a great deal more, about our ships, our guns, our soldiers, our coaling stations, our grain ships, than we do ourselves? What nonsense! Why, a hundred newspapers tell the world the whole story every day in the week. Only the other night the First Lord of the Treasury said that he hoped in three years, by God's mercy, Gibraltar would have guns. Is it possible to let a bigger cat out of the bag than that? Of course the man who encourages unfounded panic should be hanged as high as Haman; but certainly the man who encourages unfounded confidence should be elevated alongside him.

If instead of lecturing Lord Wolseley for letting the cat out at a City dinner, Lord Salisbury had lectured him for going to the dinner at all, there would have been a great deal of reason in it. All nations have objectionable " customs," civilised as well as barbarian. The " customs " of Dahomey and Ashantee are not particularly attractive, but I swear I think they are as pleasant as those of " Venter Deus," the " Great Belly God " of the City ! The high priests of " Ja-Ja," or " Jam-Jam," or whatever the monster's name is, disembowel their victims, and cut off their heads. The high priests of " Venter Deus " gorge their victims, and give them two heads. At least, that is not unfrequently the poor wretch's sensation on awakening the morning following the City "custom." How any man who can afford a chop and a pint of Pilsener beer at home, or at his club, ever finds himself at a public dinner I can never understand. I can quite understand that if a man, who rather fancies himself, thinks that he has anything that is new (it must'nt be true it appears, that is letting the cat out of the bag), or important, or amusing, to communicate to the public that he should seize any opportunity of saying it; but when he has nothing to say, absolutely nothing, either important, or amusing, or novel, I cannot understand his subjecting his vile body to a surfeit of turtle, venison, and the " Boy," in order to say it. I declare I do not believe that at Dahomey's worst " customs " you could see more complete misery stamped on the faces of those awaiting execution, or more hopeless depression on the faces of those looking on, than you do on the faces of the speakers and listeners at the " customs " of the " Great Belly God."

Most of us, we know, are extremists on some question or another ; and those very superior persons who tell us they can always keep mid-channel between the Scylla of optimism and the Charybdis of pessimism are almost always humbugs. Test them on matters that concern their own immediate interests, and it is a hundred to one extreme opinions will crop out. " Which do you prefer, O camel," asked Mahommed, "going up hill or down hill?" " May the devil fly away with both," was the reply. And so it is with us. We are all of us either going up hill or down hill. The camel that never goes off the flat is indeed a very fortunate camel. At the commencement of the Franco-German war French optimists had it all their own way. " A. Berlin ! A Berlin !" they shouted. The Rhine was already a French river ; the *personnel* of their army was perfection ; the equipment was complete to the last button, &c. Before the great collapse those who warned them of danger were ridiculed as fools ; after the disaster those who had assured them of victory were execrated as traitors. It is always so : let us take warning ; we are now much in the same position : there are optimists who tell us exactly the same story about our army and navy, even to the proverbial button ; and there are pessimists who tell us the exactly contrary story. The serious matter in our case is that the optimists represent the opinion of those who know nothing, absolutely nothing, whatever on the subject ; whilst the pessimists represent all the scientific and professional experience of the country.

The cause of our uneasiness can be easily explained ; it is a very simple sum. We have a capital of £30,000,000,000—that is to say, the national income is generally estimated at £1,200,000,000, which, capitalised at 4 per cent., means, of course, £30,000,000,000. Now, £30,000,000,000 is a pretty tall sum, quite worth keeping, and quite worth seizing, and, besides this capital, there are such trifles as " the flag," the "pride of race," an Empire on which the sun never sets (though, indeed, envious foreigners are unkind enough as to say, that on one important portion of it the sun never rises). Now, the national insurance on all this wealth is our army, and navy, and the reserve forces, and it costs us about £30,000,000. This seems a very high premium to pay, and so it is; but it is not extravagant on the amount insured, it is exactly £1 per £1,000 or 2s. per cent. Now 2s. per cent. is the exact rate most of us pay for insurance against fire, and it does not appear very unreasonable that the nation should pay the same rate as the individual. Owing to circumstances over which we have no control, we find that, for the moment, our risks are very much increased; and, therefore, we are asked to pay an increased premium. I believe that at this moment, there is no doubt whatever that the country is insufficiently insured; but whether the premium is too small, or whether the amounts are improperly distributed, I cannot say. I am inclined to believe there is a great deal of both. I believe that, for the moment, we should insure for a larger amount; but I also believe that the premium we have been paying has been most stupidly and most disgracefully wasted. We have covered by insurance four or five times over, things that are not worth insuring at all; and we have left quite uninsured things on which our very existence depends. There are now three courses open to us—to remain as we are, to increase our premium, to readjust our present insurance. Of course, if we are in danger, we must try and get out of it; to remain in danger is an act of madness. If an army and navy are necessary to our safety, we must have them of sufficient power to protect us beyond the possibility of doubt. It is childish to say we won't spend more money because we have not got full value for the money we have already spent.

It is not what we ought to have that concerns us at this moment, it is what we actually have got. No doubt our money has been wasted, shamefully, incredibly, with a stupidity without example; but because we have lost a score or two of millions, are we there-fore, in a fit of the sulks, to decline to secure the thousands of millions that remain to us ? It is childish. We must have what we want now, but we must take steps at once to make the control of our spending departments more effective and more reasonable for the future. England risks more by war than any other nation in the world. It is therefore of more importance to her to preserve peace than to any other nation in the world. Well, her chances of preserving peace rise and fall exactly in proportion as her ability to defend herself rises and falls. So long as it is believed that she can easily beat off all attacks and turn the tables on her assailants, she is perfectly safe from attack ; but if it is seen that she lives in a fool's paradise, and has neglected to keep her arms bright, and cannot defend herself, then sooner or later she is certain to be dragged into war. Nobody knows, not even Prince Bismarck himself, whether the clouds that now threaten European peace will roll by. Nobody knows whether in case of a European war England will be allowed to remain out of it. Nobody knows; nobody, actually nobody. There are lots of very wise men who will tell you they do know, but they don't, no more than the child unborn.

Nothing points the moral of Lord Wolseley's strictures on party government so much as the fact that in this country the national defence can be made a party question. In no other country in the world is this possible. Those who presume to put the interests of party before the interests of the nation are very short-sighted, and very disloyal. It must be so. If our grain ships are driven from the seas, and the price of wheat goes up to 300s. a quarter; if our colonies are conquered, our Empire broken up, our shores invaded, our capital threatened, a fine of £1,000,000,000 imposed upon us,. do they suppose they will not suffer with the rest? Will it be a party question then? If it is, it will be a very awkward question for the party who prevented the county placing itself in a position of security. Optimists do not deny our inefficiency; they do not say we are prepared to defend ourselves if attacked. They traverse the whole question by saying it is impossible that we shall ever be attacked; but this is absolutely untrue. There is only one reason why we should not be attacked, and that is our evident power to defend ourselves; but there are fifty reasons why we should be attacked, if it is seen we are not in a position to defend ourselves.

"The French have loved us like brothers for sixty years," says Mr. Gladstone, ever since Waterloo, in fact; and we have loved them with equal devotion, of course, during that long period. What nonsense! Nations that are opposed to each other do not love each other any more than individuals who are opposed to each other. It is not human nature. Did Mr. Gladstone love Lord Beaconsfield? Does he love Lord Salisbury? No, of course he doesn't. Why should he? Then why should the French love us, or we love the French? The French will never love us, but they will respect us if they know we are strong enough to defend ourselves—not an hour longer. But this position is untenable; those who advance it are on the horns of a dilemma. Our army and navy are either for use or for show. If for use, they are manifestly too weak; if for show, they are evidently too expensive. If it is impossible that we shall be attacked, we don't want an army and navy to defend us; if it is possible we shall be attacked, we want an army and navy that can defend us beyond the possibility of doubt. If our army and navy are for show, we ought not to spend £30,000,000 a year on them; if they are for use, we ought to spend on them as much as will make them effective for the purposes for which we want them. There is panic in the air—there is no doubt of it—and the only way of meeting it is to tell the truth, the whole truth, and nothing but the truth. It is the only way of avoiding exaggeration on both sides. Anything like concealment, anything that resembles that popular little game of the pea and the three thimbles, will certainly make panic more intense.

Now, what the Government, any Government that does its duty

to the country, should say is this—" War is possible. In case of war your army and navy will have to guard your coasts, your harbours, your colonies, your Empire, your grain ships, your coaling stations, perhaps even your capital, and this is its present efficiency. Are you satisfied? Is it sufficient?" If the country says Yes, the responsibility no longer rests with the Government. At present it does. It is of no use trying to swop horses whilst we are crossing the stream; no use changing our system when the danger is upon us; it is no use arguing now that for the money we have spent we ought to have more guns, and ships, and men. If we have not got them, somebody is to blame, no doubt— somebody ought to be hanged, perhaps—but it is cutting off our nose to spite our face to expose the country to the risk of disaster because some individuals have neglected their duty.

There is another point that seems to be over-looked, but which, to my mind, is very important indeed, and that is the obligation of the nation to its soldiers and sailors. We keep a certain number of thousands of men to defend us, and fight our battles in case we are attacked. The moment the blast of war sounds in our ears we say, " Now, my brave boys, now's your time ; show us the metal of your pastures," &c. This is all very well, but it is of much more importance that our soldiers and sailors should be able to show the enemy the metal of their guns. If we give them no guns, or only inferior ones ; if we arm them with rifles that jam, bayonets that bend, swords that break, we are sending them to certain defeat and death. We have no right to do this. It is a breach of faith, a breach of honour, a breach of humanity. We are traitors to our soldiers and sailors, we are betraying them into the hands of the enemy. It is a shame. It is true we do not engage to arm them as well as those they will have to fight, but it is understood that we shall do so ; to send infantry into the field with only half its complement of guns, cavalry with only half its complement of horses, to put our sailors in great iron coffins, without proper guns and means of coaling, is wilfully sacrificing their lives, and is a disgraceful breach of faith. Of course, a nation must defend itself with any arms it can get, but England ought to have as good arms as its neighbours, or better. There is no doubt of it, we can have them if we take the proper means to get them. To neglect to do so is not only incredibly stupid, but it is dishonourable and disgraceful.

1888.

PARTY GOVERNMENT.

FOR thirteen consecutive winters an acquaintance of mine went to Egypt for his health, and every spring wrote to his sisters in England, saying that the east wind was worse than it had ever been known before. Certainly, if I were writing to a friend abroad to-day I should tell the same story about Party Government. I should say Party Government had been getting worse and worse every year, till now it was actually quite "beyond." Of course, I know that grumbling will no more get rid of Party Government than it will of the east wind; but still, grumbling enables one to bear many ills that without it would be intolerable—Party Government amongst them. Lord Salisbury scolds Lord Wolseley for saying that Party Government is responsible for the miserable condition of our national defe..ces, and is quite shocked that any one should suppose that Party Government stands in the way of useful legislation. But isn't this indignation absurd? You have only to listen to the charges and counter-charges party men bring against each other to feel that in such hands useful legislation must be a very improbable event.

What is Party Government? A hundred men out of a population of 34,000,000—that is, one in every 340,000—become politicians, God only knows why, as others become soldiers, sailors, tinkers, or tailors. "*Nascitur, non fit*, say these modest mortals; "we were born so; we require no preparation. We are the superior human article. We are the leaven that leaveneth the whole mass." Fifty range themselves on one side and fifty on the other, and then the game begins. It consists in abusing, misrepresenting, discrediting, and finally replacing their opponents. They call this the game of "Haute Politique;" but the vulgar herd merely call it the game of "Dishing." "We will govern the country," says one fifty; "you are more or less a set of vicious incapables. The loaves and fishes shall be ours." "We'll be hanged if you shall," say the other fifty, "if we can help it; your principles are atrocious; the loaves and fishes shall be ours; we will fight you for them." And, by Jove, they do fight, tooth and nail—*unguibus et rostro*. Talk of the Rugby rules, the Queensberry rules, Heenan and Tom Sayers, Smith and the Elastic Pot-boy, why, these are gentlemanly contests compared to the wordy battles that are fought between party athletes.

At football and in the prize ring there are rules, and those who break them lose the game; and the spectators insist on a certain amount of fair play; but in party fights there are apparently no rules, and no fair play. The combatants hit below the belt, stab in the back, exchange accusations and insinuations that are shameful, and that they know are false, and the spectators encourage them by word and action, and howl at the referee if he tries to

R

enforce the most ordinary rules of fair play. Of course, men of the same profession must know each other pretty well—better than the outside world can know them—and therefore they ought to be a little more careful of what they say of each other, lest the public should take them at their own valuation, and that would be very awkward. It is certain that if they are one-hundredth part as bad as they represent each other to be, they are more fit for a reformatory than for a Legislative Assembly. The Radical members of the House of Commons are very fond of throwing dirt at the members of the House of Lords. "You are a spendthrift," they say, "a gambler, a loafer, and altogether a 'mean cuss.' Make way for honest, enlightened citizens like us." This is all very well. When they denounce the House of Lords they make them out to be a very poor set; but when they denounce each other they make themselves out to be very much worse! "You are a cheat," they say; "a liar, you suborn justice, put pressure on judges, pack juries, condone murder, encourage revolution, perjure yourselves," &c. Really, when one recalls the charges the Irish members brought against Sir William Harcourt, Sir George Trevelyan, Lord Spencer, and Mr. Gladstone, and those more recently brought by Mr. Gladstone, Sir William Harcourt, and Sir George Trevelyan against Lord Salisbury and Mr. Balfour, it becomes evident that reform should begin at home and the real Augean stables is in the House of Commons and not in the House of Lords.

The House of Commons is an epitome of the nation. It is composed of a majority more or less with common sense, and a minority more or less without it. If Party Government meant that the men with more or less sense competed with each other to give the country reasonably good government, all right; the system would be an excellent one. But when the men of sense fight amongst each other and bribe the men of no sense, by reckless promises of support, to come and help them, the country is no longer governed by the men of some sense, but by men without any sense, and in the present exaggerated condition of party contests this is what actually occurs. If the majority with common sense said to the champions of contagion and drink and total abstinence, the sour Sabbatarians, the cheap and nasty humanitarians, the faddists, the fanatics, the impossible persons of all kinds, "Cart away your pernicious nonsense, and let common sense govern the country," we should get on; but, unfortunately, the necessities of this cursed party system compel them to say exactly the reverse. "Dear faddists," they say, "dear worshippers of contagion and drink, of cold water, and sour hypocrisy, we know that you are fools and humbugs, and that all that you advocate is pernicious and absurd, and injurious to the country, but only give us your votes and we will support all your fads, and a great deal more;" and they do. In this way the interests of the country are put up to a Dutch auction. Party Government becomes a competition for the support of the nonsense men; folly reigns supreme, and common sense is flung to the Devil.

Now, when I see population rapidly increasing; cultivation rapidly diminishing; land relapsing from tillage to grazing; from grazing to prairie value; agricultural wages declining to 9s. and 8s. a week; farmers and country tradesmen ruined; landowners everywhere becoming absentees; ships alongside each other embarking our best operatives, and disembarking the very articles those operatives manufacture; capital everywhere withdrawn from British agriculture and British industries in order to be invested in foreign agriculture and foreign industries; the able-bodied, the intelligent, the manhood, the bone and sinew and brains of the country emigrating, and leaving the old, the infirm, the women and children, the paupers, the loafers, the lunatics, and criminals at home; capital passing from the hands of those who employ labour into the hands of those who employ no labour; every year the interests of capital and labour becoming more distinctly separated; the distribution of wealth diminishing, and the accumulation of wealth increasing; the interests of labour everywhere subservient to the interests of capital; the awful abyss that separates rich and poor; inconceivable squalor and fabulous wealth; ruinous railway monopolies; the closing of canals; judges, doctors, ministers, police, poor-law guardians, telling us that 90 per cent. of our crime, insanity, pauperism, vice, sickness, results from drink, and Government afraid to touch it; more female drunkenness than in the whole world together; the abject nonsense of the discussions about the social evil, and the deceased wife's sister; the employer of false weights and measures, the seller of adulterated drink or food, fined 10s., the starving beggar who steals a loaf imprisoned for five years; the cure of human souls bought and sold in the open market to the highest bidders; all places of amusement and instruction closed to the public on the Seventh Day, and only the public houses left open; the Government saying to the public on the Sabbath Day, "This is the day sacred to the great god Bacchus; on this day you shall neither sing, nor dance, nor hear music, nor study paintings. or sculpture, or natural history: you shall only drink:" hundreds of thousands of men employed by the railway companies, the omnibus companies, the publicans on Sunday. without complaint, and the employment of 50 men in museums and galleries denounced as desecration of the Sabbath; pauper children set to the impossible task of learning lessons on empty stomachs; the absence of technical and useful education: voluntary military service, the duty every man, yeoman or noble, duke or dustman, owes his country, denounced as compulsory service; an expenditure of £30,000,000 giving us only ships without guns, soldiers without muscle, cavalry without horses, rifles that jam, bayonets that bend, swords that break; our absolute dependence on foreign nations for food, and in the event of war our absolute inability to protect our grain ships; enormous life pensions given to men who have done the country less service than a crossing sweeper: men made hereditary peers for giving money to "the party;" for resigning a safe seat: because they are old: because they are foolish; men in opposition denouncing as the tyranny of the majority what in office they declared was the protection of the minority: boycotting. the "plan of campaign," complicity with murder excused and condoned: the ordinary party "disher" laying claim to Divine inspiration; the name of the Almighty invoked in miserable party contests; a whole party turning slap round on the arguments and professions of their lives, in order to gain votes; the man who tells the truth denounced as Ananias; the man who stands by his faith denounced as Judas: Politicians throwing double somersaults and swearing they have not moved; whirling round like dervishes and declaring it is their opponents who have gyrated; cynical repudiation of pledges and principles; Jesuistical explanations and hair-splitting definitions; the want of backbone and moral courage; everywhere the interests of party preferred to the interests of the country; the leader of a party calling on the enemies of his country, men who blow up our ships, our buildings, threaten our lives, to come over and help him to coerce his own countrymen; the disgrace of Majuba Hill; the desertion of Gordon; the slaughter of Arabs and Egyptians till the very land smelt of blood; the Budget of £100,000,000; cant paying better than truth, hypocrisy than honesty, profession than practice, verbosity than sense—when I see all these things, and remember that we owe the extraordinary profusion of this rank growth to Party Government, I cannot avoid the conclusion that, according to the standard of common sense, England is the worst governed country in the world, that Party Government has utterly collapsed and the governing classes failed in their self-appointed mission.

1888.